Chapter One
The Volcano

Ezekiel Raroso was beaming, standing proudly next to his science project. Dozens of perfectly lined tables in the gymnasium showcase the hard work of the Winfrey Elementary fifth graders. He felt that his project truly had the wow factor and although he never won anything in his life he had a good feeling about this year. He took extra time to add dirt crumbles to the paper mache hill to give the volcano an earthier look. The aroma of detergent and vinegar-filled his nostrils. He fiercely studied videos of Eugene Stude, The Science Dude on YouTube to get it just right.

"No more participation ribbon this year," he thought. As he started to smile to himself, he caught the stare of Bradley Butt Face, notorious school bully who is the size of an eighth grader with a reputation for the world's wedgiest wedgie. To Ezekiel's misfortune, Bradley happened to be on his baseball team, so avoiding him after school was difficult. His real last name wasn't really Butt Face, but it was what Ezekiel wished he had the nerve to call him because of the two years of wedgies, ear flicks, head slaps, spit wads and arm punches he got every day. On this particular morning, Ezekiel had the displeasure of running into Bradley and his cronies in the boy's bathroom. Before Ezekiel could make a run for it, the Neanderthals had him upside down over a toilet. He tried wrestling free but there was easily 500 pounds of bully holding him tight.

"Hey loser, time to go for a swim!"

As Ezekiel was dipped into the toilet, he was appreciative that it smelled of lemon scent. At least it was clean.

Rrrrrriiiiiiinnnnnnnnggggg!

"Saved by the bell this time loser," Bradley said. They released him but not before they whipped out their phones to snap photos of him sopping wet. "I can't wait to post those!" Bradley boasted.

Lucky for Ezekiel there was a hand dryer for him to dry his hair before having to get to class. Although effective, he could smell the lemon fresh scent of the toilet water on him.

•　　•　　•　　•　　•

Ezekiel wanted to barf seeing Bradley put on a fake show of sweetness for the teachers who were judging his off-the-store shelf solar system. He'd fixed tiny lights around the painted foam balls and rotated the planets around the sun. The judges applauded and immediately jotted notes on their clipboards. It frustrated Ezekiel that the teachers never seemed to realize how awful Bradley was. This made him the worst kind of bully because if you were brave enough to tattle, like Santiago Cano was one time, you would find out that not only did the teacher not believe him, the principal didn't either. Santiago tried to convince them that he was a victim of daily wedgies. He even brought in proof. He brought in his torn tidy whities and even a picture he had his pal Tony Johnson snap while he was getting wedgied. Principal Pullman laughed so hard his often-crooked toupee nearly came off. He accused Santiago and Tony of Photoshopping the picture because there was no way that Bradley, with straight A's, being the star baseball player and Boy Scout would do such a thing. Aside from this injustice, word got back to Bradley and things got so much worse for Santiago. He was often seen wearing school issued P.E. shorts because his pants and underwear were frequently stolen out of his locker. He also frequently had the lemon fresh scent that Ezekiel was now familiar with. Ezekiel had not seen Santiago since last year. Rumor had it that Bradley flushed him down the toilet.

His eyes stayed fixed on the group of teachers as they approached each table. Bradley's smile shifted as he scrunched his face scoffing and then whispering into the ear of one of his cronies. Ezekiel wiped his hair from his brow, "I should have gotten a haircut," he thought changing his focus to his shoes then scanning his outfit choice upward. "Well, at least I wore a bow tie." It was an important day, and his grandmother always told him "dress to impress."

The teachers were coming closer and his heart fell into his stomach. His stomach felt queasy like he ate bad cheese. He smiled at the three teachers holding their clipboards, jotting notes, judging him. Mr. Lee, the beloved friendly teacher who wore a bit too much cologne probed him with a grin, "Tell us about your project." Ezekiel was distracted by his cologne cloud and Ms. Flagrin's gum chewing. Her glasses danced on her nose with each *smack, smack* that at this moment, reminded him of Bradley. Every game he *smack, smacked* yelling at him to be better, faster, taller. Ezekiel wasn't very athletic and was regularly sitting on the bench. He was pretty average at school too. This was his chance to bring home a trophy. Winners earned trophies. Losers didn't.

"Yes, er well this is my volcano," he said nervously. As he was reaching in his pocket for his flashcards as he began sweating so much that his hands couldn't grasp all of them, dropping them as he pulled them from his pocket. With just one card stuck to his hand which appeared to have smeared blue pen ink, he flung it to the floor. Trying to play it off, he kicked the cards under the table with his sneaker and said, "Look here. With this measuring cup of simple household items, I can create a volcano eruption." He walked behind the table holding his cup in both hands tightly as his brow seemed to be sweatier. A bead of sweat trickled down his nose and landed into his cup. He scanned fast to make sure the judges didn't notice, he wiped his brow and poured the solution into the spout of the volcano.

He was sweating to the point he could feel his shirt sticking to his armpits. The judge's eyes were focused on the volcano spout waiting for something to happen. Ezekiel looked at his hands. They were moist with a rainbow, sparkle hue.

"Great, I must have got the solution on me. Now I look like I have Jackie's fluorescent highlighting powder on. More ammo for Bradley to tease me with," he thought. Living with a teenage girl cousin who took over the one bathroom in the house exposed Ezekiel to more girly things than he cared for.

Ezekiel fell over. It felt as though his feet gave out under him. Instantly realizing he wasn't just lame and clumsy he caught himself and pulled away just in time before Ms. Flagrin fell on top of him. The ground was trembling. Mr. Pullman, holding onto his shifting toupee, announced over the intercom, "Stay calm kids. It's just a small earthquake." The ground seemed to grow in its tremors. Students grabbed hold of their precious, time-consuming projects to save them from crashing to the ground. Ezekiel noticed his volcano was solid to the table as if fixed by the world's strongest super glue. It may have been in his mind but he could swear that the trembles were coming from the table where his volcano sat.

"Stay calm!" announced Mr. Pullman, then the sound of crashing thunder sounded, exploding red from the volcano. Red foamy magma sprayed hitting every student, teacher and wall in the gymnasium. For just a moment, Ezekiel's panic was overcome with satisfaction as he saw the red magma strike Bradley right in the nose like the punch he wished he could give. The explosion to his face sent him crashing into his solar system, causing a chain reaction that knocked into each project nearby. Projects were flying into the pool of foamy magma and students were frantically diving in after them.

Mr. Lee stumbled up. "Make it stop!"

"I, I can't. I don't know why it is doing that."

Ezekiel ran to his volcano stepping onto Ms. Flagrin's back as if a step stool to reach his volcano. He balanced placing his hand over the spout but it only seemed to make the volcano angrier, sending fierce sprays of magma everywhere. A blast hit students trying to retreat on to the auditorium stage. The lava flow was spraying so hard it was hitting the ceiling creating a sensation of red rain. The stage drapes looked like red waterfalls and the windows had a scary familiar look he had seen in a gym scene from a horror movie his mom forbid him to watch.

A group of girls was huddled together screaming while another was on their backs making magma angels giggling. Students were tripping over each other to turn the soapy, slippery red covered door knobs.

"Please stop," Ezekiel plead with his creation, holding it's spout in his hands.

The shaking calmed down a bit and the intensity of spray slowed. The magma puttered sounds of defeat that sounded like strong armpit farts.

"PLEASE STOP!"

And then, it did.

Chapter Two
The Bow-Tie

"So, tell me again how you did at your Science Fair so Nan can hear", Uncle Mark said amusingly stroking his large black mustache.

"Ugh!"

"Come on. It's not that bad. Sounds like a fun time to me. It's always the same boring projects; foam ball solar system, grow a plant from a lima bean, blah, blah boring. Our Ezie brought some action to the fair. That's the closest them kids are ever going to get to-"

Nan shot him the side eye with her eyebrow raised so high Ezekiel swore it disappeared into her bouffant hair-do.

Trying to hide his laugh, "Tell me, did you add too much dishwashing soap?"

Nan elbowed him. "You know, that is why it's an experiment. I'm sure it's fine. Why don't you go to the den and watch some TV and wait for your mom to come home? I'll get you some ice cream."

Ezekiel plopped himself onto the dilapidated sofa. He swore that when he did he saw clouds form around him. He flipped the TV on and started to flip through the channels trying to find something to amuse him and take the events of the day from his mind. Not only did he botch his experiment, but he also ruined everyone else's before judging. He also ruined his favorite bow tie. Well maybe not. It was already red.

"Maybe it's time to tell him," said Mark

"He's much too young," said Nan

"I wasn't. You weren't. Anne wasn't".

"I don't think he's ready."

"When will he be then? He finishes elementary school in just a few months. Then it will be *summer*. Do we just wait for cam–"

Anne walked in. "Hi. Where's he at?" she asked concerned.

"He's in the den," Nan gestured while pulling Anne close.

"What is going on? You two seem like I caught you in the cookie jar", Anne joked as she opened the refrigerator to grab a soda.

"We should tell him," said Mark.

Anne froze, creeping out of the refrigerator, shutting it forgetting why she was in there in the first place. She looked at her mom and uncle as if they told her a spider was crawling on her back.

"Um, tell him what?" she said as she scurried toward the den door, slowly opening it to see Ezekiel, eyes glued to the TV. She turned to them in an aggressive whisper, "Are you guys crazy! Why are you talking about this without consulting me? He's nosey with ears of an elephant when he hears his name when the door is shut! What did you say before I walked in?"

"At school, today he had an incident with his volcano," Nan said.

"Did he not put enough baking soda in it like I told him to?" Anne said loudly still peeking through the den door. In a whisper, "What happened?"

"He only caused an isolated earthquake that was on the news. 3.7 they said. Not too bad for not trying," Mark boasted. He was proud of the natural skills of the family craft Ezekiel was starting to show.

"This isn't funny! Someone could have got hurt!" Anne protested.

"More the reason we tell him now. How many more times do we have to use Memory Meddling on the people around here."

Anne sat at the table. She stared at her uncle with a thousand thoughts on how telling Ezekiel the truth would come out.

"What did you two discuss before I walked in?"

"Nothing much. Nothing specific. Just after today's incident, in addition to the others he's experienced it may be time to let the kid know," said Mark.

"I'm not ready to talk about it. It's going to lead to talking about his dad," Anne protested.

"Doesn't he ask about him? I'm sure when he sees fathers at his baseball games he is bound to wonder about his while he's sitting there on the bench," Mark was confident this was something that needed to be shared with Ezekiel. "I mean, look how much he loves wearing that goofy red bow tie. He loves it because he knows it's *his*."

Nan's face looked as it agreed, but was sympathetic to Anne.

"It's April now. Let's have a great birthday party for him, let the school year end and then we tell him," offered Nan.

"Then?"

"Yes, then."

Anne nodded.

Chapter Three
The Best Birthday Ever

May 8th came fast. Anne had a wonderful party planned for Ezekiel at the local pizza spot, Ray's Intergalactic Play Place. Ezekiel enjoyed coming here for friend's parties although he wasn't very good at accumulating all the tickets necessary to purchase any prizes that he wanted. He always had his eye on the Super Blaster 5000, a high-powered water rifle that came with a backpack to fill with more water. He beamed at it every time fantasizing about squirting his cousin as she did her yoga poses in the yard. He always thought yoga was weird.

"Good morning sunshine! Happy Birthday!" Anne said cheerily as she opened Ezekiel's door.

"Thanks mom," he said rubbing his eyes.

"Are you excited for your party tonight?"

"Yeah, sure."

"Really?"

Hearing her uncertainty, he pepped up. "Very excited. What'd you get me?" He said jokingly.

"You'll have to wait for tonight!" she said walking out the door.

"Hey dork. Happy Birthday, "said Jackie as she passed his room on her way to the bathroom.

He wanted that Super Blaster 5000 all of a sudden.

Ezekiel rolled out of bed, threw his clothes on and ran into the kitchen.

"Where's Uncle Mark?" he asked.

"Ah, he says, 'Happy Birthday' but he had to run off to work at 5 am. He's working on some exotic plants for a client that don't do well when it's bright out, waffles?" asked Anne.

"Yes please. Thanks."

Jackie plopped onto the chair next to him, earbuds in tuning everyone out.

"Did you tell Ezie 'happy birthday'?" Anne asked her.

Jackie was far too focused on her plate of scrambled eggs, ensuring a perfect egg to bacon ratio.

"Ahem" Anne stammered, pulling a plug out of Jackie's ear.

"Huh?"

"Ezie. Birthday?"

"Oh, yeah, yeah. Did already," as she shoved eggs into her mouth, grinning devilishly at Ezekiel.

Ezekiel raised his eyebrow and gave her a side-eyed glance and shook his head as he poured more juice into his cup.

The school day seemed to take forever. He wasn't very excited to have the teacher bring attention to his birthday. When it was your birthday, Ms. Flagrin made you a paper crown with the words *Happy Birthday* across it while the entire class sang to you while you just stood there waiting for them to finish.

The lunch bell rang, liberating Ezekiel from his crown as he used the excuse to politely tell Ms. Flagrin he didn't want to ruin it during recess. She smiled happily at the thought a student could be that thoughtful.

Joey and Mike were waiting at the benches for him. "Hey. No crown?" jested Joey.

"Happy Birthday man!" Mike said enthusiastically.

"Thanks guys. No crown for me. Just waiting for the day to end. Ten was filled with fun enough. Just can't wait for what's ahead for eleven," Ezekiel said sarcastically.

"Are you still crying over the volcano thing? No one is even talking about it anymore," Mike said.

"Yeah! Everyone has been talking about the coincidence of the lunch lady's dog going missing all the while this, has appeared for three days on the menu," Joey said while slopping a spoonful of what appeared to be watery, sloppy joe.

"Ew." They groaned.

"Dude, brought my lunch", Ezekiel said grinning as he held up his brown paper bag. He glanced and noticed that his bag had hand-drawn balloons, smiley faces and the words,

"HAPPY BIRTHDAY EZEKIEL!

I LOVE YOU! MOM"

"Nice lunch bag," joked Joey.

The rest of the school day seemed to go on faster with less focus on

Ezekiel's birthday. Before he knew it, he was riding the bus home chatting up Mike about which games they were going to put their energy into that night.

"I'm going straight to skee-ball. I'm feeling lucky!" Mike said.

"I'll give it a go at the Whack-A-Mole. I'm feeling a bit stronger today being eleven now and all," Ezekiel cheered.

"I can never get those little suckers. They're much too quick."

"You're much too slow dude."

They both laughed.

The bus pulled up to the curb on 113 Bernard Street and Ezekiel climbed out waving bye to his friend. "See you tonight!"

He walked up the cracked driveway up to the old beige house. He could see his Nan through the brown shutter windows watching her stories. He stood and watched her for a moment shaded by the giant magnolia tree that stood in the yard as though guarding the house. He loved watching her laugh. Her eyes would get very small and her mouth would widen open exposing her toothless gums.

He opened the gate, creaky as it was it alerted Nan that he was home.

"Ezie!"

Ezekiel walked through the wiry screened-door. "Hi."

"Happy Birthday again! How was school?"

"Fine."

"That's it? Fine?" Nan asked in her concerned grandma way.

"He's probably still mopey cause Ms. Flagrin made him wear that paper crown while the class sang. You know how much he loves to be the center of attention", Jackie said with a chuckle in her voice.

"Well I think a paper crown is very nice. What a nice teacher you have."

"It's embarrassing Nan."

"Well I don't think it is."

"I'm just trying to lay low after, well, you *know*, the science fair." The thought of what happened brought heat to his cheeks and still made him feel humiliated. It wasn't every day you became your school's Public Enemy Number One.

Nan's cheeks glowed rosy. "Yes, well I suppose *that* was embarrassing." She looked like she wanted to avoid further discussion of it.

The awkward moment passed as Mark walked in holding a strange, tangled plant that was so large and viney it only revealed his feet.

"Look what I have! It's a Spindelous Petrium!"

"Yes, I see. Why is it in the house? Kids just got in," Nan said sternly. Mark shuffled himself and the Spindelous Petrium out leaving a trail of what looked like blue mud on the linoleum floor.

"Meh! My floor! Just mopped!"

Ezekiel ran to his room to get ready for his party. He was amped with excitement as he dug ferociously in the pile of clothes on the floor looking for his bow-tie. He realized that wearing a bow-tie to a casual fun place like Ray's Intergalactic Play Place was silly but that was all the more reason to do it. He wore the red silk bow for his class picture, at Christmas, Valentine's Day, at the science fair and now today. His friends always got a kick out of it but he loved it because it made him feel grown up. Like something a man with important, special plans would wear. An important man like he imagined his dad was. Although he never met his dad, his mom told him that he left to fight in war, making him unable to send letters or come home. When he would ask his mom about him she would look very pained and sad so he stopped asking her. The last time they chatted about it floated in his mind. He had just turned ten.

"Mom, have you heard anything from my dad?"

"Ezie. You know I haven't. We shouldn't even talk about him. I've told you why."

"No one is listening. Uncle Mark is paranoid."

Anne shot him a pressed look. "He isn't."

She looked sympathetic yet conflicted. She rose from her chair, reached up opening up one of the cabinets. She fumbled around shifting cans of soup and pasta noodles pulling out a blue tin of Danish cookies. She grinned but had a sadness in her eyes.

"Here, open it," she said holding out the tin.

Ezekiel took the tin. He was a bit confused as to why his mom would feel these cookies would appease his questions. He didn't like them but wanted to spare her feelings.

"Can I have some milk?" he asked faking a forced, hopeful smile.

"You won't need it," she said as she sat back down. She placed her pointer finger on her mouth pursing her lips motioning for him to be silent.

Ezekiel pulled the tin close to him to pry the lid off quickly realizing that there were no cookies inside. Nan regularly liked to reuse boxes, jars and tins she felt fond of to hold trinkets, sewing supplies and photos. They were hidden all over the house. Nothing was worse than finding a See's Candy box filled with excitement for caramels to find Nan's button collection.

The tin looked like the memory box of a teenage girl. Origami folded notes with the 'I's' dotted with hearts, faded ticket stubs, a dried corsage, pins and an assortment of photos. What caught his eye was a bold, red bow-tie. He picked it up to further examine it.

Anne smiled. "That was his. See." She pulled a photo from the tin. There stood two fresh-faced smiling teenagers. Anne had not changed much. She had on a long-sleeved powered blue dress that cascaded to the floor. The intricate pattern of rhinestones seemed to sparkle as though the light was hitting her now. Her long hair flowed sitting perfectly on her shoulders. An interesting shaped tiara sat up on her hair. It seemed to glow rather than sparkle like the ones he had seen prom queens wear. The boy in the photo had a caramel colored face with a large white smile just as Ezekiel had. Handsomely confident he embraced his mother holding her hand carefully to balance her wrist that featured a perfect red rose surrounded by fluffy white silk ribbons. The red rose was so vibrant yet soft looking complimenting his red bow-tie. Both had costume wings on. Anne's were soft and elegant with an iridescent glow. Her partners were rugged and red. Ezekiel thought they were kind of cool and reminded him of something a mutant in his comics would have.

"This is him?" Ezekiel asked, heart pounding with excitement.

Anne nodded.

"Sweet wings mom," Ezekiel said with a nervous giggle. "Costume dance?"

"Err, yes – a costume dance."

"And my dad - um, he wore them for you? Wow. He must have been whipped," Ezekiel joked.

Anne raised an eyebrow with a giant smile full of relief. "Yes, I suppose he was."

"You look pretty though. Dorky, but very pretty."

"Thanks sweetie. I need to go give Nan a ride to pick up your cake."

"Can't you tell me his name at least?"

"You know I can't. We've been through this before. Anyone that may be looking for him because of what he's done may come for us. We always agreed that the less you knew, the less *I knew* the better. As you get older, you will understand."

Ezekiel hated that. It made him feel like he was a baby. He knew he wasn't going to convince her but this was the most he'd ever gotten out of her. He had his picture, could study his face and hold something that was his.

"Okay mom. Thanks for this," he said raising the tin with a grin.

Anne grinned as she grabbed her purse and keys, walking out the screen door. Ezekiel kept his eyes on the door until he heard the car pull away.

He pulled out other photos. Mom smiling victoriously holding what looked like a basketball in one hand, something white crumpled up in the other dressed in an athletic blue bathing suit emblazoned with an un-deciphering crest. A small gold number 7 on the corner of her chest. Behind her in the distance he could see hand-painted banners.

#7 ROCKS!

GO Granters! Put those Flames OUT!

Ezekiel didn't realize his mom played water polo.

"Geez, mom is even better than me in sports," he thought.

He rummaged through pins which he assumed where related to her athletic success. The largest was a giant blue button with bold gold letters that read, "Granters Padsphere." It had the same crest that was on his mom's uniform.

He wanted to explore the intricately folded notes but feared for ripping them. He knew he wouldn't be able to fold it back into a heart, crane or what looked like a frog about to hop so he placed those back in the tin. He held onto the red bow-tie.

"This could work for tonight," he thought holding the bow-tie up to his neck smiling to himself. It was the best gift he had ever received.

Through the next year until now, Ezekiel didn't have the urge to press his mom about his dad. He thought if he wore the bow-tie to his party it might trigger a feeling of nostalgia in her to bring it up to him.

After giving quite the effort to find it in the pile of clean laundry on the floor in his room, he realized that he gave it to Nan to clean after the science fair debacle.

"Nan! Do you know where my bow-tie is?" shouted Ezekiel from his room.

"It's hang drying in the garage sweetie!"

"Thanks Nan!" he shouted back as he shuffled himself off the floor dashing out the back door to the garage. He opened the side door revealing the pitch dark stuffy room. It smelled like a wet dog was inside – a smell familiar to him because he has helped Joey hold down Roofus, Joey's brown spotted mutt during his bath during the summer. He had always wanted a dog but Nan was worried it would make Mr. Rogers and Darth Meowler – her rescue cats upset. Ezekiel enjoyed the friendliness of the grey tabby and the playfulness of the black kitten.

He patted the wall looking for the light switch flipping it on. He swore he heard something shuffle but as the lights turned on he simply saw what he had expected to. The empty oil-stained garage floor, his uncle's garden tools and the weird plant Mark carried into the kitchen earlier. It was ginormous, as tall as Ezekiel with coils of bluish-green leaves with magenta colored veins. It had presence sitting there giving Ezekiel the feeling it was looking at him.

Ezekiel approached the clothesline Nan had fixed over the washing machine. There was his silk bow-tie gleaming clean. He pulled it from the line, turned toward a dusty gold-rimmed mirror that was leaning against the wall on the floor. He slid the bow-tie around this neck, tightened it and adjusted it straight. In the reflection of the mirror he caught movement behind him. Whipping around fast all was still. He scanned around him looking for one of Nan's cats. Nothing. He turned back to the mirror to fix his collar. He looked at his face studying the lines of his jaw, smiling as he could see the similarities of his father's face coming in. They had the same mouth, large brown eyes and skin color. The boy he saw in the photo had much better hair. Ezekiel tossed his hair with his hand to the left. He assessed. "Nope, that wasn't it," he thought. Using both hands he started fluffing it in the front in a mohawk like motion. That was it.

Pant, pant, pant, pant.

There was no mistaking the sound of a dog. He whipped around and there sat the Spindelous Petrium at his feet, twisted and formed as though begging on its hind legs. Its front vines formed what he swore were paws, scampering for his attention as it tilted what looked like its' face.

Ezekiel leaned in. It looked friendly but he'd never seen such a thing. His uncle regularly brought strange plants home but nothing that was so lifelike. He patted the top, which seemed to please the plant into submission. It laid at his feet.

"Well, crazier things have happened," he thought to himself. He scoot away from the paw leaves to be careful of not stepping on it. It raised then lowered its' head sadly as it watched him walk out the door.

Chapter Four
The Worst Birthday Ever

Ray's Intergalactic Play Place was booming with the sounds of kids laughing, bells of high-scores being achieved on the latest video games and the *chick-chick* sound of tickets ejecting victory to its' winners. Ray's Space Raptor – a costumed teenager who preferred being the mascot to ringing at the register, walked around taking pictures with glee. Pizza was in the air. A focused man stood in the open kitchen tossing dough so fiercely it looked as though flying saucers spun around him.

Anne and Nan were there finishing placing balloons around the tables as Ezekiel and Mark walked in.

"Guests should be getting here anytime now," Anne said. "Just so you know, I invited everyone on your baseball team."

"Everyone?" Ezekiel asked with a groan.

"I'm sorry honey but we couldn't invite everyone and not *him*."

"Great."

The impending arrival of Bradley made his stomach turn. He was pretty sure he tasted the burrito he had a lunch earlier. He kept his spirits up by realizing that Ray's Intergalactic Play Place was big and he had a great chance of avoiding him once the place got more of a crowd.

Within a few minutes party guests arrived and his party was in full swing. Anne handed out small blue velvet bags filled with tokens to all of the children. Once handed out they raced to the arcade. "Be back in twenty for food and cake kids!" she shouted after them.

Ezekiel, Joey and Mike gravitated to their choice games that they felt would produce the most tickets for them. They already agreed that they would combine their efforts to get the Super Blaster 5000 and would simply share it. A detailed custody schedule was previously discussed.

"Every three days, we pass it to the next guy, okay?" reiterated Ezekiel. "In extreme dire cases, of sibling warfare or bully attacks, said partner under affliction may call for the immediate need of the blaster." He wanted to ensure he had the terms clear so he could blast Jackie when the need arose. "Agreed," they said in unison and they went for their choice games.

Ezekiel went for the Whack-A-Mole but there were players on it so he went to the skee ball. He pulled out his little, blue bag of tokens and pulled a shiny gold token out. He popped it into the game slot and out slid 8 wooden round chances for him to get more tickets. He held up the first ball, steadily aiming to the topmost hole that was worth 1000 points. He wound up and rolled the ball up.

Please go in. Go in!

The ball jumped right in flawlessly. A red light above the game swirled sounding off a cheerful alarm. Several tickets shot out of the game creating a long chain next to his feet. He took another ball up.

Yes! Follow your buddy in!

It hopped right in, as did the next and the next. A massive pile of tickets continued to shoot out of the machine. A small crowd of kids surrounded him, astounded by his success.

"You sure he wasn't climbing on the game to toss the ball in there?" asked a skeptical boy.

"No! I saw him throw it up there! Ten times in a row it went in!" shouted a pig-tailed girl.

"Time for food and cake!" yelled Anne, waving her arms to motion for the kids to come back to the table.

"Sorry all! I gotta go!" Ezekiel was ecstatic. He collected his ticket winnings which were by far too much to simply carry. He had to twirl them around his neck as though they were a giant scarf. When he approached the table his friends were in awe.

"Whoa! What did you play?" inquired Joey.

"Hmphyeah?" asked Mike with an entire slice of pizza stuffed in his mouth.

"I just was giving it a go at skee ball. Got lucky I guess," Ezekiel said with a giant smile as he too shoved pizza into his mouth.

He had been enjoying himself as he just realized that Bradley was a table over. Bradley caught Ezekiel's glance.

"Oh crap, he saw me make eye contact with him," Ezekiel said.

"Dude I'm pretty sure he knows you're here. It is *your* party," Mike said.

"Just don't look over there. Maybe he'll stay away."

"Happy birthday loser," Bradley said as he hovered behind Ezekiel and Mike.

"Great, thanks," Ezekiel said avoiding further eye contact with him.

"Nice tickets. Did your mommy help you wimps get those? I know you couldn't have managed those on your own since you can't throw a ball to save your life."

As if on cue Anne approached with a tray filled with goody bags. "Are you boys having fun? Here's a bag for each of you!" she said as she handed each boy a small bag covered with tiny green aliens and filled with candy.

"Thanks, *so* much Ms. Raroso," said Bradley with a sugar sweet tone that made Ezekiel want to barf. "I appreciate this so much."

"You're so welcome sweetie!" Anne replied as she continued to walk down the table to each child.

"Sweet alien bags. Didn't know you'd want to feature your kind as your birthday party theme. With luck, they'll phone you home and beam you back to the mothership so we don't get stuck with you wasting space on a perfectly good bench during our next game." Bradley was pushing all of Ezekiel's buttons to have a response. He was saved by Anne approaching again and calling for everyone's attention. She waved the Ray's Play Place employees over. She positioned one directly across from Ezekiel with a camera to snap pictures. Ray the Raptor stood next to him waving his little clawed arms back and forth. The rest of the staff surrounded as one blew a whistle and shouted:

"Hey Ray's Play Place! We have a very special birthday today! Today is Ezie's eleventh birthday and we want to make sure that we sing so loud that aliens on Mars hear us!"

Bradley chuckled. Ezekiel began to feel heat fill his face. He grit his teeth to hold back from saying something that would get him punched in the face. It was his birthday, but that wouldn't stop Bradley from seizing the opportunity to get a lick in.

"So, on the count of three, let's sing as loud as we can to Ezie!" she motioned for Ezekiel to stand up. Now standing he smiled but was starting to feel that moist, sweaty feeling he had at the science fair.

"1...2..3! Happy birthday to you!"

Ezekiel tried his hardest to hold his smile for the camera holding employee. He wiped his brow and looked down at his white frosting cake. Green frosting that was starting to smear from the heat of eleven burning candles read *Happy 11th Birthday Ezie.* Watching the flames flicker and seeing the amount of warm light they produced to the surface of the cake took him away from the moment of embarrassment and taste of burrito that was still lingering.

Eleven candles. That's a lot of fire there. So, hot...

"Honey are you going to blow them out?" Anne tapped him on the shoulder with an encouraging smile.

"He's taking his time to make his wish!" shouted Mark.

Ezekiel pulled air into his chest, holding it for just a moment as he caught the eye of the Super Blaster 5000 on the prize wall. He closed his eyes and blew hard, eyes focused on getting each candle. As his wind hit the flame it bunched up the fire and stretched cascading over the camera boy causing him to jump to the side, knocking into Ray the Space Raptor. Flames instantly erupted on the dino's face, chest and tips of his claws. Shocked he spun around hitting Bradley with his tail knocking him over. The other children screamed and jumped up out of their seats, subsequently knocking each other over with a domino effect. Mark ran over with a pitcher of soda pouring it onto Ray. The commotion caused Ray to fall over unable to get up. The poor Space Raptor rocked back and forth making a motion with his tiny hands that reminded Ezekiel of a swimming dog.

Ezekiel stood there for a moment. The candles were out in one shot. He looked up at Anne's shocked face. It made him flee.

He didn't look back. He ran straight into the arcade hiding himself between the basketball hoops and Whack-A-Mole. This was a moment being a bit smaller came as useful. He couldn't explain what happened. His lifetime of strangeness started to come back to him.

There was the time when his class went to the zoo and they were observing the monkey exhibit. Hoping to get a closer look he walked up next to the rail of their enclosure. Two mandrills instantly ran over seeming to observe *him*. At first their red blue faces terrified him. They seemed to smile and call to the others. A few more joined them. He tried to back away as this startled him but before he knew it, they pulled him into their enclosure, sat him in the center of a soft spot of grass while another brought him bananas and groomed him by licking his hair. It was gross and Ezekiel reeked of bananas for a month.

Then there was the time that they went camping at Great Falls for a week. During the first day, he enjoyed frolicking with Jackie in the water but at night the crashing water was so loud it made it hard to sleep. The next morning when they went out to the waterfall it was gone. He remembered laughing to himself thinking, "Good. Now I'll be able to sleep!"

Ezekiel always wrote these strange happenings as coincidence. Bad luck even. Today he had enough. He was ready for summer to come so he could escape seeing the kids he went to school with. There was also relief knowing that next year he wouldn't have to return back to Winfrey. He'd be off to a middle school of his choice. He was definitely going to choose somewhere he didn't have to see Bradley Butt Face again.

He slowly climbed up to peek out the scene he fled. From what he could see everything looked normal. *Normal?*

His party guests were sitting happily eating cake. Some were already cashing in their tickets at the prize counter. Anne, Mark and Nan were chatting and smiling with the parents who arrived a bit early for pick up.

Maybe what happened just played out worse in his mind? He peeked again. Ray the Space Raptor was posing for photos with the camera boy he was sure would have needed a visit to the emergency room. He calmed himself down as he assured himself that he must have exaggerated it. Imagined it even.

He stood up pulling himself right in front of the Whack-A-Mole. He was tempted to give it a try. He pulled out a coin and popped it in. A pleasant musical tune filled the room. The tiny, purple moles started to pump up and down. Their menacing smiles seemed to mock him. Ezekiel seized the padded mallet and swung as hard and fast as he could. The frustration he felt powered each swing. Harder and harder he hit each flash of purple that popped up. He found a rhythm. He didn't miss a single one. He visualized himself with all the tickets he needed to get the Super Blaster 5000. He saw himself holding it, jetpack filled with gallons of water as he held a fierce steady shot at Bradley's face.

The game was over. The scoreboard on the game was flipping numbers so fast they were ineligible. His chest felt excited as he saw the points climb and climb. More points meant more tickets. Joey and Mike caught notice and ran over to his side.

"Where've you been? It's like you just ran off after you blew out your candles," said Joey.

"Yeah, your mom said it was time for gift opening and then you were gone," said Mike.

"Wow look at all those tickets!"

Shooting out as fast as the machine could handle, tickets flew out.

Chick-chick-chick-chick-chick...

"Whoa!"

Tickets were everywhere. They rapidly piled up around the game, faster and faster filling the arcade room pushing the boys out. They walked back, eyes on the arcade as the tickets continued to grow into a mass with hanging tentacles trying to escape the room.

Chick-chick-chick-chick-chick...

The ticket mass spilled into the dining room. Parents looked on with horror, scrambling after their children to pull them off the mechanical horses and out of the ball pit.

Chick-chick-chick-chick-chick...

Ezekiel saw his mom looking panicked. She ran to him grabbing him and shoving his friends toward the exit door.

"What about his presents?" Mark asked. "Plus, I just got a refill on my drink and I left it on the table."

Anne shot him a look. He made his way to the door with the boys.

Chick-chick-chick-chick-chick...

The ticket mass had taken over and the entire restaurant of cooks, staff, Ray the Space Raptor and all guests stood at in the parking lot as the tickets started to push out the windows and front door.

Chick-chick-chick-chick-chick...

Ezekiel didn't want to look at anyone. There was no way he could convince himself that he wasn't a big weirdo with the worst luck. Strange things just kept happening to him. His friends sensed it in him trying to assure him that the machine was on the fritz.

"That thing had to be busted dude."

"Yeah. They still owe you the tickets in my opinion. I'd wait here until they count them for you."

He felt a tinge better, then Bradley walked up to him, face to face. Looking around to ensure no adult was paying attention he turned to Ezekiel with a fake smile.

"You really are a freak," looking at Joey and Mike, "You both can do so much better."

Joey and Mike exchanged a glance then stood firm with their friend.

Chapter Five
Disappearing Act

The next few weeks passed quickly. Ezekiel was able to lay low. He avoided situations with large groups of people and especially avoided the bathroom just in case of a Bradley run in. Ezekiel's hair was just starting to not smell of lemon freshness. Today he arrived at school just in time to get in his seat by the ring of the bell. He timed his pre-lunch escape by watching the clock carefully for the time to approach 12:29 PM. He made sure his cheesy math worksheet was complete before then. Ms. Flagrin tried to make learning about angles, perpendicular lines and vertexes fun by having them draw lines on pictures. He rushed through today's assignment of *Draw a right angle on the mountain in the picture below*, so he could create a diversion which varied day by day – he'd drop his pencil, break his pencil, forget his eraser, need to wash his hands, blow his nose and many other clever excuses to be near the door so when the bell would ring, he would race out to the cafeterium. He made the line usually trying to blend in with the crowds of straggling third graders who were still hanging out. He'd grab his lunch and hide within the winter play props that were behind the curtains of the small stage of the cafeterium. He'd found himself a small wooden stool to sit on as he was surrounded by giant snowflakes, ice skating penguins and a smiling snowman who made him feel as though he wasn't sitting alone.

He felt bad that he was ditching his friends. He was still embarrassed about how his birthday party turned out and was starting to believe they were better off without him. His family never mentioned the incident and a few days after the party, the Super Blaster 5000 was sitting on his bed with a red bow.

His friends were both in the other fifth-grade class so it was easy to avoid them during the day. After school was a bit trickier. He usually rode the bus home but took to walking the seven blocks home taking the back gate exit to avoid being seen.

"Getting in a bit later now?" asked Mark.

"Uh, yeah. Bus is taking a different route," Ezekiel said making a dash down the hallway to his room.

"Wait!"

Ezekiel pumped his breaks just steps from his door. "Uh, yeah?"

Whispers could be heard from the kitchen he was hoping to avoid.

"Babe, can you come here?" Anne asked.

Ezekiel threw his head back and stared at the ceiling exhaling at his defeat to escape. "Coming." At the pace of a turtle he flung his backpack to the kitchen floor.

"Hi."

"How was your day?" Anne asked.

"Uneventful so it was pretty good."

"I know you've been bummed out lately, but I thought I'd tell you something that may cheer you up!"

Ezekiel sat down trying to hide his skeptical face.

"Well, you are eleven now and on the way to middle school."

"Yeah."

"It may be good for you to go have some fun this summer. Spend some time outdoors."

Ugh. It was coming. She's going to make me go to some nerdy camp where I'll spend my days whittling soap, eating slop and trying to not get eaten alive by mosquitos, bears or lions, he thought.

She could see the apprehension in his face but maintained her positivity. "So, we signed you up for summer camp."

"Which camp? Most kids I know go to Camp Half Moon at Big Bear Lake." He paused. "Not that I want to go where everyone I go to school with goes," he said dropping his glance to the floor.

Anne smiled. "It's a great camp and a good place to be social and make friends."

Ezekiel paused. She said "make friends" as though he didn't have any. "Are you trying to send me to some socially challenged camp for social lepers?"

"Both me and your uncle went there as kids. We had a blast."

"It's that old?" Ezekiel had to hold in his giggle.

"Ha, ha funny guy. I'm serious. I spent every summer there, made a ton of friends, memories and it's where I met your dad."

Ezekiel automatically perked up. It had been over a year his mom mentioned his dad.

"Remember that photo in the tin of me? The one in the blue bathing suit?" He nodded. "That's at camp."

"And the one of you in the fancy dress and dorky wings?"

Anne laughed. "Yes. That one too. That photo was taken at the Summer Solstice Bash my last year of camp." There was that smile he had seen with eyes that could not hide the sadness of her memories.

"Thanks mom. I'm sure Camp Loser is great."

Anne hugged him, then kissed his forehead. She held onto him. "You are not a loser."

"Uh mom. I'm not leaving right, now am I?"

"No silly. Of course not! I'm just thinking of how fast you've grown up. You'll be going on your own all summer – having your own adventure. Maybe even meeting a *girlfriend*?" She released him.

"Mom! No way!" Ezekiel's cheeks flushed warm. There was just something gross about his mom talking about him having a girlfriend. He was still operating under the impression that girls had cooties. He wasn't sure what a cootie was, but based on how kids wanted to avoid catching them, he was pretty sure it was best to stay away from the risk.

"You never know!" she chuckled. "I did."

"When do I go to Camp Weirdo?" he asked enthusiastically trying to change the subject.

"The day after your promotion day and don't call it that."

"Wow. That's quick. Waited no time to get rid of me this summer? Off to Camp Strange you go huh?" he joked.

"I already can't wait for you to come back."

She hugged him again.

"One more thing. Did you want to buy something special to wear tomorrow for promotion day?"

"No, I'm good. My suit still fits." He would have liked something new but really didn't want to put in the shopping time. Plus, the thought of running into anyone he knew at the mall was as pleasant to him as brussel sprouts.

The morning of promotion day was a sunny, blue-skied one. Ezekiel had a feeling of dread and excitement for this day. Although he had to see everyone in fifth grade out on the field, so out in the open when he'd have to walk up there to receive his certificate from Mr. Pullman, he also knew that would be the last time he had to see them look at him like he was a sideshow attraction in a circus.

He rolled out of bed to see his navy suit and white collared shirt pressed sitting on his desk chair. His bright, red bow-tie sitting on his desk gave him a bit of a boost knowing that he would be dressed similarly to his father the night of the Summer Solstice Bash. He got dressed quickly then stood in front of the mirror taking great care to adjust his tie. His hair seemed to just flop to the side emphasizing his extreme bed head and preference for sleeping on his left side.

"Nothing a bit of sculpting glue can't handle," he thought.

He squeezed the sticky goo into his hand, kneaded it a bit to soften it, then combed it into his hair, fluffing it up in the front, then the back. Now looking like his dad, he was happy. He washed his hands, dashed to toward the kitchen drying his hands on his pant legs. A bad habit he's always had.

"Oh no!" he said as he caught a glance of himself in the hall mirror. Two long, dripping water dribbles appeared on his pants.

"Oh, you'll be fine," Jackie said. "Those are water repelling to avoid stains. Nan picked those 'cause she knows you don't believe in using a towel."

Ezekiel ignored her as he grabbed a breakfast pastry from the cabinet. Anne walked in wearing a pale, pink dress Ezekiel loved. He thought it made her look like a princess.

"Good morning Mr. Graduate!"

"Hello Princess Mom!"

Jackie rolled her eyes. "There is so much cheesiness in this room, someone get me some crackers," she said as she hid beneath her latest tween, girlie magazine.

"Are you ready to go?" Anne asked.

"As ready as I can be," Ezekiel replied.

•   •   •   •   •

The parking lot at school was packed. Rows and rows of cars flooded the lot and playground. After parking, what seemed to be a million miles away Anne and Ezekiel made it to his school ground field. The lush green grass was freshly cut creating an earthy aroma in the air. Several rows of chairs were set leaving an aisle down the middle toward a five-level set of bleachers. In promotion rehearsal, you had to walk down the middle of the aisle toward the bleachers, approach Mr. Pullman (not get distracted by his crooked toupee), shake his hand, receive your Promotion Certificate, then take a spot standing on the bleachers, smiling to pose for photos.

"It couldn't be over fast enough," he thought.

Ms. Flagrin called the children over to organize them by alphabetical order. Parents took their seats. He tried not to make eye contact with anyone and could tell that Alan Rachoor and Mia Rodgers weren't too thrilled to be stuck next to him. Sitting next to them he could sense that they were on the opposite edge of their seats to avoid being as near to him as possible. Mia leaned over to whisper in the ear of Zoey. Ezekiel only heard "strange" and "weird" when deciding to avoid looking at them, he looked outward where he found Nan and Mark waving at him. Anne was adjusting her camera lens ensuring she had the perfect shot. He gave them a little wave. As he lowered his hand he realized he caught the attention of both Mike and Bradley simultaneously from across the way. Mike smiled and waved at him motioning his hand like a phone holding it up to his ear mouthing "call me" then placing his hands together as though begging mouthing "Please."

Before he could feel horrible he realized Bradley was mocking him. He had stolen the pink bow off of Penelope's head and he was holding it up to his neck shouting, "Who am I, guess! Watch out! I'm coming! Something bad is going to happen because I'm a loser!" Several kids were laughing. Mr. Lee wasn't paying attention to his class as he was assisting parents to their seats. Ezekiel's face fell and he just stared forward. For just one second he felt ashamed in his skin and considered taking off the bow-tie before walking up there. He touched the corner slightly pinching it, prepared to pull it down. He paused thinking of his dad and he stopped. The boy in that photo had this tie on, was strong, handsome and confident. He definitely would have kicked Bradley's Butt Face's butt and here he is wearing it. He then felt ashamed he considered removing it.

"Why does it have to be this way?" he thought. He scanned the audience looking at all the moms and dads cheering for their boy or girl. He caught a glimpse of a father holding his toddler boy above his shoulders likely cheering on his older sibling in the audience. The man was beaming with pride. This made Ezekiel wonder if it was he who made his father never come back.

Perhaps his dad saw what was wrong with him and did not want anything to do with him. Maybe his mom lied to him to spare his feelings. The thought of this made him begin to tear.

Stop thinking like this or you're going to start crying.

Thinking about it only made him more upset. He knew he had a lot more than other people had. This made him more ashamed to feel as though he wasn't grateful for the family he had. Giant tears swelled his eyes and dropped down his face. He wiped his eyes with his hands, then on his pants. He felt a cold chill in his hands despite it being a beautiful June day.

Lost in his thoughts he had not realized that the principal had already finished going through the Q's and several promoted fifth graders were standing up there. Tightness in his stomach hit him as he realized that he would have to walk that aisle soon. An overwhelming surge flowed through him making his heart beat a bit faster. The coldness had left him. He rubbed his hands together to make the balmy feeling go away. He could see that iridescence again.

Oh no. Please don't let me be noticed!

"Ezekiel Raroso."

He jumped up, trembling as he began his walk down the aisle. As he passed the row Bradley was in he could hear whispered shouts.

"Dork!"

"Loser!

He felt heat in his face but he still walked forward. Anger swirled in his mind but he still pressed forward, pressing each step harder and harder into the grass. It felt as the grass was building up around his feet at each step like small fingers trying to clasp his shoes. Down his line of sight, he could see green embers develop around the podium, alongside the bleachers and around the chairs and music stands of the band. He stopped in his tracks frozen at the sight.

More and more lush green came up from the ground pushing the bleachers up, then in. Once realizing this, the children who were so proudly posing, presenting their achievements were screaming frantically to get off the top rows. Crashing into one another, falling and disappearing into green. The podium disappeared and the abandoned musical instruments were left behind to be consumed by sprouts of grass. Still standing just steps from his destination, Ezekiel looked out to where he last saw his family sitting. They weren't there and he didn't blame them.

Sullen, he walked back down the aisle, through the field, the black top and out the side gate of the school.

He walked home and cried a hard cry wishing he could disappear from the world.

Chapter Six
The Tragic Tale

Anne, Mark and Nan came home exhausted after assisting with the mess at the school. Memory Meddling was no easy task. It left you feeling starving and extremely thirsty. Mark chugged down a full gallon of chocolate milk lapping up the dribbles in his mustache. Nan started pulling ingredients from the refrigerator to prepare Ezekiel's favorite shortbread cookie drops. A batch of cookies always made the adults feel better after producing such a strong enchantment.

"I'll go check on him," Anne said.

Ezekiel was lying in his bed on his side, staring at the wall still dressed in his suit. He could sense his mom was in the room.

"I don't want to talk."

"Honey I'm sorry things went crazy at school today and you didn't get your chance to get your moment up there. Apparently, the groundskeeper used too much fertilizer and over watered the night before. The sun made the grass have an extreme overgrowth overnight! I meant have you-." Ezekiel cut her off. "You can save it mom. You and I both know it's me. There is something wrong with me. Bradley is right. I'm a freak and a loser. Even the grass didn't want me there. These weird things keep happening to me and you all just act like it isn't happening."

"Bradley called you those things?" Anne quickly pivoted the subject. "Why didn't you tell me? You have to know those things are not true. Kids that act that way are unhappy about themselves and they take it out on others."

There was a pause as Anne was searching for something more to say.

"Never let anyone take you to a dark place where you feel less than who you are and what you're worth."

She walked to the side of his bed where she could see his face. His cheeks beneath his eyes were puffy as though cried out of tears. She stroked his cheek and gave him a kiss on his forehead. He knew if he wasn't receptive to her attempts at making him feel better she would worry.

"Should I pack for Camp Strange?" he asked with a hint of a scowl.

"I've taken care of it for you. Uncle Mark has your suitcase by the door downstairs. I received your camp list and went shopping for all your supplies. They give you a camp uniform when you get there."

"A *uniform*? Well it might as well be called Camp Strange then," he whined.

"It's a cool one. I promise."

"Says the cool lady who wore wings to a dance."

"Anddd he's back!" she joked.

"I'm just saying. We have a different sense of style." He fought a smile back as hard as he could. He wasn't ready to not be upset.

"You may have so much fun there, you'll find yourself in your own wings," she teased.

"Right," he said sarcastically. "I'm stoked for a summer filled of popsicle stick arts and crafts and singing around the campfire."

"There is so much more there than that. I may not have mentioned it, but the village on the outskirts of the camp is wonderful. It happens to be where I was born and grew up. The camp instructors will take you kids out to go shopping on Murlock Road. There is a bakery with the best custard-filled pastries. The shops there make for a super, fun afternoon. Off the road there is a wonderful bazaar."

She continued. "And at camp you sleep in cool barracks on bunk beds! There are fantastic campfires and storytelling after a long day at the lake, riding and shooting."

"Sounds wonderful mom. I'm stoked to go and get away from here."

She shot him a look with a raised eyebrow.

"Not from you guy's mom. From everyone else and maybe Jackie."

"Okay buddy. Are you good?"

"Yes mom. I'll be fine," he said as he removed his bow-tie and started to unbutton his shirt. He reached for his dresser drawer to find his pajamas.

Anne hugged him again. He forced a smile for her.

"Okay honey. I'm going to double check your bag. Don't stay up too late."

She walked out of his room as he climbed back into bed with a book. Mark and Nan were sitting at the kitchen table enjoying freshly baked cookies.

"Can I take him some?" asked Nan.

"Sure. He's up reading a book," Anne replied.

Nan piled a dozen cookies on a small plastic plate, grabbed a cold glass of milk and walked to Ezekiel's room. She happily returned with a smile of satisfaction.

"So, he wanted the cookies then?"

"He sure did. Apparently, I'm the 'best grandma ever' too," Nan said beaming.

"Well the cookies are that good," Anne said.

"So, let's cut to the chase ladies. Today was a close one. I'm glad we were able to work together to fix what happened but what about Ezie? He's over there thinking this is all his fault," Mark said abruptly.

"Well, we know that it is sort of his fault," Anne replied as she looked down as a terrible feeling fell over her.

"He goes to camp tomorrow. They will tell him everything. Teach him everything. You know how kids are. You tell kids something and they think parents are pulling the wool over their eyes. To show them, let them live it freely is how they learn. It's how they grow."

"And what about his dad. Are you afraid he will find out the truth? You're sure the Magnus Magister has taken all the necessary precautions?" Nan asked. She was very concerned.

"I spoke with the Magnus when I registered him a few months ago. He's aware and fully supportive. The Faerman Guard is stronger than ever and still being led by Dux Diego. The Council's new Praeses, Amare Lumiere has been wonderful to work with. The new focus on passport regulation, Color Records and human relations advocacy has greatly improved general welfare and safety," Anne said proudly.

"Yes, well when you took that position in the Praeses office we thought we'd hear more updates on progress regarding Hematite activity. Are they any closer to ending the conflict?" Nan asked. "I hate sending him over there knowing that on top of everything else he is going to learn, he will be fearful of the political climate.

"I work in the Grant Department. It's not part of the Strategy of War Council," Anne said.

"He's a boy Phyllis. I don't think he will be concerned with politics and what the Praeses is doing. He's barely going to wrap his mind around it. Most kids who crossover know they will live here in secrecy. They are trained to manage themselves in their homes as soon as they can walk," Mark said firmly. "Plus, I know them Lumiere's. Good family, but Diego was a bit of a hot head. He's still running the Guard?"

"Yes, well if you remember what happened to his poor family," Nan said.

"What happened?" Anne asked.

"I'm surprised you were never told during one of those Fire Tale sessions. Well, maybe it was too close to when it happened, too fresh for good taste. During the height of conflict with the Hematites, Dux Diego received a tip from his second cousin – I believe his great-aunt's son Uriel, that the Hematites were going to attack Murlock at night. Uriel had overheard some known loyalists having a conversation over some drinks at the Gargoyle. The Dux sent his men secretly into town during the day to warn the families to evacuate or go into hiding. Aaron Lumiere, Diego's cousin was working late at the Council Hall and was not informed that this evacuation was going to take place. Neither did his wife or two-year-old son who happened to come across for the day. When Aaron entered town, he saw that it was surrounded by the Guard. They would not let him enter. He protested and insisted that his family was still inside their home. He demanded to speak to his cousin. Unable to pull Diego from his post, the Hematite arrived as he was told. He deployed his men from hiding around dark corners of the homes and they went into battle. I can still remember the screams and begging of Aaron that night."

Mark closed his eyes rubbing his brow.

Please! They're all I have. Let me go in to get them!

"After what seemed like eternity a few loyalists were caught and jailed. Diego was most upset he did not catch the Malum Coacter."

"Isn't that just a story? About the Malum they tell at Fire Tales?" asked Anne.

"I'm afraid not," said Nan. "Each generation of Hematite have a new Malum Coacter to lead their cause. They've grown weaker and are less active obviously but I'm sure there is one out there. Your dad always kept up with the news."

"Yes, Ladir kept me most informed. He had many friends in the Guard who filled him in. Anyway, after allowed, Aaron runs to where his home is. Many of us who grew up going to camp with him followed. We found rubble, crushed walls and roof. We tried to pull and dig to show him they weren't there. Aaron was insistent that they were as he was frantically pulling up debris. Then we all saw it. There was a tiny stuffed troll doll still being clutched by a tiny, little hand."

"How terrible!" Anne began to tear.

"A few years later Hematite activity slowed down. The Dux settled down, married and had two children, Susel and Spero. On the day of Spero's second birthday, the Dux was likely off strategizing with the Guard on a mission and his wife was at home with the children preparing for a party. When he returned for the party he found his wife Hope and Susel bound and tied. His son was taken. The Guard searched everywhere, even crossed over, put out a child abduction with the local police. He was never found."

Anne was in full tears sobbing into a cloth napkin. "I see him almost daily in passing and had no idea he even married, let alone had children."

"After the disappearance of Spero, Hope was never the same and just seemed to disappear as well. It's all gossip what happened to her. I did hear that Susel ran off to Bulgaria to study abroad and married never returning. Diego has been alone most of his life. Many have said they believed that Diego had it coming because of what happened to Aaron's son and that it could have been prevented had Diego simply listened. Many also believed it was orchestrated by the Malum as revenge for his loyalists who were captured that night they attacked Murlock."

Ezekiel was lying on his floor, ear pressed as close to the gap of the door to the floor.

What truth?

Chapter Seven
Off to Camp

Ezekiel stood in the dark. All around him were tall pines that let out powerful scent. The only thing illuminating his path was the haze of a cloud covered moon. He looked all around for him. He knew he was there. The air was cold making his steps feel as though they were being pushed back as his knees stiffened. After long, the trees around him began to lessen in number and he stumbled upon a pasture with houses on the horizon. The moist haze of fog surrounded him making his path disappear. The uncertainty of where he was made him feel the need to run toward the town. He found himself surrounded by roads of cottages that were silent and still. He felt alone but knew he had to continue on. *He* was there.

He found himself in front of a small yellow house. The only house to have a light on.

This must be it.

He opened the white, wooden gate that surrounded several bushes of white roses. He walked up to the door to discover it already cracked open. He pushed it open and entered the house. The inside of the home seemed to stretch larger than it appeared outside. In the far corner of the room Ezekiel could see a tall figure in black. The light in the room did not stretch to the figure and the shadows cover his face.

Dad? Dad is that you? Dad!

The figure turned away from him.

Ezekiel charged forward. His shadow emerging ahead. His shadow reached the figure and the darkness combined.

He spun around. He reached into his shadow. Nothing.

Dad!

He ran back out the door into the darkness and plummeted, down deep crashing to the ground.

Ezekiel awoke empty to the sound of his alarm. He was sweaty and his legs ached as though he had just got out of his PE class running laps. He looked out his window and glanced at the clock. 5:48 AM. It was still dark out with the slight radiance of the morning sun begin to make its' peak.

He groaned but knew he had to get up. He sat up and rubbed his head. He caught a glimpse of himself in the mirror. His hair was sticking straight up in the front just like he liked it. He pulled the covers off, changed fast and headed for the kitchen. He could already smell bacon and coffee.

"Good morning camper!" Mark was used to waking up early. He was usually at work at this time had it not been a Saturday.

"Morning," Ezekiel yawned.

"Eggs?" Anne asked even though she was already plopping them onto his plate. She looked nervous.

"Yes please.

Everyone ate in silence still overtaken – Ezekiel by sleepiness from staying up too late pondering over what truth he had not known about his dad, Nan and Anne were worried about him being all on his own even though they knew how necessary it was for him to go.

"Ready?" Anne asked with a heavy sigh. They all jumped into her car to head to the park.

"The camp buses depart from McMasters Park at 8AM. The ride to the campgrounds can be a bit, um, bumpy as they wind the hilltop roads so don't get scared."

"Mom I'll be fine. We've been out to the lake before. All those twists and turns to get to Lake Arrowhead remember?"

"Yes, well this is a bit bumpier."

"I'm sure he'll be *fine*," Mark pushed.

During the drive, Ezekiel reflected the details of his dream. It felt so real to him. The cold he felt in his slumber left his lips weathered.

What did it mean?

After passing the gated entrance to the park he decided he'd write his mom during camp and ask her about what he had overheard. He didn't want to get stuck in an embarrassing family discussion among strangers. His hope was to be low key, make a possible friend or two and survive the summer.

"We're here!" Mark exclaimed.

Lines of blue buses were parked perfectly in a line. Children were gathered around their parents toting luggage and eager to find their bus assignment. A group of girls squealed in glee as they jumped holding each other's hands discovering they were assigned to the same bus. Ezekiel scanned around and noticed several kids seemed to know each other, yet none were recognizable to him.

"Ezie over here!" Anne called as she planted herself in line. "This is where you find out which bus you're on!"

Ezekiel joined her blushing as he had to pass through the crowd of girls he was just observing. He made sure he didn't look back at them as Anne seized him into a great big hug.

"I'm going to miss you so much! Be sure to write me every week." She clung onto him tightly as they stepped forward closer to the table with the cheerful brown-haired girl.

"Okay mom. I'll write every week," he replied, thinking about how it would surprise her to know he had been spying in on their conversation and that he had overheard them talking about his dad and this place he was going to. He wasn't very good at geography and wasn't particularly familiar with the forest areas so he wasn't quite sure where he was headed for the summer. Anne was very vague about it when he asked.

"Hello!" said the cheerful, brown-haired girl. "Name?"

"Ezekiel Raroso."

"Is this your first session at camp?" she asked with a giant smile.

"Uh, yeah."

"Well a big welcome to you! I'm Sam. Full name is Samantha but if you want me to respond, call me Sam."

"Sure. Nice to meet you Sam."

"It's his first time traveling to Faera and he's never been to Murlock," Anne interjected suspiciously.

Sam's eyes lit up. She seemed surprised like she was full of wonder. She tightened her lips as if to hold back what she really wanted to say. She shifted her gaze and looked down at her clipboard and scanned.

"That will be bus #13." She looked at his face and sensed his apprehension. "You know, my little brother is also new this year. He is also on your bus. Maybe you can do me a favor and keep an eye out for him. He's a bit short, brown hair with thick glasses."

Ezekiel stood for a moment staring at her white name badge. S. Teardhmen. He wanted to memorize his exchange if the possibility could lead to a friend.

"Sure," he replied.

"His name is Kalos. Please don't' tell him I asked you to be nice to him. He's just very, well, nervous about his first session being away from mom and dad. I don't want to embarrass him. You seem like a nice kid."

"Thank you. I'll keep an eye out for him."

Anne assisted Ezekiel with his suitcase. She waved Mark and Nan over to the side of bus #13.

Campers! This is your one-minute warning! We will begin loading the busses in one minute!

"Well buddy, have fun," Mark said. "I have something for you."

He pulled out a dark grey rectangular box from his pocket.

"Here. You'll need this."

Ezekiel took the box and opened it. Inside was a small dagger similar to one his uncle had. He always had it on him as it was a useful work tool as a gardener. He also recalled seeing him use it during some of their family campouts. Ezekiel always thought it was very cool. The blade was short and curved like a miniature pirate sword. The handle was bound with dark brown leather and it was accented with small bronze studs. The dagger in the box was plain and as he stared at it more he realized how different it was than the one his uncle had. It was plain silver with a solid metal handle.

"Thanks," Ezekiel said. "They ran out of Swiss Army knives?"

"Ah those are for rookie campers! A real camper needs something more!" Mark exclaimed.

"You'll see that come in handy for, uh, whittling wood and soap figurines." Nan said.

Ezekiel couldn't help himself. He couldn't wait all summer to ask about what he had overheard them talking about in the kitchen. A lot of adult type stuff very similar to the things he tuned out when his uncle watched the news.

"Is it meant for me to protect myself if something bad happens?"

"Where ever would you get an idea like that?" Anne said with panic taking over her voice.

It is now time to report to your bus assignment. We are set to depart in 5 minutes!

"Looks like I better get going. Don't want to get a bad seat," Ezekiel said trying to avoid responding.

Nan hugged him, Mark gave him a nod and wink. Anne flung herself onto him despite his attempt to make way for the bus.

"You'll be fine. I wouldn't send you somewhere that wasn't safe. You'll see that the camp list calls for you to have a dagger of your own. Your uncle was very excited to buy that for you because he remembers when our dad gave one to him. You will be out in the wilderness. Things are different there. You won't have TV, air conditioning or video games."

"Mom I *know*. I really gotta go. I promise I'll write in a couple days."

"I'm counting on it mister," Anne said smiling as her eyes became misty.

Ezekiel kissed her on the cheek and walked to bus #13.

Chapter Eight
The Bus Ride

Ezekiel stepped onto bus #13. In the driver's seat was a very small, old man with tiny almond eyes. His wrinkled, sandal covered feet just barely reached the pedals. His Hawaiian floral shirt and puka shell necklace put him at ease.

"Hello Ezekiel," said the friendly bus driver.

"Hello. Um, how do you know my name?" Ezekiel said trying to hide his concern.

"Ah! I am Mas! I've been driving for more years than I could count or remember for that matter. I know all my kids, their kids and their kids. Never forget a face."

"You know my mom?" he asked inquisitively.

Mas leaned toward Ezekiel closer, straining his eyes to get a closer look at him.

"Ah yes. Little Miss Anne. Pretty and good at Padsphere. Her father was the good Ladir."

Ezekiel was still skeptical. His mom was just there at the park. She could have easily spoken with Mas prior to him getting on the bus. Then the idea hit him. His dad also attended camp. If he literally never forgot a face he'd surely know him.

"Hey buddy you're holding up the line out here!"

Ezekiel turned to see that there were a few children waiting to come onto the bus. Wrestling her way directly behind them was the same brown-haired girl who assigned him to this bus, Sam.

"Oh, sorry. Nice to meet you Mas."

Ezekiel was disappointed that he hadn't reacted faster. He figured he could always chat with Mas after they arrived at camp. He knew it was a long way, Mark had warned him that the ride would be very bumpy, windy up mountains, then windy down mountains and would take a couple of hours. At least he would have time to think of all the things he could ask about his dad.

He walked down the aisle of the bus. Most of the children had taken their seats and seemed to be already exchanging exciting plans on what they were going to do once they got to camp.

I can't wait to go riding at the stables!

I hope to be in the archery tournament!

I wonder if we have to wait for the Bonding Ceremony?

Not sure. I forgot to ask my mom.

It seemed like everyone had a clue except for one boy who was sitting in the very back seat alone. He was very small and could easily pass for a third grader at Winfrey. He had an overly full head of thick sandy brown hair that seemed to hide his face. He had black rimmed glasses that seemed too large for his face. His little face stared out the window.

"Um, hi. Can I sit here?" Ezekiel asked.

The boy looked up surprised. "Yeah go ahead."

"Well if you'd prefer to sit alone I could go and-"

"No, it's fine." The boy scooted over to give Ezekiel extra room to sit. Being closer to the boy Ezekiel could see a familiar sadness in his eyes. He sat down.

"So, what's your name?

"Kalos. Yours?"

"Ezekiel, but my friends call me Ezie."

"That is a cool nickname. If I had friends I'd want them to call me Kal. My sister calls me that"

"Kal is really cool." It dawned on Ezekiel that this was Sam's little brother. He had now realized why she asked him to 'look out for him'. He seemed shy, and uncomfortable in his skin.

"So, is this your first time at camp?" Ezekiel asked.

"Well, yeah. It's everyone's first time on this bus. They'll keep us all together until the Spectrum – didn't your parents tell you that?" Kalos seemed very surprised that Ezekiel was so clueless. It seemed to give him confidence.

"My mom didn't tell me much except all the activities that are there. I mean, I've been to camp before, just not *this* camp. I was thinking my mom was sending me here because, well you know. It's a camp for strange kids who are kind of weird. I mean, not that you're weird." He felt warm in the face. He didn't want to offend Kalos.

"My mom and dad went here…I don't know my dad, but I know that's how my parents met."

"I'm sorry."

"It's okay. I've never met him."

There was a pause of silence. Both boys wanted so badly to have something to talk about and were worried they would say something to the other to jeopardize the likelihood of friendship.

"Looks like we're out of the city," Kalos said adjusting his glasses, peering out the window to the emerging earth mounds covered in green lush.

"I just hope there isn't any bus ride singing. Ugh. If I have to sit through an hour of *100 Bottles of Beer on the Wall*, I think I may jump out of the window."

Kalos burst out laughing. "I'd join you, but being that we can't fly yet that might be a problem."

"Darn. You and your technicalities." Both boys laughed.

The ride was long and the boys enjoyed chatting about all they were seeing. They passed open plain fields of wheat, groves of citrus fruit that filled the bus with the smell of fresh oranges. The children enjoyed passing through the small hills of green covered with cattle. The cows seemed so still they looked like the props in the cafeterium from the spring play. These fields also had a strong smell that filled the bus.

"Ew! Cow doo!" shouted the boy who was sitting in front of them. Ezekiel and Kalos burst out into a gut-wrenching laugh that gave the boy more energy. He had a warm brown face and very light eyes that seemed to disappear when he smiled. Ezekiel immediately thought he was cool.

"The conjury of my sister!" the boy declared preparing his hands up as though to defend himself from the curly haired girl sitting next to him nose deep into what looked like a textbook. She looked at him giving him a fierce eye roll.

"I'm writing ma when we get to camp. Let's see how much you're laughing then," the girl replied calmly. The boys were clenching their giggles in.

The cow doo boy crossed over his sister and slid to the back seat with Ezekiel and Kalos.

"Hi! I'm Ethan LaVie. That's my lovely double Dara."

"Fraternal. Not identical," Dara said without lifting her head from her book.

"She never misses a moment to tell everyone that," Ethan said with a mischievous smile. Can't say I'm not happy about it. Can't imagine how cool I'd look with all that hair," he said rubbing his very short kinky hair. That struck a nerve with Dara as she closed her book sitting up on her knees to turn back at the three boys.

"I'm telling ma' about that too. When I do learn how to conjure that, it will be in your hair!"

Ezekiel was stunned by her snap at Ethan but more so by her pretty face. Her big curly hair cascaded perfectly around her dark face. He instantly liked her. She sensed it immediately.

"My brother was raised in a barn. I'm Dara," she said sticking out her hand to shake his, then Kalos'.

"Nice to meet you," Ezekiel said blushing.

"You too. Not as excited about going to camp as *him*, but I could use the opportunity to learn more history. I'm fascinated by all anthropologic studies and hear that every night there is a campfire where the Guides tell real tales from the past."

"Boring! We go to camp, she wants to learn stuff. Blah," said Ethan.

"Look! We're heading up! That means we're almost there!" shouted Kalos.

Ezekiel leaned a bit over Kalos to get a closer look out the window. Ethan jumped over Dara to get to the window. The bus was making an effortless upward climb winding up the mountain. They were going quite fast for the steep incline. Ezekiel was glad that he wasn't near the window because it made him feel like he was looking over the mountainside edge. He got a glimpse of what looked like 20,000 feet from the ground. He looked straight ahead and started to feel uneasy as the bus inclined even steeper, going faster and faster. The speed on the dirt road made the bus rumble as it accelerated. He clutched his seat, palms sweaty, heart racing. He scanned around and all the children were engaged in conversation or laughter. Some were looking out their windows with exhilaration.

Powdered clouds seemed to be within arm's reach of Kalos' window. The bus climbed and rattled going faster. Mas smiling happily in the reflection of his rearview mirror. He reached for his intercom while steering with one hand.

"We're going to take off now. Hold on!"

Ezekiel held onto his seat even tighter. The anticipation of what was going to happen terrified yet excited him. He noticed Dara was back to reading her book.

Why is no one panicking?

Both Kalos and Ethan noses pressed against the glass of the window on their knees.

"Here we go!" Ethan shouted.

Mas shifted gears up, hit the gas hard sending the bus over the edge of the mountain.

Chapter Nine
Aileron!

Ezekiel let out an ear-piercing scream as he clenched onto the back of Dara's seat. His commotion caused everyone on the bus to turn and stare at him. A group of girls snickered and giggled eying him. He startled Kalos and Ethan who was happily watching the bus ascend further up into the powdered clouds. Dara whipped around quickly to see the cause for alarm she dropped her book. Ezekiel had a moment to realize that everyone was calm.

"Why is no one panicking? Am I dead?" he said out loud.

"Uh, are you okay?" Ethan asked.

"Why would you be dead?" Kalos asked holding back a laugh.

Ezekiel, still clutching onto the back of Dara's seat, he slowly raised himself up to peek over Kalos and out the window. His heart palpitating for fear he would see the bus plummet into the ground. Instead he saw that they were floating with fierce purpose, a sight he had seen when traveling in an airplane with his mom when she was nice enough to give him the window seat. Fluffy white clouds shuffled alongside them in the bright blue sky. Below Ezekiel could see the tan patches of earth, fields of green and long stretches of lines he assumed to be roads to everywhere. They were *flying*.

"This bus flies?" he asked, feeling a bit more at ease as he studied Dara's calm face.

"Uh, yeah. How else do you think we're going to get all the way to Faera?" she replied reaching down for her book.

Ezekiel's instinct had him reach for her book first so she wouldn't have to. He turned it over.

Sapiens: A Brief History of Humankind

"Looks fun," he said handing it back to her.

"I find it interesting. I am fascinated by all species beginnings."

"I didn't know buses could fly. I guess technology is getting that good,"

Ezekiel said, playing off the fact that he was just terrified. He felt certain that he was heading to *Camp Strange*.

"Uh yeah 'technology'," Kalos said making quotations with his fingers.

Ezekiel still felt out of the loop on something but he had already made a spectacle out of himself so he decided to avoid the subject any further.

The kids chatted more about their pets, school friends and life, favorite sweets and TV shows. This helped ease Ezekiel from the brief terror he felt as they flew off the mountain. He made a mental note to research flying buses.

Just as the ride started to feel long, Ezekiel's ears started to pop as they began to descend. He looked up at Mas who was smiling as he steered and pulled levers that seemed to gear the bus lower.

"How about some landing tunes, eh?" Mas said as he flipped on the switch to his radio. Cheery music filled the bus exciting the children. Chatter of fun-filled camp activities blending with the music. Ezekiel leaned over toward the window to see the land beneath them come in clearer.

"You're not going to freak out, again are you? The bus has to touch the ground you know," Dara said with a grin.

"Um, no. I'm good," Ezekiel replied as he straightened up giving a nod to Kalos to further emphasize his comfort to Dara even though he was still dying a bit inside over the touchdown of the bus. Going forward he assured himself that he would not be the strange one here. He was going to use this chance of new friends to do everything to not be the oddball.

The bus was so close to landing he could now see the clear distinction of trees, plants and a body of water with several small boats.

"Have you ever ridden in a paddle boat before?" asked Kalos nervously.

"Sure. They have them at the lake I went camping at with my family. They're super easy and fun," Ezekiel said trying to assure his new friend.

"I'm just not that good at stuff like that."

"I'll help you. It's like riding a bike."

"I don't do bikes." Kalos was starting to look how Ezekiel first found him.

"What? Why not?"

"They're dangerous. You can fall. You can crash!"

"We'll have to work on that," Ezekiel said giving him a side grin and a pat on the shoulder wondering how he could be so happy watching the bus go off a mountainside, yet be terrified of something that is set on the ground he is controlling.

The bus continued to descend yet slowed in its speed to a gentle floating until it set itself onto the ground.

"We've arrived to the Faera cenote entrance. Your luggage will be waiting for you at camp," Mas announced.

Row by row the children stood up and exited off the bus and were greeted by Sam.

"Hello campers! I hope your ride in was great! Now is the time for some real fun. We are standing at the entrance of the Faera cenote. In an organized fashion, select your boat. Each boat seats six. Please do not run as there are enough boats for everyone. Do not paddle off until I tell you to. Stay with the group and do not wander off onto a side trail. A couple years back some campers found themselves off trail and wound up caught in a tiff with some kelpies. On my whistle, you may go and select your boat."

Pew!

Sam blew her whistle. Children everywhere walked briskly with their seatmates to select their boats. Ezekiel, Kalos, Dara and Ethan grouped together finding their boat. Kalos was a bit hesitant as he noticed the boat rock back and forth with instability. Dara jumped in taking a seat in the front. Ethan winked at Ezekiel as he took a seat in the back offering to help Kalos get in while Ezekiel held the boat steady. Once Kalos was in, Ezekiel took his seat next to Dara.

"Are there any seats available?" Sam asked loudly as she walked back and forth peering into each boat. Realizing there was Dara's hand shooting up, she walked over with two children.

"Here you go. You can join them. More the merrier, right?" she said with a big brief smile as she avoided direct eye contact with Kalos as to not cramp his style. She left behind a tall blonde girl with large green eyes, with a pair of pink bow hair clips perfectly set on each side of her hair. She didn't look like she wanted to be there as she assessed her bright pink nails. Sam returned with a boy with black spiky hair and a giant smile that made his almond eyes even smaller.

"Hi! Come aboard!" shouted Ethan.

"Happy to! I'm Miles. Miles Iwasaki," the boy said as he jumped into the back row of the boat. The kids introduced themselves as well.

The tall blond girl stood there.

"Well, aren't you coming on?" asked Ethan.

"Boats aren't really my thing," she said.

"Well they're not really anyone's thing," Dara said with a short tone. "But we have to get on to get to camp, don't we?"

The tall blond girl eyed her. She wasn't used to having other kids sass back to her. She stepped closer to the boat but stopped not wanting to get her shoes wet.

"What now?" groaned Dara.

"I don't want to ruin my shoes." The tall blond girl looked down at her sparkling light pink sneakers.

"Seriously? You're going camping. They're bound to get absolutely dirty," Dara said.

"I'll help you, hold on," Ethan said hopping out of the boat. He stepped onto the shores water holding on to the boat pulling it as close to her as possible. He stuck out his hand.

The tall blonde girl smiled. "Aubrey Walker," she said taking his hand, stepping on the side of the boat and hopping in. "Thank you. I just hate being dirty or wet."

"I'm Ethan. She's my twin sister Dara. Here's Ezie, Kal and Miles. Welcome to our noble ship," Ethan said.

"Fraternal twin," Dara emphasized.

"Yes. She never misses that," Ethan chuckled.

Pew!

Sam sounded her whistle paddling her boat out first. Each boat followed suit lining up in a cluster behind her.

"Okay! Time to peddle!" Ezekiel shouted. His boat mates pushed lining up behind the others. Once all the boats were grouped together, they all set off following Sam down the blueish green lagoon. Ezekiel was in awe of the tropical plants that seemed to engulf the lagoon framing it so perfectly. As they rode forward the trees grew taller and more clustered around shading them. Small rays of sunlight shot through tiny holes overhead.

"You good Kal?" Ezekiel asked.

"Yeah. It's not as bad as I thought," he replied as he was giving maximum effort so he wouldn't be bringing them down.

They pressed forward and their surroundings became darker as they entered a tunnel of earth. Long creeping vines hung down from above where there were openings revealing bits of sky and trees. The children were all in awe of this sight.

"This is the Passage of Navi," Sam said. "The ancient Faerman queen would come to swim here at night to gaze upon the constellations. It was believed that the stars would foretell prophecy. Let's continue on. Please use the lanterns in the box located starboard."

"Wow. Queen Navi ruled all of Faera with King Aoberon. Legend has it that she looked upon the stars and saw pain amongst the Faerman if it continued to be ruled over by a single entity. She convinced Aoberon to denounce their rule and help form a democracy like the Quotidian. This is how they formed the Council lead by a Praeses but decided by the people," said Dara proudly.

"I'm sure it's a decision he regrets to this day," joked Ethan.

"I think it's great that the King listened to her. It's nice to see that sort of equality," said Aubrey.

"I completely agree." This pleased Dara changing her initial impression of Aubrey.

"Huh?" Ezekiel was so mesmerized by his surroundings he was half listening to the girls only catching something about stars and a queen.

"Some believe that prophecy was misread then and that it was not the monarchy that was to bring pain, but the rule of the Hematite that would," Dara explained.

"It's all pish posh," Ethan said.

"My grandfather believes it. He's been saying it for years," chimed Kalos. "I don't see him much, but when I do, it's all he talks about."

It dawned on Ezekiel what they were talking about. He remembered hearing something about 'Hematite' when he was eavesdropping on his mother's kitchen conversation the night before.

"What are Hematite?" Ezekiel asked.

Dara whipped a fierce look at him. Through his peripheral vision, he could see that the others were stunned too.

"Okay, seriously were you born in a barn?" laughed Miles.

"Right?" agreed Ethan.

Ezekiel looked at them blankly waiting for the punchline. None came.

It hit Dara that something was off about Ezekiel. His reaction on the bus and now not knowing about Hematite was strange. She didn't want to make him feel bad so she let it alone and responded simply.

"Maybe your parents didn't tell you about them because we're kids and the idea of them is a bit scary. The Hematite are a group of Faerman that feel they are the next evolutionary step for Faermankind. They are violent and have been known to do horrible things to get what they want."

"My grandfather insists that they're wiped out and that there are just a few nuts running around claiming to be loyalists," added Kalos.

"You don't hear about this on the news because the Council works hard with the Guard to ensure travelers have proper passports when leaving Faera. The passports give details on the person's Spectrum and abilities," Dara said.

"My mom doesn't like us to even chat about them. She says it makes them more powerful if we do because it spreads fear. Ignoring them is best," added Aubrey.

It all sounded concerning to Ezekiel. He didn't really understand the need for passports and such since he wasn't a big traveler. He had also overheard his uncle confidently say they had them under control. He also knew how paranoid his family was and that there would be no way they'd send him if it was going to be dangerous.

They paddled deeper into the cenote and were surrounded by complete darkness. Flickers of lanterns were being ignited illuminating the cavern. Dara lit their lantern with ease revealing the glowing turquoise water beneath them. The ceiling was filled with long, dripping cascades of limestone that shimmered iridescence. Ahead Ezekiel could see where the water came to an end.

"We're almost there. Prepare to dock and carefully step out of your boats," Sam instructed.

They were approaching a monolithic wall of red rock. There was a Parthenon-esqe edifice illuminated by unknown sources of light. Between the grand ivory columns were massive sculptures Ezekiel couldn't quite make out. He could see the faces of men and women but could not recognize them as anyone he had ever studied in school. As they moved closer to the shoreline more details became clear. The monument had a peaked roof featuring even smaller sculptures that seemed to have a realistic quality to them. It was as if they could re-enact the chariot riding battle scene they were frozen in.

They approached the shore halting their paddle. Sam jumped out of her boat and faced the children to scan for the seven boats that followed her.

"Glad to say we all made it! No one went off trail! Before you leave your boats I just have a few more instructions to give you before we enter the temple."

"Please stick together with the group you boated with. This will make it easier to ensure no one gets lost. The temple entrance is chaotic and the Council is very busy with other matters. Since none of you have any bags or belongings walking through security should be easy. Once it is your turn you will walk through the detector swiftly. Once you pass you will be cleared to proceed. Once we are all through we will walk out and head into town for lunch."

The campers stuck close to their boat groupings as they walked up the marble steps. Sam opened the door and the children shuffled in. They were in a enormous buzzing room that was adorned with white walls, marble floors and fancy ivory crown molding that stretched to more long columns that curled from the floor to the ceiling. There weren't many people there, just a few uniformed employees stationed near the detectors.

"Well hello there campers!" greeted the friendly guard from behind the detector. Ezekiel could only see her face from behind the huge contraption. "Come on through!"

One by one each camper proceeded through the detector. Unable to see where each child passed through to, Ezekiel asked where they were going after the walkthrough.

"Security is always super tight if you travel in on foot. They say flying or daggering in is better," Miles said.

Once closer to the detector, Ezekiel could see the silver archway that seemed to lead to darkness, yet he could hear the voices of his fellow campers on the other side. Dara passed through quickly, then Miles, Aubrey and Kalos. Ethan said, "Woo hoo!" making a silly face and jumped through. Ezekiel walked up, last in line looking at the guard for assistance. She noticed his apprehension.

"What's the matter honey? Did you forget something?"

"Um, no. So, I just, *go in?*"

She chuckled. "Well yes if you want to get going to camp. Is this your first time traveling by foot here? Not a problem. It's best just to take it one step at a time."

She was smiling at him. He stared straight ahead into the darkness in front of him taking steps. As he passed through he could hear the guard shout, "Have fun! Bye!" all the while feeling a cold refreshing air seize him, then a warmth filled his face as he approached light illuminating a lovely courtyard filled with his fellow campers. The courtyard was filled with tropical trees, grass and stone benches surrounding a decorative water fountain of sculptures of women with wings holding jugs of water. Water flowed from their containers onto the decorative basin. White rose bushes surrounded them as did a grand bush sculpture of winged babies with floral crowns. The air was sweet.

Sam stepped forward to recount the campers. "Okay everyone. One last thing before we enter town for lunch."

She walked toward a grandiose arbor that was highly adorned with greenery, and a rainbow of flowers. It was the size of the front of his house. There was a pillar of marble with a seal Ezekiel recognized from his mom's cookie tin. In very fancy script it read:

Courtyard of the Rite of Aileron

The center of the arbor was the same seal. Sam waved the children into one line making eye contact with Ezekiel. She approached him, gently holding him by the shoulders and said, "Ezekiel will go first. Those in his boat grouping please follow." She winked at him as she leads him to the first step of the arbor.

"Many of you may have heard about the Rite of Aileron from your parents or older siblings and may be prepared for this. Those who are not listen. When it is your turn, you will approach the arbor, bow to it with respect, enter it standing on the seal. When you are ready, shout 'Aileron!'"

The children excitedly surrounded Ezekiel and his friends as close to the arbor as possible. He wondered what strange camp ritual this was and recalled some of the weird ones he had faced in the past. There was a time when everyone wrote their parents to send gum so you could chew and assemble the world's most stupendous gum tower alongside your cabin. Another was a trust fall off a log that didn't go so well for him. His favorite was the booger wall his unit started a few years back. Some of their finest picks displayed there.

"Go ahead," Sam said giving him a gentle push.

Ezekiel walked to the first step. He bowed feeling a real level of respect for such a nicely kept arbor. He thought of his uncle and how hard he knew it was to maintain such a natural piece of art.

He stepped inside the arbor gentle placing his feet on the bronze seal. He looked out to the crowd of smiling eager faces that offered him encouragement. He took a deep breath and shouted, "Aileron!"

He immediately felt a warmth and strength build in his back. Cheers from the crowd burst. Genuine cheers, not the kind he was used to back home. He must have done something right. He looked at Sam's face, it was beaming. She waved him out. He took a swift step forward and felt himself bump the pillars of the arbor. He looked up and saw his sheer wing caught on hanging greenery.

Wait! My wing!?

Ezekiel began to panic reaching for his back to pull them off. He spun around trying to grab for them and they flapped as though they had a mind of their own. The crowd backed away allowing him space to create his own personal tornado. Sam ran over and grabbed his shoulders pressing down.

"It's okay! Look at me! Look at my face. Think *down*."

She had him firmly so he wasn't going anywhere. Her eyes put him at ease and he thought, *down* like she said. His wings relaxed and flapped down folding into themselves. He could *feel* them and it was weird.

"See, I knew you could do it!" She turned to the crowd who still seemed in awe of him. "Next!"

Sam and Kalos approached him as Dara went up next, then Ethan.

"Are you okay?" Kalos asked.

"This may be a surprise to you, and I'm sorry I'm the one who has to break it to you, but you're a Faerman kiddo," said Sam gently. "I had a feeling your mom didn't let you know once I checked you in today. She kept emphasizing it was your first time coming here. Like, ever. That is strange for most Faerman. Even if you're not old enough for camp or the Rite of Aileron, most Faerman have at least visited family or been to town."

Ezekiel was stunned. Kalos wanted to offer his support.

"Did you really not know?" he asked.

Ezekiel's blank face told him more than words could have. He looked at his sister for help.

"I feel like he's remembering all the times weird stuff has happened, or stuff he thought he made happen was really him making it happen," Sam said with a smile.

She was exactly right.

Chapter Ten
The Gorging Gargogle

A million thoughts swirled through Ezekiel's mind.

Is this real or an effect of a head injury caused by the bus reeling off the mountain?

I knew I was different. I knew it!

Ugh. The science fair. My party. The Promotion Ceremony!

He covered his face with his hands realizing all the signs that had been there, how his mom, Nan and Mark had been so secretive. The picture of his parents was right in front of him.

They have wings too.

The thought of his parents having wings gave him comfort. He realized that his mom was trying to tell him. Remembering the look in her eyes it all made sense to him now.

He felt someone touch his shoulder. He looked up.

Smiling Kalos, Ethan, Dara, Miles and Aubrey stood in front of him, wings out proudly. Dara stepped closer to him.

"You want to grab some lunch? Talk about it with us? I-*we* can tell you anything you want to know about being a Faerman kid." She smiled at him. She felt bad for him not understanding how his family could have hidden this from him.

Ezekiel nodded. He could see Sam smiling at him from afar. She gave him a thumbs up. Her cheesiness amused him. He wasn't sure what a Faerman was but knew he wasn't going long without finding out more.

"Hey so it may not be what you want to hear right now, but man, your wings are awesome," Ethan said.

"Wings," Ezekiel scoffed glancing back at himself.

"Yeah, well everyone gets them and they all look different," he replied turning so Ezekiel could get a better look at his.

"They have tiny markings that are unique to you. Kind of like a fingerprint," Dara said.

Pew!

Sam stepped forward blowing her whistle.

"Wonderful job campers! Your wings look great! A few rules to cover before we head into town for lunch."

"No flying. No attempting to fly or spreading your wings fully. Stay together in your boating group."

She proceeded to lead the group to a grand ivy-covered wall with a single wooden door. She pushed the door open holding it to allow for the group to pass through. From a short distance, Ezekiel could see a sleek grey street adorned with light posts surrounding colorful storefront shops. The street was buzzing with many people with vibrant shopping bags, baskets of bakery goodies and exotic produce. Flickers of colorful specs jumped into the air from the far distant end of the street. As the children walked closer he could see the specs grow larger. Fluttering groups of Faerman swirled in the air. Some hovering engaged in happy conversations. A blue-winged teenaged girl stood next to an orange winged man. He picked her up tossing her into the air and joyously applauded as she fluttered down. He handed her a small blue velvet pouch then filled it with gold coins. He kissed her on the cheek and she ran off with a group of girls all adorned with various colors of wings.

Sam led the group waving them to assemble in a tighter line. "Stick together to the right. There are many great shops to check out but you will be free to do that on the weekend. Today we will be stopping for lunch at the Gorging Gargoyle."

She stopped at the entrance of a stone cobbled storefront. There were huge clouded windows making it difficult to see inside. What was most unusual was the hefty stone gargoyle perched upon the rooftop. Its face had large eyebrows that emphasized its unpleasantness. The mouth was downturned as if it ate something bad.

Bluuuuurrrrrppppppp.

The gargoyle let out a enormous belch and smacked its mouth with displeasure. Its eyes widened as it turned to look at the children.

"Ew," said Aubrey. "If the food wasn't amazing here I would never come back.

"He's so freaking awesome!" said Ethan.

After learning he had wings, Ezekiel wasn't surprised at the existence of moving burping statues. He was focusing on all the questions he was about to ask his new friends.

The children entered the restaurant. It was a dimly lit place filled with many mismatched linen covered tables. Plaid, paisley, seersucker and floral patterned. A single, drippy wax candlestick was centered at each table illuminating the guests who sat there. Ezekiel swore he walked past a half man half horse but refused to turn around to confirm it as he was feeling bewildered enough.

"This way!" Sam shouted leading the children into a back room. A faded wooden sign nailed overhead that read:

The Pantry Room

The room had several long rectangular banquet style tables covered in the same mismatched linens and drippy wax candles. The stone walls held portraits and oil paintings of random household items. A fancy golden framed portrait of a green and yellow sponge was perched above the mantle above the fireplace. Next to it were paintings of an empty red bowl, a can of beans with a toilet plunger and lastly a cat litter box that had obviously been used.

The children were swift to find their seats and Ezekiel's boating group sat at the orange striped table closest to the can of beans and toilet plunger. The table was set with a small metal stein that had the image of the Gorging Gargoyle grumpily set. Ezekiel realized it had been hours since he had something to drink and the sight of the stein made him yearn for something to quench his thirst.

A towering cyclops walked into the room. He was wearing a wine-colored smock with a black and white sneaker on his right foot and a tan construction boot on the other. Sam walked over to him calling everyone to attention.

"I would like all of you to meet Everett the Great, culinary master and owner of the Gorging Gargoyle."

"Welcome to the Gorging Gargoyle," said Everett with a subtle bow. "The pixies will take care of your drinks in just a moment. He raised his arms and clapped his hands twice. Immediately dozens of tiny, golden pixies came flying out of the kitchen flying over the children hovering over their steins. In their tiny little hands, they held small white pitchers. Synchronized, they all poured a honey, sweet mead into each stein. As each filled, it chilled forming a frosty froth on top. They quickly flew back to the kitchen leaving their luminescence behind.

"Honey mead!" Aubrey cheered as she took a big gulp, then licking the creamy froth from her upper lip.

Ezekiel grabbed his stein. It was cold to the touch. He took a sip. The honey mead was refreshing, bubbly and sweet.

"Do you like it?" Kalos asked trying to lighten his mood.

"It's good," Ezekiel replied ready to break the ice about everything. "Can I ask you guys something?"

They all nodded.

"What the heck is a Faerman? Sam said I was a Faerman. What does that mean? Is this why weird things happen to me and my mom sent me to Camp Strange? What do I not know and what do I need to know?"

They all looked at each other, then at Dara.

"Well I guess I'll give it a go," she said with hesitation. "Trying to keep it simple, you're what Quotidian call a," she looked around, then whispered, "fairy."

"I thought that only girls could be fairies," he said louder than expected. The children at the table next to them gave scowling glances at hearing what he said.

"Shhhhh!" Aubrey and Dara said at the same time in a whisper. The boys held in their giggles. Ethan keeled over, hands over his mouth so his laugh didn't escape.

"Faerman don't like that word. It's the slang name given by Quotidian or Quo's for short – people who are not Faerman and do not have the ability to produce charms or fly. The word goes back many centuries connected to a time when people were scared of the Faerman abilities and they would actually try to trap us. Even harm us."

Ezekiel liked when Dara explained things. She said things so plainly he had a hard time being upset with her being so calm. "Okay, so how is it that I didn't know I had *these*," he said tapping on the edge of his wing.

"We're all able to produce them when we're in Faera after we've performed the Rite of Aileron charm. There are strong enchantments amongst the exits of Faera to prevent the exposure of wings outside of here. Generations of

Praeses – our leader *here*, like the President we have at home have spent life time's ensuring Faerman integrate with Quotidian, promoting human relations. There are not enough jobs or resources here in Faera so we have to cross over to survive."

"Why do you think my mom wouldn't tell me about this? All of you seem like you've known and it's no big deal. It *is* a big deal. I've had so many weird things happen I couldn't explain. Then off to camp I go to find all this!"

"Is that why you call it *Camp Strange?*" Aubrey asked.

"Well what else would you call it?" Ezekiel said.

"I think that is a cool name. Sounds mysterious. That's how things get trending. We should all call it *Camp Strange*. We should give it a hashtag," Ethan started before getting elbowed in the rib by Dara. "Ouch! Well it's better than Camp Faerman."

Dara paused. She didn't know the answer to Ezekiel's question because there wasn't a good one she could think of. The boys shifted in their seats. They could hear Everett the Great's voice shout, "Plates out!" The herd of pixies flew out circling the room like a light show. With them in each hand were tiny stacks of white plates the size of a penny. Their flight pattern was impressive as they issued the plates to each camper. As the plate landed on the table it grew in size displaying delectable meals of the child's desire. Ethan had breaded chicken strips with a towering fruit platter. Dara's spaghetti and meatballs arrived alongside, Aubrey's sushi, Kalos' pork chop and apples, and Miles' curry and rice.

"Crave plates are the coolest," said Miles who was ready with his fork in hand.

"Crave plates?" asked Ezekiel.

"Crave plates are pixie enchanted. They have the ability to detect what its holder wants to eat and produces it for them," explained Dara.

Ezekiel thought for a moment. Suddenly a pile of sugar drop cookies piled up on his plate. "No way they are like Nan's," he said as he took a nibble out of one. His eyes lit up in reaction to their warmth and flavor. Buttery with a sugary crisp just like his Nan's.

"So 'Faera', that is what this place is called?" he asked. "You've all been here before?

The children all nodded mouths full of food.

"Yeah, I mean most Faerman live in Quotidian cities but regularly come to visit their relatives or to vacation. Adults come in regularly to shop because there are things sold here they can't exactly get once they cross over," Kalos said. "I come a few times a year to visit my grandfather. He never leaves because he's the leader of the Guard."

"Really?!" Dara said over her large bite of meatball. "Your grandfather is Dux Diego Lumiere?"

"Yes, that's him. Don't see him much since all he cares about is work. Mom thinks he's a bit obsessed with it."

"He's been the Dux for like ever!" Aubrey said.

"My Pop Pop went to camp with him. They played against each other in Padsphere. It was mega ultra competitive," said Dara.

"Yeah! Pop Pop was the Celerpoint on the Granters. One of the best Blue Faerman teams ever. They had a rivalry with the Flames – the Red Faerman team. Dux Diego was a well-known Sphere Guard in his day," Ethan said.

Ezekiel realized that he had heard of Kalos' grandfather before. Mark was talking about him and it wasn't good. Knowing this and that this wasn't the place to ask about what he had overheard, he changed the subject.

"I think my mom played Padsphere. I mean, I saw a picture of her in her uniform. She was a Healer I think? It looked like she won or something," he stammered trying to fit in.

"Whoa that's cool. It's a really tough game. You can't make the team until your colored and even then, you have to beat out everyone for a spot cause the team is exclusive taking just six players!" Ethan added.

Ezekiel smiled at the thought that his mom was a star athlete. She was always so mom-like it was hard to picture her as anything else.

"I know it seems crazy, but I think you'll learn a lot more at *Camp Strange*," Dara said smiling, trying to make Ezekiel laugh. "You'll learn even more than we even know. That's the reason parents send their kids there. We get to work on managing our abilities which is great when we're trying to blend in."

"Blend in? Phooey. We should be happy we have these abilities. Dara over here thinks this is all old-fashioned and would rather spend her summer" he exaggerated a gasp, "*reading in her room!*"

"I'm open to that conjure we were talking about earlier," she said giggling with Kalos.

Pew!

Sam stood front and center. "Lunchtime is over. Let's make our way out in an orderly fashion. Same rules apply as I previously announced," she turned and walked to Everett the Great to thank him for the wonderful lunch.

"I hope to see you all this weekend! Enjoy your first day at camp!" Everett cheered. "Please caution yourselves as you exit. Gorgie is quite full from all the table scraps he received today so he's a bit sour."

The children stood up and began to walk out the Pantry Room. In the corner of his eye, Ezekiel could see the pixies make their way into the room circulating with such aerial choreography to remove each plate and stein from the tables. They walked through the main dining room and he was able to get a clear look of the horse man he knew he had seen. He had the upper body of a muscular man wearing an orange shirt with smiling faces that said 'Mmbop, Hansen' in rainbow letters. He was sitting with a very tiny person who was the size of a toddler who was wearing overalls with no shirt. As the first group exited the Gorging Gargoyle they screeched.

"Ugh! Disgusting!" said a boy who was first out the door and was covered in what looked like chunky, pink slime. With him stood four others who were also slimed.

Bluuuuurrrrrppppppp.

Gorgie the Gargoyle who sat perched above the children was burping up a fountain of pink all over the shop front entrance. He blinked then chuckled at his slimy, pink victims. Everett came running out with a mop and bucket. He gave Gorgie a fierce look with his one eye.

"Gorgie! I said to wait for the campers to leave you naughty boy! Look what you've gone and done to our new friends. No more scraps for you!" Everett shouted.

Bluuuuurrrrrppppppp.

Gorgie gave one last loud burp then settled his sour face to a stubborn pout. Several pixies came flying out winding themselves around the campers who were afflicted. Their golden sheen swirled taking away the pink mess.

"Well glad that was taken care of!" Sam said. Stick together to the right and let's move on. The path to camp is at the end of the road."

Chapter Eleven
Camp Strange

Sam led the children along the street. There were many shop fronts with colorful canopies, open glass windows and vibrant colors alluring in several passing by.

"Look there's Pop Pop!" Ethan shouted waving through the window at a smiling very well dressed man. "This is his shop!"

Ezekiel looked closer at the elegant painted script on the window.

Gastelum Tatters

Finest Faerwear Since 1928

The walls of the shop were marbled and the entryway was an emerald green canopy with the same shop script in gold. Through the window, Ezekiel could see suits and coats hanging mid-air. Fancy frocks of every color and texture danced in a circular fashion allowing for each to have its chance to be in front.

"Everyone gets their Solstice Bash outfits from Gastelum's. We should stop by this weekend. We'll have our dresses before anyone else," Aubrey said to Dara.

Dara blushed. "That's assuming we're asked to go," she said.

Aubrey glanced at Ezekiel then at Dara. "I'm sure you'll be asked."

The air filled with a sugary sweetness that filled Ezekiel's nose and warmed his belly as they approached a pink shop. Through the glass window he could see elaborate decorated, towering multi-tiered cakes, powdered sugar puffs and stacks upon stacks of colorful macaroons.

"I can't wait for the weekend! You haven't lived until you've had some sugar puffs from Dulcebus' Bakery!" Miles said eyes glued to the presentation display in the window of colossal, round puffed pastries sprinkled with mounds of confection.

The row of shops made Ezekiel feel normal. There was something he liked about them. He wasn't sure if it was the shops themselves, the fact his parents likely walked these same steps or the fact he was having fun with new friends.

The group continued to walk until the pavement ended and the road forked. To the left of them in the distance there were several rows of brightly colored tents. A few of them puffed colors of pastel every few seconds. Ezekiel must have paused for a moment to take what was in front of him in because Miles said, "It's the Bazaar. Quo's have them and call them swamp meets or farmer's markets."

The children followed Sam to the right path through a green pasture that seemed so familiar to Ezekiel. The long grass swayed in the breeze. Peculiar little insects buzzed along. They hadn't walked for long and within the distance he could see what looked like a long wide wall of green bush. There was an opening amongst the bush wall with a where the path continued. Hovering above the opening was scrolled banner.

Camp Faerman
Educating, Peace & Harmony of All Kind

A wave of excitement pushed through the crowd of children. The campgrounds were well in view. Monumental four-story structures of logs were assembled creating towering sleeping quarters. Swirling wooden staircases were stationed alongside.

"That is where you Fledglings will be quartered," said Sam pointed toward the towers.

She continued to lead the group to a grand outdoor amphitheater. The staging area was shaded by a spherical moss formation. Centered was a podium similar to what was left of the podium at Winfrey after the Promotion Ceremony. It was covered in a growth of green and colorful florals. Tiered rows of logs with colored pads for seating.

"Seating is organized by color unit. The Magnus Magister will explain this further. Fledglings are seated here," Sam said pointing to the first rows of logs directly in front of the podium. The children found their seats upon tan colored pads. Before they could engage in their inquisitive chatter, several campers entered the stage holding an assortment of unusual instruments. A lanky, orange winged camper held firmly on what seemed to be a golden horn with a keyboard attached. Several campers had long, odd, silver tubes with multiple mouthpieces and several keys the pressed as they switched the mouthpiece they blew out of as they warmed up. The sounds of pipes and strings filled the air in a pleasant tune. The band swayed to the beat building the energy amongst the children.

"I'm totally going to learn how to play colossal pipe," said Miles beaming at the silver tubes on stage.

"That's cool. I think I'm more of a Padsphere guy myself. If I start practicing now, I might have a chance in say, four years to make the team?" chuckled Ethan.

"Sure. Keep dreaming," Dara shot back.

A group of white-winged campers entered flying in unison. They swirled around plopping into each of their seats. They began a rhythmic clap and then began a repetitive chant.

We are (clap, clap)
The Healers! (clap, clap)
We are (clap, clap)
The Healers!

A luminescence shot from the group as they spun into their seats.

Without haste, a group of orange winged campers entered chanting repetitively.

Hey, hey, get out of the way!
The Elements are here to blow you away!

They blew wind that circulated a small funnel in the middle of the stage as they took their seats.

A wave of green campers hovered above, spreading themselves all around the amphitheater chanting.

Who rocks the house?
The Arbors rock the house!
And when the Arbors rock the house, they rock it all the way down!

All together they flew down hard just inches from the audience in the crowd, landing in their seats. Many Fledglings ducked cover.

The amphitheater started to mist. It was refreshing on this warm day. Rainbow colors refracted off the misted air. The blue campers entered in all angles releasing sprays of water onto the crowd. The patterns of their sprays reminded Ezekiel of those water fountain shows he'd seen at fancy hotels.

Everywhere we go, people want to know, who we are.
So, we tell them!
We're the mighty, mighty Granters!
The mighty, mighty Granters!
If they can't hear us, we'll shout a little louder!

They all sat celebrating their entrance.

Lastly a cluster of red campers hovered in with their red hood over their faces. From the center of their cluster each camper raised their hand creating a flame in their palm. They brought the flame together forming a large ball of fire. They quickly separated circulating the area, flames in hand chanting repetitively.

We're fired up!
We're sizzling!
We're turning up the heat!
When it comes to everything, the Flames can't be beat!

Each of them threw their flame into the air as they took their seats. The flames rose high in the air and fizzled out as they fell from the sky.

The crowd cheered and applauded the grand entrances of all units. On stage, seven people entered that made the entire place go silent. A stalky, tan man with a scruffy peppered beard took to the podium. He wore a navy blue athletic vest with the camp crest emblazoned on the left side of his chest. He was rugged and athletically built.

"Welcome campers. A great big welcome to this year's Fledgling's," he said with a nod to the front rows of campers which followed with mild applause.

"I am Nelson Aguirre, the camp Magnus Magister which is just a fancy old-fashioned way of saying 'Dude in Charge,'" Giggles came from the crowd. "It's actually 'Head Instructor'. Those who are joining us for the first time and those who have not colored are placed in the Fledgling unit which is overseen by myself. You will attend courses with the other instructors you see here today. Each of them specializes in their spectrum's focus and will prepare you for the day your color comes in. Now while we encourage you to learn as much as you can about the enchantments, conjures and charm specialties of all, be aware that some, all or none may be within your ability."

"Now you may wonder, why come to camp to do this? As many of you know, Praeses Amare stresses the importance of maintaining Faerman culture and practices while integrating peacefully in the Quotidian world. The Praeses feels that by training you at a young age you will build the knowledge and skills you need to protect Faera, build human relations and be a proud Faerman who contribute a greater good to the world."

The crowd applauded. As Ezekiel scanned the crowd it reminded him of a sporting event with a massive rowdy crowd dressed in its team colors and apparel. What made this different was that there were six different teams sitting here.

"It also doesn't hurt to have you kids unplug from having your faces inserted into those Quotidian devices. It's a shame to hear that kids are preferring these instruments to playing outside to find adventure. I encourage you to enjoy all the camp activities, swim at the lake and visit Murlock."

"Now for some simple housekeeping. Curfew for all is 9 o'clock every evening. You must report back to your unit grounds by this time every night. Campers found outside this time wandering the grounds will earn their unit a demerit. Every three demerits will result in a unit consequence that will vary from Feasting Room duty, collecting algae from the Padsphere Pond and stable dung clean up."

Many Fledglings looked around with concern.

"Demerits can also be issued by instructors if you are late to a course, not following directions or are engaging in horseplay. Wandering off grounds is forbidden at any time."

"Now not all is lost. We believe in redemption. To err is to be human and we have all lost our way at one time. If you find your unit has earned itself a demerit, you can have it erased by various good deeds. Our community has a great need for volunteer assistance. To work off a demerit, you may volunteer in the Relic Room, The Book Chamber or Green Pastures Retirement Village during the weekend. Your service must be at least five hours. You will never find yourself in a situation you cannot choose the redemption."

"Lastly, you may write your family as often as you wish. The Pixie Post is located in town but we have a Pixie Post Pick-Up box just below the Astro-Observatorium."

"Now off you go. Follow your unit leaders. Fledglings, follow me."

The band picked up a cheery tune as everyone exit. The Fledglings followed the Magnus out of the amphitheater back the way they entered. Ezekiel could see that his wings were blue. He led the group to the large four-story log structure and up to the winding staircase at the center of the compound.

"Here are your unit grounds. This is the main staircase. The girl's quarters are to the right and the boys to the left. You are free to choose your bunkmates. Each room settles four as you will find each room has four hammocks and trunks. You will find that your luggage is in the den space. I will return in an hour so we may walk to the Feasting Hall as a unit."

The children made a mad dash for the staircase. Worse than a pile-up on the interstate kids pushed through to try and sort their luggage and made a mad dash to find the best room to bunk in. Smooshed shoulder to shoulder Kalos had an idea.

"I'll squish my way to that top room to call dibs. If you can bring my luggage we can claim that highest room."

"Genius!" Ethan said.

Ezekiel wiggled his way through spotting both his and Kalos' luggage tags. Ethan was helping Miles retrieve his case from beneath a pile of others. Within moments the den was clear and the kids had shuffled up the stairs to find each other.

The boys checked each level calling for Kalos. "Kal are you in here?" They peaked and he wasn't found on the first few floors. They made it to the top and there was Kalos at the very top room hovering in the top bunk of the enchanted hammock. "Took you all long enough!" he joked.

Ezekiel was amazed at the room. There were no walls, just a sheer, sheath that floated along the supporting logs. The room had two sets of floating hammocks filled with the most, lush bedding and pillows he had ever seen. Each boy had a trunk to place their personal belongings in. When Ezekiel opened his trunk, he found himself several sets of the camp uniform. A navy blue hooded vest with the same golden camp emblem as the others. A belt with a pouch, plain white shirts, cargo shorts and pants. He placed his other camp items inside remembering his dagger placing it right on top.

Chapter Twelve
Feasting Hall

"Let's get our uniforms on," said Ethan.

"Um, can't everyone see us?" asked Ezekiel as he poked at the sheer drapery that tented their room.

"That's an easy fix," Miles said. He cleared his throat, touched the drapery with his hand and said, "Swathe!"

The drapery turned solid and lost its sheer.

"Coolness! You know some charms already?" Ethan asked.

"They are Enchandrapes. We have some at our house," he replied smiling.

The boys got dressed in their hooded vests. Standing in the official camp wear Ezekiel felt important, like he belonged to something bigger than he could ever imagine. He had felt cool in his baseball uniform, but knew he wasn't very good so the thrill didn't last long. With this uniform, he felt like he could do anything.

"All done?" asked Miles. "Expose!" The drapery returned back to its sheerness.

Ezekiel was fine with a bottom bunk so he walked to it and plopped himself down careful not to kick over his neatly folded camp pajamas that were placed at the foot of his hammock. He rocked himself back and forth.

"Cool! Said Ethan, "It doubles as a swing!" He pulled the hammock climbing on top above Ezekiel. Miles and Kalos did so on their side of the room the boys rocked back and forth.

Ethan stood up as he balanced, rocking back and forth. He positioned his hands waist level and said, "Dude! I'm surfing!"

Kalos laid horizontally and opened his wings wide, riding the swaying as he motioned his arms forward. "I'm flying!" Miles got on his feet in a crouched down position, rocking, then standing like Ethan. "I'm surfing too!" When he stood, his head pushed little Kalos off his hammock and through the drapery plummeting four stories down the side of their log compound.

"Kalos!" Ezekiel shouted as he went plunging through the drapery wall. All he could think about was catching him. He felt the heat in his wings as they spread fiercely, beating faster and faster allowing him to pass Kalos' fall. He opened his arms seizing Kalos' hood, then the chest of his vest into his chest, clasping him in a bear hug. His heart was racing and he slowed himself down allowing them to safely touch the ground.

The Fledgling's compound roared with cheers and applause. Everyone caught witness of what happened through their Enchandrapes. Unfortunately for the boys, so did the Magnus.

"What do you think you are doing?" he asked sternly. "How did this happen?"

The boys looked to each other for words. Ethan and Miles dropped their faces. Kalos was on the verge of opening his mouth when Ezekiel interjected, "It was my fault. I was rocking on my hammock and accidentally bumped into Kalos who was on the top bunk. He went flying through the drapery so I dived after him."

The boy's mouths all dropped open, yet remained silent.

"That is disappointing to hear. You are quite lucky that your instincts allowed you to come to the aid of your friend. Most Fledglings would not be so lucky. I'm afraid I have to issue this session's first demerit to your unit Mr. Raroso."

The Magnus blew his whistle calling all the children to line up. Dara and Aubrey quickly joined the boys to inquire what happened.

"I'm sorry," said Kalos to the group.

"No, it's my fault. If I didn't stand up and bump you, you wouldn't have went flying out," said Miles sadly.

"It's fine guys. It was an accident. If I do some community service I can erase the demerit," Ezekiel said. "I'm just glad you're okay."

"Are you guys nuts?! Someone could have been killed! You're going to get us into trouble and our unit is going to spend the weekend cleaning up dung in the stables instead of having fun in Murlock!" Dara shouted at them.

"It was an *accident* Dara. Miles just stood up in the bottom bunk and bumped Kal in the process. It was totally an accident," Ethan said defensively.

"*Accident-schmackcident.* I saw the whole thing from our side of the compound. Everyone saw the whole thing. You were all swinging up there. It's a surprise you all didn't go flying off the bunks." Dara scowled at them.

"It was pretty wicked," Ethan whispered nudging Ezekiel. The adrenaline of the flight pumped through him.

"Everyone assembled then? Let's go! Off to the Feasting Room we go!" the Magnus said.

In a clustered group, the children walked along the path. The sun was almost set, beaming just a glimmer of light in the distance. The sky was a watercolor wonder of radiant pink, blue and orange. The Magnus plucked a sunflower from a stalk. He looked at it as he placed it into his palm. "Thank you sunflower. Light please." The flower's petals shone light, brightening up the dark path.

"Awesome," said Aubrey in awe. "I can't wait to learn how to do that."

The Magnus led the group up to a giant oak tree. The trunk was fat and stout with towering branches of green. It did not look like the Feasting Hall they were looking for. A single wooden sign was nailed to the trunk.

Feasting Hall

"Well here we are," said the Magnus. He knocked on the trunk. The outline of a door formed and he pulled it open walking the children inside. From where Ezekiel was standing he could see that the hall had more depth on the inside than it appeared on the outside of the tree. Once all the way inside he could see several wooden benches. The high ceilings were a grey painted wood with arches that reminded him of a cathedral. The hall was illuminated by glass lanterns with a single sunflower head. The main wall of the hall had a colored banner hovering for each color unit displayed and beneath hovered smaller banners indicating the year of a Padsphere tournament win.

The children formed a single line to enter the food line. Ezekiel and his friends grabbed a tray. Once closer to the open kitchen he saw a broad, bulbous creature with huge eyes and brassy, blond curls. It was scooping food amongst a flurry of pixies onto the camper's plates. As he got closer he could hear the pleasant cute giggle it had when a red-winged camper exchanged playful banter. He was close enough to see that fried chicken, honey biscuits, mashed potatoes and colorful mixed vegetables were on the buffet. He approached it noticing it's white apron and gloves. It seemed to smile at him batting its' long eyelashes.

"Hello sweetie. Whatcha havin'?" It asked in a sugary, sweet voice that did not match its pungent exterior. Ezekiel didn't want to be rude so he forced a smile as awkward as it felt.

"Everything...ma'am," he replied realizing it was a she. She placed a bit of each food item in such a loving way as though she had made the meal just for him.

"Fledging I see. Hold on baby." She leaned below the counter placing a fluffy, sugared pastry on his tray. "Home-made custard puff. To sweeten your first day." She winked at him.

"Thank you," Ezekiel replied, again forcing out his smile to be polite as he continued on the line grabbing a goblet and utensils. He could see in the side of his eye that all his friends had also gotten the custard puff. As they all came out holding their trays of food, they were beaming at their plates.

"Sweet Sally is so nice!" Aubrey said.

"Sweet Sally?" asked Ezekiel.

"The Feasting Lady. Everyone calls her Sweet Sally. She's been here forever. My parents and grandparents have the fondest memories of her."

"Yeah, she never lets anyone leave this room hungry. She will walk around checking everyone's plate to make sure they ate enough," said Miles. "I love her already." Miles was always thinking about food.

The children sat down. Immediately a group of pixies approached them with their pitchers filling their goblets with orange nectar. With his cup in hand, Ezekiel felt the cup get ice cold. He was starting to love that. The meal was delicious. Every bite of juicy chicken and buttery potatoes filled their tummies. The vegetables were teal and root like with the texture and sweetness of a jelly bean. He had never seen such a thing. "What is this?" he asked.

"Jelly root of course. What does it taste like?" said Miles the food connoisseur. "Grows only in Faera so you wouldn't see it in a Quo grocery store."

The jelly root was so good but he didn't want Sweet Sally to find that the custard puff was still sitting on his tray. It took two hands to hold and take a bite. The sweet custard oozed out the sides hitting his tongue and making its buds explode with happiness. It was the best thing he had ever had in his entire life. He was so full but could see Sweet Sally making her way to their table. He wanted to make sure she saw him enjoying her special dessert.

"You, kiddos get 'nuff to eat?" She asked. All the children nodded as they continued to nibble on their custard puff. It satisfied her to see Miles lick the powdered sugar off his fingers as he chomped the last bite. "Goodie. You kiddos enjoy your night. I'll be sure to cook you all up a great breakfast."

"Oh, my gosh. I'm going to explode," said Kalos. He hadn't said much over the meal still plenty upset for getting his friends into trouble.

"Dude I need to loosen my belt. You're going to have to roll me to my hammock," Ethan said.

Ezekiel stuck out his belly and rubbed the bloated ball it appeared to be. He let out an exaggerated groan. "Just leave me here guys. I'll be fine all night cause I'm not going to make it. Go on without me." Aubrey giggled.

The Magnus blew his whistle. "Please be sure to throw away your trash and to bus your tray to the kitchen for cleanup. We don't want to leave Sweet Sally a mess."

The children gathered their trays taking them to the kitchen line. Large soapy tubs with fluttering pixies waiting to collect the trays waited. Before the children walked away, the pixies already had the trays, plates and utensils spotless clean.

The Magnus assembled the children in a group leading them out of the Feasting Hall door. As they walked out, the sunflowers behind them went out as the Magnus began to thank his. The flower in his hand lit the way leading the children back to the Fledgling compound.

The walk was short. Ezekiel could see the campfire area on the Fledgling grounds lit as though waiting for them to arrive.

Chapter Thirteen
Fire Tales

Around the stone fire pit were various stools of nature. Spotted mushrooms, tree trunks and floating swings of vine that fell from the surrounding trees.

"Gather round and take a seat," the Magnus said as he took the center red, spotted mushroom. The children followed suit selected their seats. The fire was warm generating a soft glow that spread as wide as the circle casting shadows of their wings onto the landscape.

"Every night we will gather here for a Fire Tale session. I will share with you some of the greatest Faerman lore. While many of the tales may seem to entertain you, some may be frightening. As with all fables they are meant to serve a purpose and provide a lesson learned."

"Let me take you all to a time long ago. The Oscuridad family was a Faerman family who was very wealthy. They were the land shareowners of the mines and the main creators of dust. As you all know, the mining of stalactite crystal is what provides us the essential foundation to our enchantments. The patriarch of the family, Jareth enjoyed the riches of his profitable enterprise and overindulged his two children, Naya and Jareth II. They were given everything they wanted. Multiple colored pony Pegasus, exotic, custom-made clothing and lavish birthday parties filled with hundreds of guests. The eldest, Naya was beautiful, enjoyed the jewels, gowns and grand life, but enjoyed it most when she would carriage into Murlock with her maid-servant to parade her fortune amongst the common folk. When she colored, she loved to dress her bright red wings in dainty strings of diamond-encrusted chains. Many would admire her beauty as she strolled into town, yet too intimidated by her grandeur to ever approach her."

"Her brother Jareth II was quite the opposite. He was known to all as Deuce and he appreciated the comfortable life but desired the simple things. His gold wings were often seen hlyking, reading, or volunteering his time at the Relic Room. He had a passion for Faerman history. His father was quite proud that he had a gold Faerman in the family."

There was an awe by the children and several mouths dropped open.

"What's hlyking?" Ezekiel whispered to Kalos.

"It's when you go flying in the woods or up the hillside," he whispered back. "He had gold wings! That's super rare!"

"Their father was getting old and was ready to retire his post as the dust business leader. He wanted to keep the business in his family as his father did for him. He loved both his children equally and could not decide between them, deciding to have them share the duties."

"Jealous of her brother's gold wings and abilities that came with those wings and wanting to prove herself, Naya desired more profitability. She proposed that the Faerman work harder and faster or be replaced with pixies. She wanted to increase the cost. Deuce disagreed. He sought out ways to give back to Murlock, the town where the miners lived. He wanted to grant leisure days and gold to thank the miners. When conflicted, they approached their father and he did not advise them and he encouraged them to work out their differences."

"Deuce reached out to the community of miners. He used profits to restore the Relic Room and to build the Green Pasture Retirement Village. Most noteworthy was his sizable investment into this very camp. An experience he wished he had, had. Being a wealthy son of a business mogul was quite lonely. Having a sibling who wanted nothing to do with him was even lonelier."

"Naya, filled with envy of all the attention her brother was receiving for his good acts. She was livid when the Praeses awarded him the Medallion of Faera, the most prestigious recognition a Faerman could receive."

"Blinded by her feelings, she sought assistance from another great power in Faera. A darker power that she knew could help her rise above her brother. She requested a meeting with the leader of the Hematites, the Malum Coacter. Pleased to meet with the daughter of the richest Faerman in the land, a meeting was arranged. In the middle of the night, the Hematites came to her home, blindfolded her and took her to their palace. When the bind was removed, she was presented to the Malum. The Malum agreed to assist her but only if she arranged a meeting with Deuce. He convinced her that he admired all her brother had done for the Faerman. He instructed her to bring him to the woods to meet privately."

"Naya approached Deuce asking him to show her how to hlyke. Surprised and happy his sister wanted to spend time with him he agreed. The two soared into the skies amongst these very trees we sit beneath landing in the outskirts of the woods to break. As they rested, Hematites surrounded them, trapping them by the very same dust they produced with a binding charm. Blindfolded and afraid they were taken to the Malum."

"The binding charm wore off allowing them to remove their blindfolds. They realized they were in the infamous Collection Room. Horrified, they were surrounded by walls filled with hanging wings. The Malum pulled his dagger and instructed his followers to hold them both so he may add to his collection. Not having gold wings in his grand collection was and continues to be a desire. The seizure of the wings of another is a most unspeakable act as it renders the Faerman powerless – a shell of the living."

"Betrayed, Naya begged for her release. Deuce used her distraction to pull his dust laced with rohan root to form protection around them both. He seized his sister and flew out casting powerful charms to avoid capture. He held his sister tight delivering her safely to their father. Crying, she threw herself at her brother's feet begging for his forgiveness. He pulled her up handing her his dagger."

"Confused she accepted it. He told her. 'I'd rather you stab me in the front than in the back.' Naya was shocked and having just been on the brink of death, all that had mattered to her – the parties, diamonds and lavish frocks did not matter at all. She begged for his forgiveness. She insisted she would give up all her beloved belongings. That she would change."

"She gave her chains of diamonds to her maidservant. She gave gowns away to Faerman girls attending the Solstice Bash who could not afford to purchase their own. She was regularly seen with the large pink boxes filled with goodies from Dulcebus', handing them out to the miner children in town. Both siblings worked very hard together to make Murlock a better place."

The children were completely silent. The story was much scarier than Ezekiel had anticipated.

"The moral of the tale is within each of you. Take what you will."

The Magnus stood up. "It is now time for bed. Please make your way to your sleeping quarters and enjoy your first night. We have a lot of fun planned for tomorrow." With dust and a sunflower, he threw it ahead of the children. It hovered dreamily waiting for them to follow. As it floated along the path to the compound it expelled a soft glow that seemed to touch the other flowers along the way, illuminating the path as they passed. Once they reached the staircase, the glow faded. The children walked up the wooden spiral staircase to their rooms.

Realizing he was sleepy, Ezekiel was happy to change into his camp pajamas. They were navy blue and as soft as a baby blanket. Once dressed he climbed into his hammock, along with his new friends to settle for the night. Miles started snoring immediately.

"Crazy story from the Magnus huh," Ethan said. "I've heard it before from Pop Pop. He was a little boy when it happened so I know it's true.

"It sounded like a fairy tale. I mean, no offense but come on. Gold wings," Kalos said.

"Just so I understand, is that okay to say 'fairy tale'. Dara said that was a bad thing to say," Ezekiel inquired.

"He's saying it's a dumb story," Ethan shot back. "Dara is right. Don't tell her I said that."

"I remember the tales of the Gold Faerman. I liked them even though the stories do get a bit unbelievable but my Pop Pop would tell me that there was a little bit of gold in all of us we just need to bring it out. In a true Gold Faerman, they have the capabilities of all colors making them the most powerful. It was believed that the world needed one to balance out the rising evil," Ethan explained.

"The Hematites?" Ezekiel asked.

"Yes. The Hematites were known to kidnap young Faerman and enchant them to do their bidding making them forget their parents. They wanted to be the most powerful and they found a way to achieve more capabilities beyond what they were born with."

"Are you sure you want to tell him all that?" asked Kalos. "It's scary."

"He needs to know," Ethan said plainly. "The Hematites get the capabilities of other Faerman by using their dagger to take the wings of another. They then obtain the power of that Faerman leaving that Faerman powerless."

"Are you sure you guys aren't trying to scare me?" Ezekiel said with a skeptical tone.

"No. They say they have a palace, where they keep the wings of their victims to please their leader," Ethan said.

"My grandfather said that the Guard has kept the Hematites under control. They are weak and rumored to have lost the Malum," Kalos fought back.

"Malum?" Ezekiel

"The Malum Coacter is their leader. They select a new one when the one dies," said Ethan.

"Well isn't there a Gold Faerman to you know, help out with that?" Ezekiel asked.

"He hasn't been seen in years," said Ethan with a disappointed tone. "I've never seen him."

"It's also been rumored that the reason why we have this camp is to train us to protect ourselves from them. We learn protective enchantments to stand a chance against getting swiped," Kalos said.

"That sounds wonderful. And I thought that the Magnus' story was scary," Ezekiel said. "You guys really know how to tuck a guy in for bed."

"You've got a lot to learn about being a Faerman. Just trying to help," Ethan said.

"Thanks," Ezekiel said.

"Swathe," Kalos said as he took off his glasses, setting them on his trunk. The moonlight was then shielded and the boys fell asleep.

Ezekiel awoke in pure darkness. He stood at a long familiar dark path leading to a yellow house surrounded by a white, wooden fence. He recognized the white rose bushes and quickly felt a feeling of anticipation rush over him. He knew his dad was in there. He had seen him there before.

He reached for the latch on the gate, pushing it open. A force in his body pushed him on to the porch and gave him the bravery to enter inside and confront this stranger who had abandoned him. The room was dark and lit by a single, candle flame. His shadow was vast and dark as it shot up the glowing wall. Amongst the shadow, across the long room he could see the dark outline of a man.

Dad! It's me! Turn around!

The figure jolted, turned but he could not see his face clearly. The figure ran further into the room. Ezekiel was not going to let him go without trying. He urged his body forward to his fastest run, but his legs felt as though he was running through deep sand. He pushed his legs hard and could hardly inch forward. The black figure had disappeared.

Dad! Why don't you want me?

The shadows answered back.

I do.

Chapter Fourteen
Camp Tour

Ezekiel woke up to the sounds of an energetic trumpet. He felt rested, but recalled his dream and it left him bewildered. Miles stretched letting out a loud yawn.

"Morning," Miles said as he jumbled out of his hammock.

"Morning," the others replied back.

"Expose," grumbled Kalos revealing the rising sun. Surrounding their compound were bronze colored horns with fluttering wings and small beady eyes. They had grumpy expressions on what seemed to be their face.

Once the horns saw that everyone was up, they fluttered to the ground transforming into the cutest, furry, little puff balls. They had tiny hands and feet which helped them roll expeditiously down the path toward the campground knoll.

"Changelings. Gotta get me one of those to terrorize Dara," Ethan said.

The boys quickly dressed in their uniforms to race down the stairs to meet the girls. It seemed as though everyone was excited to start the day. Chatter amongst the children was just as jovial as it was on the bus the day before. Before Ezekiel could check in with Dara and Aubrey the Magnus approached them from what seemed to be out of thin air.

Pew!

The Magnus blew his whistle. "Good morning campers! Glad to see you all out for morning orders on time. I will lead you to the campground knoll for flag salute and the daily schedule."

The children followed him down a dirt path surrounded by rows of unfamiliar plants. Small wooden stake signs plunged into the dirt labeled the vegetation. Ezekiel squinted to get a look at what was growing.

"Jelly root," he said to himself as he eyed the blue tipped leaves emerging from the earth. "Ornsicle Stalk," he read as he passed lengthy green stalks that looked like corn. When staring closer he could see the giant kernels of tangerine-colored cobs emerging from the stalks.

"Those are so good!" Miles said pointing them out for Ezekiel to see. "They taste like orange cream!"

Several strange, teal feathered, chicken-like birds ran across their path with a side to side type hobble. Their bright pink beaks showcased a set of rather big white bucked teeth.

"What is that?" Ezekiel asked. "Not that it's shocking for Camp Strange I'm sure," he added.

"That's an Eurp! Their eggs are delicious!" Miles said.

"Eurps are indigenous to Faera so you wouldn't know about them. They have evolved in both color and tooth size according to Shantelle Simonette's, *A Faerman's Guide to the Evolution of Indigenous Creatures* book. It's been an amazing read," Dara chimed in.

"Sounds so much fun," Ethan said sarcastically. Dara ignored him.

They halted once reaching the large circular patch of dirt that surrounded and an intricately stacked pile of rock with a flagpole emerging from the center. Colorful florals bordered the pile and were outlined with more rock, then more flowers, then more rock creating a mesmerizing ring pattern. Five teen campers held in their hands a folded navy colored cloth. The color units joined them reciting their cheers from the night before. The Fledglings were excited to see them at it again.

The Magnus and color unit instructors stood up front. The five campers centered by the flagpole began their ceremony.

Colors presented!

They lifted their feet off the ground as they fluttered forward in sync. They surrounded the flagpole and attached the large navy material to the clasps of the ropes. The material shot up revealing the navy camp flag emblazoned with the camp crest. They formed a line facing the campers still hovering.

Wings up!

All the color unit campers lifted up hovering just slightly over ground with one hand behind their back and the other touching the shoulder of the person next to them. The Fledglings looked around for direction. The Magnus gestured his hand up onto the orange winged instructor next to him, nodding for them to follow. Once all connected, the flag leader led them in the camp salute.

I pledge to try my best,
In all the camp tests.
Enchantments and charms,
To protect, not harm,
To create Faera peace,
I will never cease.

The colored units pulled their hands from each other's shoulders into a fist they pulled into their chest over their heart, then down. The Fledglings were a beat behind but followed suit. The color unit leaders pulled their groups into smaller meetings to discuss the day's schedule.

The Magnus approached the Fledglings. "After breakfast, your day will be filled with a campground tour. Each of you will be given a map and compass to help you navigate the grounds. After your tour, you will break for lunch. Before returning to meet, be sure to grab your daggers. We will be heading to Seers Lake for your Dagger Bonding."

Ethan motioned to Ezekiel mouthing, "Yes!" Naturally he had no clue what this meant.

The Magnus continued. "Dinner will be served at the lake tonight among the stars as we will not have enough time to walk back to the Feasting Hall for dinner. Miss Sweet Sally has been kind enough to arrange for a meal flight from our pixies."

"There will not be a fire tale tonight as the Dagger Bonding and night picnic will take most of our time. We have a full day for you tomorrow so it will be important for you all to get your rest tonight."

Breakfast seemed quick. Sweet Sally had prepared a full buffet of multiple flavors of sausage, eggs, ham, pancakes, waffles, crepes filled with chocolate, fried jelly root, butter muffins and bagel crisps. Ezekiel was not that hungry and still felt satisfied from his large meal the night before. Naturally, Miles was in heaven enjoying his third butter muffin.

"What is the Dagger Bonding?" Ezekiel asked as he took a gulp of honey mead.

"Only the moment I have been waiting for!" Ethan shouted.

"Ugh. Great, you with a knife. Just what we need," Dara replied.

"A knife? I brought one that my uncle gave me. Am I supposed to bring that with me?" Ezekiel asked.

"After the bonding, you will always have it on you. It has magical properties. It will come if you call it. It will transport you where you need to go. It's your way to protect yourself against losing your wings!" Ethan said enthusiastically catching the attention of a few Fledgling girls sitting nearby. They had concerned looks on their face.

"Excuse my brother for being a bit over dramatic. He believes too much in all that Hematite nonsense. Don't let him bring you down with him."

"Down with him?" Ezekiel asked.

"Yeah, down with him to crazy town," she replied.

"She's just scared to do the bonding. You have to swim in the lake!" Ethan said.

"I *can* swim," she said annoyed. "I just don't want to with a dagger. Who *knows* what lives in that lake."

"I'm sure there is nothing as creepy as you," he shot back.

Aubrey giggled. Dara shot her a look of surprise. "Oh, I wasn't laughing at you. I was thinking it would be quite funny to cast a floating charm on the boys while they try to swim in the lake. That would be hilarious!"

Dara grinned.

After breakfast, the Magnus accompanied by several pixies assembled the Fledglings. "Campers, my friends here would like to hand you all a campgrounds map and compass. Both have enchanted properties that will help you on your way. Your map will always lead you in the right direction to where you need to go."

"What about the compass?" Ezekiel asked realizing he actually said that out loud.

"It's a compass my dear boy. It points you in the direction your map tells you to go. They're like a team. North, south, east or west," he replied.

Ezekiel's face turned pink and filled hot. He heard some giggles in the crowd. How was he to know it was a plain ordinary compass. Everything else around here was not as it seemed. Hiding his face into his map trying to shuffle behind his friends, he hoped not being directly seen others may forget what he just asked.

He led the children on the worn path to an open area with wooden picnic tables and stools. The area was covered by arches of interwoven tree branches. The arches cast a nice shade over the area. Various color splatter was on the floor. "Here is where you will meet with instructor Kunal Veer. He is a master of the Faerman Craft and unit leader to the Arbors. Here you will learn how to grind elements with nature to make your perfect dust. You will start your first session tomorrow."

The children continued along the path enjoying the colorful insects that jumped from flower to flower alongside them as if to get a better look at them. They approached an open green field with five skyscraping poles. Each pole had a wooden platform above with a different color unit banner hanging from it. Below each pole were clouds so soft they looked like giant cotton balls. A wooden staked sign read, *Flight Field*. The Magnus turned to the children smiling.

"Here you will learn the fundamentals of flight by instructor Trav Iocus, unit leader of the Elements. He will show you the steps to proper hovering, take off, soaring, and of course landing while maintaining humor despite your falls and bumps along the way. Also, this is the very spot our fastest fliers compete in Flight Tournaments."

Ezekiel was most excited to learn to fly. If he was going to be a kid with wings, he felt he should master this. With hope, he wouldn't be awful like he was on the baseball field.

The Magnus waved the children to follow along the path. They were quite a distance from where they started and the Fledgling compound was just a tiny square in the distance. Faded, sun-weathered stables housed horse like creatures in colors Ezekiel had never seen. They had wide strong wings. One was seen happily trotting along, stretching out his wings as though showing off for the children.

"Here you will learn to ride a Peggie. The flight of a Pegasus is quite a remarkable one. Note they really enjoy wild asparagus so I recommend bringing them some before you ride. They will be more likely to bring you back," the Magnus said with a chuckle.

"They might not bring us back to the stables?" Miles seemed concerned. He more than anyone appreciated good food but was concerned where he'd be taken if he didn't provide an ample offering.

"It's not that big of a deal. They may drop you off at the lake or another unit's compound. They don't leave the campgrounds or anything – I think," Ethan said.

"I don't know if I'm going to want to take that chance," Ezekiel said.

"They are amazing. I can't wait to learn more about them!" Dara said surprising everyone. She realized their shock and quickly added, "What? I'm fascinated with creatures that are so intelligent."

Wanting to be brave, Ezekiel added, "You're right. I'll have to give them a go." He smiled at her.

"Just over here around the corner you'll find the archery lanes," the Magnus pointed out toward several campers who were out on the lanes very attentive to the instructor. "You'll get to spend some time with Mateo Conti, unit leader of the Flames.

The map in Ezekiel's hands illuminated the path to a location labeled, *The Pond*. "There is a pond here too?" he asked his friends. "I mean how much swimming are we expected to do around here? He was more concerned with his flight lessons.

"It's the Padsphere Pool! That's where the teams play. I can't wait for the first game!" cheered Ethan.

"Oh, yeah, Padsphere. Still don't know what that is," Ezekiel said.

The group stood at a large stadium like structure. A bright blue gate lead to the Pond. The Magnus had a giant smile across his face. "Here my friends, is where we come to enjoy the athletics of Padsphere. Let's quietly peek inside and we may see a bit of practice going on."

The group walked in. Ezekiel's heartbeat and anxiety built up in him stepping into the facility. He knew his mom was quite the player and he was literally walking the same steps she had. He quickly recognized the scene from his mother's photo. There were stands on all sides of the large oval pool of water. An orange rope laid in the middle of the pool hovering on its surface. Beneath the surface, plunged several feet under were a pile of balls that seemed unmoving. From his view, he could see two campers on each side of the pile underneath the water. They popped up every couple of minutes for air and down under they went. Each side of the dividing line also had two campers out of the pool hovering attentively with their eyes on their third player who held a ball firmly to their chest. Lastly there was a player on each end of the pool who hovered as though protecting the large green lily pad with a netted stick just underneath them floating on the pool. The lily pads had a few balls placed on them neatly.

The campers out there were from the Arbors. Their unit leader, Kunal blew his whistle. Suited in green suits, players dived into the pool trying their best to grab a ball from the pile on each side. Beneath the water, you could see the difficulty to retrieve and defend a ball. "Those are the Retrievers! They have to pull a ball up from the pile to pass to the Celerpoint – the player hovering above. He's waiting to get the ball so he can cross the centerline, pass those Sphereguards and the Padguard onto the pad. That's how you score!" Ethan exclaimed. His face was elated with excitement.

Watching it was a bit chaotic as each side had to simultaneously defend, retrieve and attempt to score. They popped in and out of the pool attempting to pass the ball to each other trying to avoid being slammed into the pool. Ezekiel had a new respect for the game. Despite being told they had to be quiet, the children were cheering as the Celerpoint bested the Padguard scoring a point. It did look like fun.

The Magnus waved the children over and they reluctantly followed. "The first game will be at week's end. Until then, let us allow our Arbor friends to focus on their practice. Maps out."

The map illuminated the path to the lake. As they walked along the trail, a large swampy area caught his eye. Wide trees stood tall with wispy trails of green. Upon the trees were platforms of floating hammocks covered by sheer drapery. There were streams of water that flowed every which way alongside small leaf topped cabins. A blue painted sign was staked into the ground that announced this space as the Granters unit.

The children were led to the lakeside. The sun was warm glistening sparkle off the surface of the blue lake. The lake was framed by monolithic, green, towering trees.

"Gather around," the Magnus said calling the children over closer to the lake. "This is Seers Lake. We will report here after lunch. The lake is known to have magical properties and has been known to show visions of the past, present and future to those who are worthy to see it. Living in the lake are many peaceful creatures. Be respectful of their living space and they will be respectful of your presence."

"No way am I coming to swim in there after today," Dara whispered to Aubrey.

Ethan formed wings with his arms and whispered a silent cluck at her. She stuck her tongue out at him.

Ezekiel checked his map to see how far out they were from the Feasting Hall. The map glowed showing he was a five-minute walk away. His compass spun to the north-west.

"Your maps should be alerting you just about now to report to lunch. Enjoy and I will see you all back here shortly. Be sure to bring your daggers with you." The Magnus dismissed them to lunch.

Chapter Fifteen
Dagger Bonding

Sweet Sally never ceased to disappoint. Lunch was a widespread variety of triple-stacked grilled cheese sandwiches, fried orsicle, and felly weed noodles. All of these things were much different than what Ezekiel was accustomed to, but to his surprise, he really enjoyed them.

With much excitement, the children rushed to their compound not even needing to rely on the guidance of their enchanted maps. Ezekiel felt a bit intimidated of his dagger. The idea of having a weapon on him at all times was odd to him. His uncle referred to it as a "tool" but Ezekiel assumed that was just more fluff to conceal the details of the truth.

Ezekiel lifted the latch on his trunk. There was his straight edged dagger sitting right on top his extra camp pajamas. He pulled it out, carefully ensuring that it stayed in its protective leather casing.

"Hey cool! You have a new edition Cantata!" Ethan scared the crap out of Ezekiel as he seemed to pop up from behind him like a well-trained ninja.

"Not sure. My uncle handed it to me just before we got on the bus."

"Well that is supposed to be a limited-edition blade. I got mine from Tabernam's." Ethan held up his curved leather dagger case. "It's not as fancy as yours, but I always liked the curved blade. It reminds me of those cool Arabian night's battles. Ma says it would give me more personality cause no one would have the same one." He attached the dagger holder onto his leather belt adjusting his empty dust pouch.

"I have a Tabernam too!" Miles chimed in as he was finishing the last bites of puff pastry he snuck from the Feasting Hall. He held up his wide straight edge dagger case. "I went for a jagged edge. I wanted mine to have more *umph*." He dusted crumbs from his hands and fixed his case to his belt as fast as Ethan had. Ezekiel was careful to observe how they did this so he copied their steps. The case had a leather-bound ring that looped right into his belt.

Timid, Kalos fixed his dagger case to his hip. Ezekiel wanted to include him in the excitement as he seemed a bit quiet this morning. Ezekiel assumed he was still shaken a bit by the four-story fall.

"I like yours Kal. It's fierce. Suits you well," Ezekiel said.

"Thanks. My mom picked it out."

"Can I see it? I bet it's great." Ezekiel was trying to be encouraging.

Kalos seemed reluctant but his strong desire to be liked talked him into it. He pulled it off his hip, then presented it in his palm. The case was a red leather and a bit worn. The dagger itself had a unique curl to the handles.

"That case was my grandfather's," Kalos muttered.

"It's cool. I like the handle," Ezekiel said eying Miles and Ethan to chime in.

"Yeah man, can't wait to see how you personalize it," Ethan said.

"I like the red case. Was your grandfather a Flame?" asked Miles.

"Uh, yeah. He's super proud about it. Mom and great-granddad were too. It was kind of a disappointment 'cause mom married a quo. Grandfather was not happy about it. Sam was kind of the weirdo who sprouted as an Arbor. There's a lot of hope in the family that I'll be a Flame too," Kalos said. He seemed to be apprehensive about it.

The boys head down the winding staircase where they quickly found Dara and Aubrey. Both girls were sporting their distinctive daggers on their left hip. Dara caught Ezekiel's stare at her dagger. He was trying to see what kind she had so he could bring this up as a point of conversation later. Maybe even compliment her on it even though she certainly was not a girl who fell prey to such admiration. She beat him to it. "Nice dagger," she said.

Ezekiel blushed. "Thanks. It's a-"

"It's a new edition Cantata!" Ethan interjected.

"Wow, very nice," she said mildly impressed. "I think you'll find the bonding cool. A Faerman relies on it to get around. You're not allowed to have one or use it until you're age ready for camp."

"I'm so going to decorate mine with the greens and blossoms of foxglove," Aubrey said cheerfully.

"I'm still not sure about how I'll decorate mine. I'm thinking binding the handle with clover root and a magnolia. Or maybe a gardenia. Once we're bonding, I think I'll know," Dara replied.

"We decorate them? Like with flowers and stuff?" Ezekiel asked looking down at his hip. The thought of making his manly tool look girly disappointed him.

"No silly! Unless you want flowers that is!" Dara replied looking up from her map as she glanced at her compass.

"I see nothing wrong with it if he does want flowers. I think a strong succulent could be very masculine," Aubrey said.

"Yeah, a strong *succulent*," said Ethan mockingly, emphasizing the 'suck' in the word.

Both girls rolled their eyes at him.

"Off to the lake then?" Kalos offered trying to keep the peace.

Dara had her map out which gleamed with the steps needed to reach the lake. She wasn't scared to swim but was a bit nervous about any water creatures they may run into. Although she was very interested in the studies of science, origins of species and just a general desire to know more, she knew there were things in there she could not control or see coming.

They passed swiftly through the eurp path walking carefully to avoid stepping on them or the mother hen's eggs. She eyed them meticulously with warning.

"Stubborn buggers!" Kalos said jumping over a snuggled group of them who lay in the middle of the path.

"Well we are in their home," Aubrey said defending their stubbornness.

The boys slowed a bit as they passed the Pond. They all stood up on their tippy toes with hope to catch a glimpse through the side columns of some action by the teams practicing for an upcoming game. Ezekiel was just shy of seeing the water. He could make out the bold red swimwear.

Dad was a Flame. I wonder if he played Padsphere?

He wanted to see more as his mind wandered a bit fantasizing about his parent's successes on these very same grounds. His feet began to lift off the floor. He could now see the practice action clearly. The Retriever flourished with success from the water throwing a ball to the Celerpoint just before being slammed into the pool. The Celerpoint advanced across the pond nearly getting tackled by a Retriever. Once he crossed the defensive line he faced a lone Padsguard.

"What are you doing?!" shouted a red-haired, blue-eyed, pretty lady. She had a white cardigan with the camp crest neatly embroidered on the chest. Her bright blue eyes were very familiar to him. He tried placing where he knew her and lost his concentration, plopping to the ground clumsily when Aubrey spoke.

"Hi mom."

"Hello. May I ask why your friend thinks it's okay for him to fly when that is not permitted until he's practiced on the Flight Field and has been cleared by Mr. Iocus?"

Ezekiel scrambled up. He had not realized his clear view of the pond was due to his hovering. "I-I'm sorry ma'am," Ezekiel stammered. "I didn't know I was, um, flying."

"*Really* mommy. He's just found out he's a Faerman and he's never been trained. He can't help it," Aubrey defended.

The kids all wondered why Aubrey's mom was at camp. She must have sensed it and calmed her demeanor.

"How rude of me. I am Dr. Allyssa Walker, unit leader of the Healers, Campground Physician and Aubrey's mom."

All the children offered introductions and pleasantries.

"Now you must be Ezekiel Raroso," she said.

"Yes. That's me," he replied, a bit nervous about where this was going.

"I heard about yesterday's incident. That paired with today seems like I should issue another demerit." His face fell further than it had been. "But, being that I know your parents well, and understand your circumstances, I am willing to turn a blind eye this one time." She smiled at him hoping to warm him up.

His nerves forced a smile back. "Thank you so much."

"You'd better hurry. I'm sure they are expecting you at the lake if that map is any indication on your time frame," she said giving a glance toward the map in Dara's hand that was now glowing red footprints urging them to hurry.

"Nice to meet you!" the children called to her as they ran to the lake. She waved them off.

·　　·　　·　　·　　·

When they approached the lake, the Fledglings were all surrounded on the shore barefoot. The children hurriedly kicked off their shoes and blended themselves into the crowd as if they'd been there on time. The Magnus emerged from the lake walking simply onto the shore.

"Welcome to your Dagger Bonding! I just spoke with the tandos. They are aware of our need to use the lake and have agreed to maintain their dolphin-like shape in order to keep you all at ease. Everyone loves a dolphin, right?" he chuckled. "Tandos are shapeshifters who use this ability as a defensive mechanism. They shift into something that is more scary or intimidating than what they are facing. Being that there will be the presence of you harmless Fledglings, I was able to convince their leader to allow us access."

"Now, you will see a lot of fresh water ivy. Please do not pull on it as it provides sustenance to the locals. Be as swift as possible in your swim to the bottom of the lake. Hold onto your dagger tightly. Once you've placed yourself firmly to the ground, plunge your dagger into the lake floor and think firmly about standing on the shore in fresh, dry clothing. Any questions?"

There weren't any. Just excited smiling faces and chatter. Ezekiel had about a thousand questions but thought he'd save them for later.

"One more important note before we get started." This silenced the crowd immediately. "Seers Lake gets its name for its enchanted properties. Should the lake deem you and worthy of needing some insight, it may provide it. Do not be alarmed by this vision for it is simply an illusion. Do not allow it to distract you from the magical pull of your bonding. Once you are all done, I will allow you time to personalize your dagger. Now on my whistle, *pew!*"

The children spread across the long lake deck to find a spot to dive in. Ezekiel looked and saw that only a handful of children did not jump in. Dara being one of them. He looked at her with encouragement. She seemed to avoid his eye contact.

The Magnus approached. "Ah, I always have a handful who need a bit of extra encouragement. Well, off you go then!" he said parting his hands. In that motion, the children left standing were tossed into the lake on each side.

Ezekiel plunged into the warm water taking in as much air as he could. He opened his eyes. In front of him he could see the long lengths of freshwater ivy swaying to the beat of the water. Below several children disappeared in the darkest part of the water, at least 15 feet from him. He felt his hip to ensure that his dagger was still there. Once he felt the hard leather handle, he swam down underneath the deck he was just plunged from to look for Dara. He didn't want her to be alone. He saw someone swim alongside him. He whipped to that direction. Nothing.

He proceeded to swim scanning the lake floor. His sight was blocked by vegetation. Where was Dara? Where was anyone?

How am I breathing underwater?

Not a naturally good swimmer, but good enough to pass the swimming test at his old camp to be in the 8-foot deep section of the pool, it had just dawned on him that he was effortlessly swimming without need for breath. He figured Dara must have mustered up the courage to just go for it. He began an effort to plunge himself downward to the lake floor. He passed through tendrils of lake ivy careful to not wade or kick them. He started to get closer to the darkness. He gave himself an extra push of energy. It was so dark. He stopped, placed his hands in forward to feel out what was in front of him. He focused on placing his feet down to feel for the lake floor. Once he felt the cold sand between his toes he knew it was time to sink further. He unclipped the latch on his dagger, pulled it out and with both hands plunged it into the ground.

Nothing happened. He removed it from the floor. Perhaps he did it wrong. He tried again. Nothing. He held tight staring into the darkness of where his hands would be he could see a handsome man remove his crown. He seemed happy to do so. He stared into the joyous eyes of his beautiful young wife who also removed her large, diamond encrusted crown. They embrace. She leaves the room and never returns. Ezekiel could sense the heartbreak in the man. He cannot see them it is all black. Still holding onto his dagger thinking fiercely about being dry and standing on the shore the image of a figure in a black hooded cloak, with beautiful hands stood afar. It seemed to see that Ezekiel was looking at it and it ran. Guards ran after it shooting out chants and charms to catch it.

He could hear eerie whispers chanting, "Take the fall. Take the fall. Take the fall." He spun around in the darkness trying to find light then gravity fell beneath him. He was falling. He tried pulsing his wings hard to fight the fall but it was as though they were covered in concrete. As he approached the ground he could see a faint light appear suddenly where he could see a crying toddler standing in the corner of a dark room. Large swelling eyes with tears streaming down his face he begged for his 'mama'.

Ezekiel stood on the warm sand clutching his dagger tightly. The brightness of the sun blinded him.

"What the heck took you so long!" Ethan shouted as his friends surrounded him. The other Fledglings stared too.

"Um, not sure. It wasn't working," he replied nervously. He felt as though he was in trouble.

The Magnus ran over, kneeling down to his level, examining his face. "You okay buddy?"

"I think so. I mean, yes. I'm sorry?"

"Did you run into trouble down there? Stuck in some lake ivy? Upset a tando?" The Magnus was very concerned.

"No, I mean, it didn't seem like it took long."

"Ah, I see." He turned to the children. "Campers. Looks like we're all good here. Please proceed to the grounds to find what you must to personalize your daggers. Dinner is in an hour. Please report back here for a meal on the shore to celebrate this achievement. Remember, daggering is restricted to the campgrounds and within Murlock. With practice, we will be able to achieve travel outside of Faera. Travel into our camp is forbidden and we have special enchantments protecting our grounds."

The children seemed to hesitate. The Magnus widened his eyes as if to say *go* as he held onto Ezekiel's shoulder to stay. The children received it and dispersed. Ezekiel's friends walked away giving him glances of support. When the crowd was far enough, the Magnus smiled at him.

"The lake has granted you with a vision I assume?"

"I think so. I mean, I could have been hallucinating because I was underwater so long."

"Perhaps. Most who are not gifted in the unit of Granter find it difficult to be underwater any longer than a well-trained quo. Being that you spent an hour down there may be a strong indication that you will sprout blue." He smiled. "Blue Faerman are highly skilled in aquatics making regulating them in Padsphere quite the challenge. Anyway, what else did you see?"

Ezekiel had experience with being strange. It seemed to be happening even in the strangest and most unbelievable place he's ever been. He knew all too well that even admitting to a hallucination would be a cause for concern in this world too. He didn't want to lie and perhaps if he was meant to see these insights, the Magnus could be of assistance.

Ezekiel proceeded to describe what he had seen in great detail. The Magnus listened attentively with no change in his expression. This calmed Ezekiel.

"Well, for reasons that cannot be explained, the lake felt you needed that information. It only presents insight it feels the receiver needs to know. Much of what you described sounds like the past. Perhaps these reasons will reveal themselves in time. Until then, is there anything I can help you with? I understand that you are new to Faera."

"Why do I have to carry this?" Ezekiel asked freely holding his dagger.

"Well, that is your magical property. It allows you to transport as you did today from the lake dry. It allows you to connect to the enchanted elements of our world, nature, elements all living things. You'll use it tomorrow to make your first dust which will allow you to cast simple spells. You will learn how to transport through earth mounds. When camp is over, you will be prepared to travel home, leaving Faera by dagger. As you and your dagger experience more life, the stronger your bond becomes, so strong you can call upon it for help and it will come to you."

"I guess I just always thought daggers were for weaponry reasons. Bad guys and robbers."

"Ah yes. You are a smart one. Well, since you ask, yes, our dagger is our form of wing protection. There are forces out there that desire what is not naturally theirs for the taking. Once your color sprouts, you will be placed in your unit to train on specific skills to enhance your craft and protect yourself against dark Faerman."

More Hematite stories came. Their existence was becoming more real to him. The children began to make their way back to the shoreline.

"Well it seems I've taken your entire hour to personalize your dagger. Several apologies." The Magnus scanned around and patted his pockets. He looked at his wrist. He had a dark brown leather woven bracelet with a few amber colored beads. He pulled a bit of dust from his pouch, releasing it onto his wrist. The strands of leather unbound, twisting magically off his arm, then onto Ezekiel's dagger, winding, crisscrossing and then tying itself onto his handle. The strands of amber hung off the side.

"Amber is known to have strong protective properties against dark forces. Plus, it looks wicked cool." The Magnus smiled looking for Ezekiel's response.

"Thank you. You didn't have to do that. I could have thrown something together," Ezekiel responded with a big grin. It did look pretty cool compared to flowers or succulents.

"Anything worth doing is not thrown together. All our moments happen for a reason. I believe this one will serve you well."

Chapter Sixteen
The Aoberon Tale

The sun had set behind the lake and horizon casting a purple haze in the sky. The children had soft picnic blankets, woven by the most skilled Faerman. They were made in such a way that they deflected the sand of the shore allowing the campers to dine comfortably. Sweet Sally sent pixies over to the lake with baskets filled with a delicious roast chicken, honey biscuits and berries. The pixies released tiny bottles of honey mead from the air as they spun around in their patterns of service. Once Ezekiel caught the bottle in his hand, it engorged to a full size.

"Okay, what happened down there?" asked Ethan who wasted no time to inquire once he noticed the Magnus occupied by the arrival of the unit instructors.

"I saw something. Maybe it was nothing. I dunno. The Magnus thinks I may be an early sprouter of blue," Ezekiel said stuffing biscuit into his mouth.

"Well that would explain how you managed to hold your breath underwater that long. Most of us were down and out in less than a minute," Dara explained.

"Why didn't the Magnus just go and get you? Summon you out. He has the ability," Kalos said.

"Now that I think about it, he didn't really seem surprised about it. Happy even," Ezekiel replied.

"I was scared you drowned," Aubrey muffled.

The dreary undertone of her words was mulled over by the entrance of dancing fireflies that circled around them illuminating the darkening sky.

Ezekiel shared with his friends everything he saw at the lake floor in detail as they continued to eat their dinner.

"That sounds like the Aoberon Tale," Miles said. "My grandmother would tell me the story before bed."

"I know that one!" Kalos chimed in. "It's the one where the king decided to not be king anymore. The queen convinced him to end the monarchy. Then she went missing."

"Yeah. The elders believed it was a punishment for ending it," Dara said. "Something I don't understand because it created the democracy and leadership of the Praeses. Faerman got to vote and decide on stuff."

"Yes, but a lot of Faerman didn't want things to change. They liked things the way they were. My grandfather told me the one thing that stayed was the Guard. They worried that the Hematite would rise up against the start of the new leader who happened to be the daughter of the king and queen. She was the newly elected Praeses," Kalos said. The group was surprised at his level of knowledge on the subject. "Hey, my grandfather can go on and on about these things. I'm not a nerd or anything."

"I think that is a pretty common story," Aubrey offered. "It's a major part of Faerman history. It changed the way things were done for those crossing over to live among quo's. The Council encouraged it but many Faerman were against cross-breeding, learning quo customs or even worse – that quos would learn about Faera."

More surprised faces that Aubrey didn't seem to notice. The others were amused by how surprisingly smart their friend was.

The pixies soon arrived and removed their plates leaving behind floating sunflowers that offered more light. The Magnus approached as the unit instructors left in a hurry. Mateo Conti turned back for a moment to face the children as he threw a fire charm in the center of the beach. The Magnus opened his dust pouch, grabbed a pinch of dust in each hand. He flung out both his hands releasing the fine iridescent powder over the children. It seemed to float like a sheer haze as it spread amongst them with a trail of fog to his palms. He lifted his hands raising the children and picnic blankets up in the air. He pulled them closer forming a crescent circle.

"Let us meet for our next fire tale. Mr. Conti was kind enough to cast a fire for us to enjoy." He cleared his throat and seemed a bit hesitant to begin.

"Today's tale is one of Faerman history. Many of you may already be familiar with it but I was recently inspired to share it with you. Typically, we do not discuss such politically filled tales in the first or second years at camp, but after discussing it with the rest of the unit instructors, most agree that it should be fine."

Ezekiel knew immediately where this was going. It had been his vision that had "inspired" him. In his gut, he knew that there was more to this story than his friends had shared or that the Magnus let on.

"Many years ago, all of Faera was ruled by the Aoberon family. The King had a wife, queen Navi who was adored by their people. She was beautiful and smart and a good mother to their three daughters, Gilla, Gabrielle and Geneva. Their leadership was fair and they were liked by the people they ruled over. King Aoberon had a strong Guard that let his followers feel protected, even under the uprising of the Hematite."

"As you may all recall during your travel through the cenote, passing through the open valley, pool to Queen Navi and named after her. Legend has it that she had the gift of a seer and was able to look upon the stars, read them and foresee the present future. The King heavily relied on her star reading to make decisions for the people."

"The Queen looked upon the stars for the last time seeing the pain of the Faerman, the fall of Faera and the uprising of evil if the monarchy continued. She shared this with the King who was devastated with concern. The Queen had never been incorrect in her predictions. The King insisted they call upon the Gold Faerman, Herc Oscuridad to work with the Guard, to help protect their followers and their way of life. The Queen plead with him to not place all their hope in one individual. How could one person make a difference? Depressed, yet convinced he agreed. He sought her counsel on how the land should be ruled, for surely someone had to be in charge. The Queen offered the details of a democracy – where the people used their voice to vote and select who they thought should lead the people. This was modeled off of the Quotidian system. The Queen was clever. She encouraged her middle child, Gabriella to run for Praeses as she was most like-minded like her father. The Faerman were very apprehensive and skeptical of her ability to be a leader and make wise decisions."

"A week before the election, as a symbolic gesture, the King and Queen met with the Praeses candidates and removed their crowns as means to pass the torch of leadership. The King wanted to offer words of appreciation and advice before parting the palace that would soon be the site of the Council. Navi left them and was never seen again."

Ezekiel shifted in his seat. He felt warm and sweaty. He looked down at his hands and could see the beads of iridescence forming.

"Aoberon was devastated. Gabriella led the Guard in the second largest Faerman hunt of all time. They were unsuccessful in retrieving any sign of where Navi went. Gabriella's leadership during this devastating time won the Faerman people over. She was elected the first Praeses."

"Now Praeses Gabriella Aoberon had a strong desire to do well but it was quickly obvious that she lacked the intellectual bandwidth to manage the job. She was accustomed to the life of a princess. She was not entirely familiar with Faerman Law. She elected her friends and family members to take high powered positions. Her biggest failure was her appointment of Puck Lumiere as the Dux. He was her father's friend and advisor but actually more of a humorous companion. Through their lack of leadership, wise counsel and connection with their people, the Hematite were able to act freely. Children just your age were frequently kidnapped from their homes. They were then enchanted to do the bidding of the Hematite and would be found by the Guard after committing their crimes to be confused. Most had their memories of their parents removed and many could not be cured or restored even with the work of the best Healers. Herc could not battle the numbers he was against."

Ezekiel had broken out into a full sweat. He was hot. He wiped his forehead with his sleeve. His mouth felt like the driest desert. All his friends had their eyes locked onto the Magnus as to not miss a single word he was about to say.

"Lucky for us, the position did not fit Gabriella long. The Faerman protested, used their voice and she was removed. This was a pivotal moment because it forced the people to use their voice and vote to elect leaders who could represent them. The Council was formed to protect the people from this occurring again and they worked closely with the Guard and Herc to ward off the Hematite."

"So, see. Some tales do have an obvious happy ending. I implore you to think about this tale and how it can relate to you. Learning about history is beyond the purpose of storytelling. It is to enhance the mind to make greater decisions for tomorrow. With that Fledglings, I dismiss you to your compound and trust you may find your way back quickly if you all dagger there. Please concentrate your magic on your hammock, and only your hammock. We certainly do not want boys popping up in on the girl's floors."

He seemed to give Ezekiel a wink as he pulled his dagger out, plunged it into the ground and disappeared.

The children were eager to travel by dagger and many were gone before Ezekiel or his friends could stand up. His friends seemed to wait for him to say something.

"I don't know about you, but I'm so hot. Must have been the fire. That Conti guy gave us a super hot flame huh," Ezekiel said to lighten the mood.

"I'm fine," was replied back in unison from the others.

"Well I think I'll just grab a sip from the lake if you don't mind. It's freshwater and all. I used to do it all the time at my other camp."

He approached the shore of the water cupping his hands, bending down to for a scoop. His hands entered the cold water. Something grabbed his hands, pulling him down into the darkness.

He was completely submerged in the lake. He could not see but he could feel the freshwater ivy brushing against his arms and legs. Although terrified, he remained still to not disturb them. A soft glow presented just slightly illuminating the outline of what appeared to be a dolphin.

Oh crap. I upset the tandos and now I'm a goner.

"I'm sorry I drank your home. I really am. I was just so thirsty-"

It's okay, and you're not a goner.

"Wow I didn't know you could talk."

I'm not. You are.

For just a second Ezekiel was confused. He realized that he was hearing what the tando was thinking.

You can hear me. It makes me glad to run into a land dweller who can. I do have to tell you that I can sense that you attract what I am naturally afraid of, what would typically make me shift. I wish I could offer you more detail, but I can only feel it, not see it. Be cautious while here in Faera.

Ezekiel thought back.

Am I in danger?

I can't be sure. Just be careful.

Thank you. What is your name?

My name is Furwat. Nice to meet you Ezekiel.

Ezekiel was pulled from the lake. Standing there was Mateo Conti.

"Late night swim?" he asked.

"No, I uh, slipped," he responded nervously.

"I see. You should make your way to your compound. We wouldn't want anyone to worry, eh?"

"Right." Ezekiel slammed his dagger into the ground thinking hard about his warm hammock and pajamas.

•   •   •   •   •

"Dude! What took you so long!" Ethan shouted.

"I met a mind talking dolphin named Furwat, got weirded out by the Conti guy and then used my magic dagger to appear here. Seems pretty normal for around here." He plopped himself onto his hammock and hid under his blanket.

Miles burst out laughing.

"You're hilarious," Kalos said.

Chapter Sixteen
Craft & Flight

The morning trumpet woke the children to a bright sun. Ezekiel dressed and sprinted off to the Feasting Hall and ate breakfast so fast his stomach started to cramp. He wanted some time to write his mom as he was sure she was eager for a letter. He pushed his plate aside and pulled out a folded piece of paper and pencil from his pocket.

Dear Mom,
Camp is great. Made friends. Thanks for never telling me I'm a Faerman, can do magic and fly.

He erased the last sentence. When he re-read it, he felt bad that he was being so mean and she wouldn't have the chance to talk to him about it.

Dear Mom,
Camp is great. Made friends who have helped me A LOT. I'm not mad at you. Padsphere seems cool. There is a game tomorrow Arbors verses, Flames. Maybe you can teach me how to play so I can be good.
I like the food here even though some of it is weird. I'm excited to go back to Murlock. The Gorging Gargoyle was cool. He barfed on some kid.
Tell Nan and Uncle Mark I said hello. I really like my dagger.
Love,
Ezie
P.S. I got in trouble for flying.
P.P.S. You can't get mad at me 'cause I should be mad at you.

He folded the letter and told his friends he'd meet them at the first course of the day which happened to be Faerman Craft with Kunal Veer. He was very excited to reap some benefits of being magical because most of what seemed to happen to him was always odd. He didn't have much time to make his way to the Pixie Post and then the Craft Hut so he concentrated his thoughts on the Pixie Post drop slot as he plunged his dagger into the ground.

The Pixie post was a small hut the size of a parking toll booth at best. One window revealed the view of the fluttering chaos of several pixies sorting mail and packages. He observed other campers drop off their letters, press with the camp seal and push it through the mail slot. The pixies would retrieve the envelope that was double their size, then cast a shrinking charm to shrink them to the size of a rice grain. Ezekiel had to duck down as a stampede of pixies flew out of the slot with mail bags in hand. He approached the counter to grab an envelope and seal his letter. The wax press left a navy-blue impression on the envelope and quickly a pixie removed it from his hand to be sorted.

"Thanks," he said to the pixie. It swirled in pleasure as though it said "You're welcome."

Ezekiel pulled out his map to see how much time he had before Faerman Craft. His footsteps were still glowing with proper time but he thought it best to practice his dagger travel in order to get there faster. He focused on the details of the Craft Hut, picturing the branches that formed the canopy he plunged his dagger into the ground.

He felt the magic pull him and he appeared under the Craft Hut, shaded by the brushwood. Lines of tables and stools beneath set up in a classroom like fashion. Several campers had already found their seats in the front. Hiding behind a giant *Beginners Faerman Craft* book he could see familiar black curls pulled up into a pouf. He walked up to Dara hoping she'd see him and give him an indication to sit. At his first step near her peripheral vision she looked up at him. "Hey."

"Hey," he replied. He felt stuck now. Was he supposed to sit, or go somewhere else? She sensed his need for an invite. "No one is sitting here. I just got here early 'cause I wanted a good seat." Her cheeks got warm pink.

Ezekiel sat on the plush of the brown spotted mushroom stool. He felt shy. He wanted to say something to engage her but he just wasn't used to having friends that were girls. There were girls in his class who all thought he was strange so he didn't have to encounter them unless forced to for a group assignment. He stared at her from the corner of his eyes watching her highlight and read her book. As he dropped his gaze he noticed her dagger on her hip.

"You went with the gardenia. It looks good on you," he said.

"Oh, yes, you noticed! Aubrey and I found many different flowers to choose from. Once I saw this blossom I just knew. Can I see yours?" she asked.

He looked down at his hip as it was on the opposite side of her view. He flipped the strap and pulled it out.

"Wow. Where did you get amber stone beads here? Those are really hard to come by in Faera."

"You know what these are?" he asked.

"Well, yes. For fun, I read some geology books in third grade. Apparently, there are many stones that have enchanted properties for us. Those are known to offer protection to the owner."

"I think it was a bracelet. The Magnus took it off his wrist and gave it to me. I think he felt bad for keeping me back from the personalization search."

Dara seemed to be processing what he just said. Before she could respond, their friends arrived.

"Hey you *two*," Aubrey cheekily said. "Whatcha doin'?" She smiled like a Cheshire cat. Ethan raised his eyebrows.

"Nothing. Got here for a good seat," Ezekiel responded with a grin.

The Craft Hut filled with campers popping in out of thin air and every seat was taken. Kunal Veer appeared suddenly. His bold green Arbor vest complimented his brown face and large brown eyes. He was very handsome. The tone in the room from all the girls was that of shifting and straightening up in their seats.

"Hello! Welcome to Faerman Craft. Here you will learn the basics of casting simple charms and enchantments to enhance your life. Today we will focus on two skills. Making basic dust from stalactite and a simple spell. Let's begin." He pulled a stalactite rock from his vest, placed it on a small disc then sprinkled it with dust. "Multiply!" He threw out his hands toward the children and in a wave of shimmer exact replicas of the rock in hand appeared in front of each camper. The children cheered and applauded.

"Now with your dagger, cut the rock down the middle. Pick up one half and hold it firmly. With your dagger gently shave into your rock. Allow the crumbs of the rock to fall onto the dust dishes in front of you. The smell of magic may be usually strong the first time you sniff it, but I assure that you'll get used to it."

In unison, the children followed his instruction. The hut filled with with the various colors of the rainbow and the scent of something that hit Ezekiel's nostrils as though something was crawling up his nose. From the back of the room someone shouted, "Ouch!"

"Please be careful to not slice a finger off," Kunal said. "Dr. Walker doesn't enjoy mending appendages and you will be in the Infirmary for a few days. There is too much to learn to be lying around all day." He walked around inspecting the camper's work. The boy who came close to losing his finger was having a very hard time. Kunal approached a brown-haired boy with a freckled face. "Lucas, you need to hold the rock firmly. Gentle strokes of the dagger." Lucas' gentle stroke was more of a chop. The stalactite turned from its lime hue to a putrid brown and crumbled to rot onto the floor. He looked confused.

Kunal produced another rock and dish for him and patted his back for encouragement. He continued to assess the rest of the campers. He stopped to applaud multiple students including Miles and Ezekiel. "Wonderful texture for a first go boys. Very fine. It's all in the wrist everyone." Dara was very focused on earning that praise but Kunal proceeded to walk past her. Once he confirmed that all the children had completed a full dish of dust he called their attention.

"Now, please carefully funnel your dust into your hip pouches. This amount should be enough to last you a week. Weekly we will practice fine-tuning our skill," He approached Miles and raised his dish for all to see. "This is fine fae dust. The manipulation of rock tends to be most natural for Elements but with practice, you all can achieve this," he said raising the dish just a bit higher winking at Miles. Miles was beaming at his praise.

"Now with our dust we will work on our first simple enchantment. Please untie one of your shoelaces and pull the laces loose from your shoe."

The children followed his instructions excitedly. Ezekiel chose his right shoe to loosen and eagerly sat up for Kunal's next instruction. The confidence in him was erupting.

"Now look at your shoe. Memorize the curves and zigzags of the laces and picture how they need to be as a finished tied product without the use of hands. See it in your mind happen. Pull them tight!" Eyes of the children diverted and squinted as though to give their laces extra effort. "Now, grab a pinch of dust and cast it to your laces and say, "Bind!"

Shouts of the incantation exploded. Ezekiel's laces pulled tightly, weaved into a perfect bow as did Dara's. She looked and smiled at him pulling her hand into a fist mouthing "Yes!" to him. She pushed out a high five to him that made him feel like warm goo.

"Mr. George!" Kunal shouted to Lucas as he wound his legs up falling out of his chair. Kunal ran over to assist him as several children giggled at his expense. Ezekiel felt sympathetic as that was usually his place in the room.

"Now while I help Mr. George here, please untie your shoe and practice on your seat partner."

Partner. Gulp! Ezekiel turned to Dara. She was focused on his shoe. He was focused on her pretty face.

"You want to go first?" she asked.

"You go ahead. Ladies first," he replied.

"Bind!" Dara said firmly. Ezekiel laces wove and tied with ease.

"Awesome!" Ezekiel cheered her on.

"Thanks! Now you go!" she said with excitement.

"Bind!" Ezekiel shouted.

In less than a blink of an eye Dara's shoelace wove quickly.

"Wow that was turbo fast!" she was beaming at him with surprise.

The children continued to practice on their shoelaces laughing and enjoying its simplicity.

"Our time together is at an end. Please feel free to practice this craft. This will help for our next session, basket-weaving! An old-fashioned skill but wonderful for enhancing your craft skills for larger more complicated enchantments. Please check your maps for your next course session." He stepped off the platform of the Craft Hut and vanished.

Ezekiel and Dara both whipped their maps out. Footsteps glowed leading up to the Flight Field.

"Yay! Finally," shouted Ethan a few tables over. "Do you see what's next?"

The six friends came together filled with excitement plunging their daggers into the ground focused on the fun they were going to have on the Flight Field.

•   •   •   •   •

The Flight Field was a large open field of green. The sky was a vibrant light blue with bold white clouds powdered perfectly through the sky. The five field pillars stood tall and proud with unit banners waving slightly in the warm breeze of the summer. The fluffy clouds at the base of the pillars were no longer present as they were the other day of the camp tour.

"Hellllooo kiddos!" said the cheery, very tall Element unit leader. "My name is Trav Iocus and you get to spend the summer learning to fly with me! How cool is that?" On cue, he pushed off the ground and went into flight straight up in the air like a superhero. He wound around each of the five pillars, twisting, flipping and soaring. He came directly over their heads ruffling the hair of each child he swooped over. He made his final grand landing facing the children backward, fluttering down, then whipping around quickly. His eyes had thick black glasses and his eyes were large and glossy all of a sudden. "Whoa class. Is that you?" His eyes sprung forward, bobbing up and down like a slinky. At some point in flight he conjured some googly eyes. The children cheered and applauded his display.

Trav removed his prank eyeglasses and tucked them into his orange vest. He smiled largely which emphasized the deep dimples he had in his dark face which framed a very large smile.

"A few boring rules we have to cover for safety reasons." He really sounded sympathetic. "Flight is only permitted on this field until you have passed your flight test. Flight tests will be in two weeks. If you do not pass at this time, you will have another opportunity to retest a few weeks after. We are scheduled together daily for an hour but feel free to pop in during the non-scheduled times to get more practice in."

The children seemed nervous at the thought that they may not pass the test. On everyone's mind was the plan to practice as much as possible before then.

"Also, for those of you that demonstrate early flight skills, during the week of the Summer Solstice we host the Games. Five of you will be selected to represent your unit to compete against each other for the title of Unit Champion."

Ethan's eyes lit up and he beamed a glance at the other boys. Ezekiel began thinking of ways he could break it to him that he just wasn't athletic. Never was and wasn't showing any signs of improvement.

"Now before we work on going up the pillar beams, let us work on a basic pulse. Spread out, wings length. Let me demonstrate."

Trav spread his orange wings then pushed them down, then up in a smooth motion. He lifted off the ground and just hovered a foot off the ground.

"This is pulsing. I'm not using my full exertion just yet. Too much exertion will result in too fast a push off into flight making it hard to control your direction and speed, especially when you are just starting out." He seemed to release his pulse, landing on his feet to the ground. "This pulsing technique is what we will work to today. First let's just see a basic up, then pause, then down softly." He demonstrated. "Now let's try as a group. Focus on controlling your pulse and your body. On my count, one, two, three, up, hold, now down. Good, again. One, two, three up, hold, now down. Lucas, I said down buddy."

Lucas George started to glide upward as his wings pulsed rapidly. Trav turned to the campers, "Keep your feet to the ground. I'll be right back." He flew up after him with powerful speed. While in flight up, Lucas lost control and hit Trav coming down hard. Both seemed to be falling fast.

Where are those clouds? Ezekiel began to panic. He pictured the clouds in his mind with his hands on his dust pouch. He could try to fly and catch them but was certain he could only support one of them. Not able to choose he boldly ran forward, threw a handful of his dust beneath them and yelled, "Clouds! Please! Clouds!" He closed his eyes as he could not bear the thought of what he would see otherwise. Arms wrapped around him and he could hear sounds of jubilation. He opened his eyes and both Dara and Aubrey held onto him. Unable to bask in the joy of that moment as it was overshadowed by a flurry of "You did it!" he ran over toward the crowd of campers surrounding the fluffy white clouds. The entire green field was gone and it was covered in white plush.

"Let's run in and find them!" Ezekiel said stepping into the soft thickness of the clouds.

"I'll call my mom for help," Aubrey removed her dagger, hit the ground and disappeared. The rest of the friends followed him as did the other campers.

The fluff was thick making it hard to see. "Be careful to not step on them! They could be hurt!" Dara shouted. Kalos fell over losing his glasses. "Ouch!"

"Are you okay Kal?" Ezekiel called out.

"Yes! I tripped," he replied. "And lost my glasses." He began to feel around the floor.

"I'm coming to help you. Miles! Ethan! You guys in here?" Ezekiel called.

"Yeah bud. We're practically holding hands," Ethan said jokingly even though he was holding tight to Miles' hand.

Ezekiel kneeled low and felt the floor. "Kal!" he called.

"I hear you closer! Keep coming this direction!" he shouted back. "Ouch! My hand!"

"Oops, sorry. Glad I found you. Let's feel around for your glasses," Ezekiel said. The boys grabbed each other's hand to not lose one another. The thickness of the clouds made it difficult to see even an arm's length ahead. They tapped on the ground and felt on the cool grass hoping to find Kalos' glasses, Ezekiel felt what seemed to be leather. "Don't move Kal. I feel something. I'm going to let you go."

"Okay," he said apprehensively.

Ezekiel continued to feel around. It was a shoe, connected to a foot, ankle then leg! It was Trav. He patted him as soft as possible, squinting hoping to see some indication that he and Lucas were okay. He was able to lift up and pulse, hovering over Trav. He felt what seemed like four arms. A sense of relief waved over him. Trav had Lucas clutched into his chest before they fell.

"I found them! I found them! Help me!" Ezekiel called out.

"Stay calm! Don't panic, Ezekiel. It's me, Dr. Walker. Campers! I need all of you to get a pinch of dust. When I say, release it toward the clouds really focusing on what this field would look like on a warm sunny day and shout, "Evaporate!" With hope, some of you are destined to be Elements or have the gift. Now concentrate! On my count. One, two, three, EVAPORATE!"

Ezekiel kept close to Trav and Lucas focusing on casting Dr. Walker's charm. He was nervous standing next to their bodies and feared the worse making his focus on the enchantment difficult. Very slowly all around him, the clouds began to fade. The trail where his initial charm was cast was clear revealing half of Trav's long legs and Lucas' feet.

"Can you hear me Ezekiel? I'm going to crouch down and look for your feet. I see some clearing." Dr. Walker got on her hands and knees and crawled to where she could see the bright orange vest and wings of Trav.

"You did well," she said to Ezekiel. She placed her hands on them to separate them gently on their backs. She placed her ear to Lucas' heart. She lifted up and stroked his head. A soft, white glow seemed to generate from her hands flowing into Lucas' forehead.

"Ow," he groaned. "My head."

"Ah good. It hurts, yes?" Dr. Walker asked with a smile shift over to Trav. She placed her head on his heart. She sat a moment then placed a hand over the side of his left rib cage and the other on the left side of his temple. The warm, white glow illuminated into his chest making the bones of his ribs project like an x-ray.

"Uh, I'm getting too old for this," he groaned.

"Oh, what's that? Third time in a decade. That's not bad," she replied with a chuckle.

"Campers we have arrived to help," the Magnus said accompanied by the other unit leaders. In a moment, all the cloud fog was gone and the field was back to normal. "The flight lesson is over for today and will resume tomorrow. You are all dismissed, except you all," he said pointing to the six friends. The other campers seemed to evaporate rapidly daggering back to the compound.

"So, what happened?" the Magnus calmly asked.

"We were practicing pulsing then the Lucas kid just flew off. Mr. Iocus went after him and Lucas fell hard, crashing into Mr. Iocas. It seemed to knock him out in the sky. They just fell," Ezekiel said.

"And?" the Magnus asked with an unsatisfied tone.

"Um, I ran over and hoped that by some miracle I could cast the clouds into place to save them from, um…"

"I see. That was an awful a lot of clouds. How did you do it?"

I grabbed a handful of dust and threw it beneath them. I pictured the clouds there as they were the other day and I yelled for them to come. Then they did. There were too many of them." Ezekiel looked down. He felt bad as it seemed he was here creating the same chaos and havoc he did at home.

"Well that was an impressive display of atmospheric elemental manipulation. Especially on a warm day like this. Aside from that, you saved two lives," the Magnus said.

"But I didn't. It was Dr. Walker who saved them. She brought them back to life!"

"Ah, it seems that way, but had you not placed the cloud spell there to soften their blow, there would not have been anyone to save. You see a Healer can only heal someone on the brink of death. They cannot bring back the dead. According to Dr. Walker, she did not have to do much to heal them as they had minor broken bones and concussion. Both should be back in flight tomorrow." He patted Ezekiel's shoulder.

"As for the rest of you. Such good friends to step in and help your friend, instructor and camp mate. I applaud you all! Now please, off to the rest of your day." He turned and vanished.

This was the first moment Ezekiel felt homesick.

Chapter Eighteen
Murlock Visit

The next week flew by. The Arbors lost the Padshphere game against the Flames. Chants celebrating their first win of the summer filled the Feasting Hall at every meal when they entered. The days were filled with enhancing Faerman Craft skills – the Fledglings had worked their way up to basket weaving and placing simple objects around them in the basket with no hands. Some campers, Ezekiel included advanced to a hovering spell. Next would be pulling your hover spell alongside you. Flight Field courses continued with no incident and Trav and Lucas returned happily and fully mended. The children went on to learning proper ground push off for flight, wing technique and landing. Ezekiel and his friends felt ready for the Flight Test at the end of the week.

Ezekiel's homesick feeling went away quickly after he received a visit from a pixie delivering a large package to his hammock. It was wrapped in sky blue paper and twine.

"Mom must have got my letter," he said to himself as he ripped open the package. Inside was a plastic brown margarine container, candy bars, a family group photo from the Promotion Day, a worn blue vintage baseball cap with the Camp crest and a folded letter. He picked up the margarine container and gave it a shake. Just lifting the container, he caught a whiff of Nan's buttery, sugar drop cookies. He ripped open the lid and started to munch on a cookie sharing with the other boys as he unfolded the letter from Anne.

Dear Ezie,
I don't know how to start, so I guess I'll just get to it.
I am sorry I never told you about being a Faerman. I hope you can understand the reasons why. Nelson tells me that you are aware of the Hematite existence and their threat. Now that you know about them, I can now tell you that they are the

reason I did not tell you about your heritage. For now, that is all you need to know. You needn't be afraid. The Council and Guard are stronger than ever.

I also hear that you are performing very well, flying even! How very exciting for you. Me, Uncle Mark and Nan are very proud of you.

Of course! When you come back I am very excited to talk about my Padsphere days. You have a year or so until your color sprouts so we can get you ready to try out for the team.

Nan baked some cookies – that's not butter. Candy is from Uncle Mark. I thought you might like the cap – I stole it from your dad when I kicked his butt in the Padsphere Championship!

I'll write more later. I'm sure you have a ton of questions but enjoy your time there.

Love you!
Mom

The package and letter cheered Ezekiel up. The idea of going into Murlock today also had him excited for the day although he wasn't thrilled with having to spend an hour on community service to make up for his demerit. He had three choices; sorting books at the Book Chamber, dusting and sweeping to keep the Relic Room museum pristine or being a helper at the Green Pastures Retirement Village for the elderly Faerman who needed companionship and a bit of help around their cottage. The idea of having to be quiet and alone for an hour at the Book Chamber did not seem appealing. Ezekiel didn't mind simple chores, but the idea of cleaning for an entire hour to keep ancient art and war relics clean didn't sound fun either. He figured spending some time with an old person would be the best choice because he liked his Nan and her friends. An hour with folks like that wouldn't even seem like work he concluded.

The Magnus assembled the children in a group to walk them into town.

"Rules for Murlock visits are as follows. You must report back to campgrounds by sundown. You are not allowed to fly because you have not passed your flight tests yet. Once you are issued a clearance next week, you must keep your feet to the ground. Those of you who are working off demerits, please have your demerit sheets signed off by the community sponsor and returned to me for review. Any questions?"

As expected there weren't any. The children were eager to get into town. The crowd eagerly made their exit out of the large green wall, passing through the grand camp gates.

"Where should we go first?" Ezekiel asked the group.

"You have not lived, until you get some donuts from Dulcebus' Bakery," Miles said. All the kids agreed with excitement.

"We came ready for a stop there!" Aubrey said excitedly, turning her head for the boys to notice her donut patterned hair bow.

"Yup!" said Dara a bit more enthusiastic than normal, leaning forward so the boys could see her cupcake patterned headband.

"Wow. It must be good," Ezekiel said jokingly.

"The owner sells cute items that have patterns of his goodies for advertising. It's brilliant," Dara said thoroughly impressed.

The group of friends found themselves in a long line that flowed five storefronts from the bakery itself.

"Whoa, are they giving it away for free?" asked Ezekiel who was surprised by the long line.

"No, it's always like this," Dara replied. "It is that good and definitely worth the wait."

The bakery front was pink. The large window featuring the daily delights was canopied by a pink and white striped fabric. The smell in the air was warm like fresh baked chocolate chip cookies. Their excitement grew as they approached the large window allowing them to get a closer look at all the colorful pastries. The friends gazed in so close, their little noses and hands pressed on the glass. Featured in the window was a ten-tiered bright yellow-frosted cake. The cake had a white frosting piped trim so detailed and flawless it looked like lace. Fondant flowers of pinks, blues, purple, and orange decorated the steps of the tiers. White chocolate moldings of wings were placed delicately on top amongst more colorful fondant florals. Small multi-tiered silver tea trays displayed colorful macaroons, white sugar powdered cookies and large buttercream frosted cupcakes. The trays hovered in the window switching their place in front to be the featured star.

The children entered the bakery. The ceiling was so high it seemed to reach into the heavens. Faerman and pixies in bright pink apron dresses buzzed up and down carrying pink and white striped boxes along a donut filled wall. An infinite number of wooden pegs stuck out of the wall. Each peg had at least a dozen freshly baked donuts. As the pixie would grab a donut from the peg, place it into the box, the remaining donuts on the peg would push forward and a new freshly baked one would appear in the back. The entire process reminded Ezekiel of a vending machine. The pastry wall was very similar. The pixies and Faerman working the pastries flew up and down with gold tongs opening clear doors to pull out various cupcakes, cookies, fritters, popovers, loaves, scones, cannoli, eclairs, pies, cakes, muffins and Danishes. Each completed box was sealed with a gold bow.

Genery Dulcebus, the bakery owner himself was a large man with pink flushed cheeks and white hair, always wearing a smile that made his eyes close. He had a white chef coat, pink apron and hat with a happy gut chuckle that all the children loved. He was working the coffee station and was assisting a few campers with their ice-blended Decuple Chocolate Confection Mochas with whipped cream drinks. He finished them off with a cookie crumble sprinkle, a chocolate candy bar, a swirly lollipop and a pink candy straw.

"Ten different chocolates go into that drink!" Miles said excitedly as he ran over with Ethan and Kalos to get in line to place his order with Genery. The others walked to the donut wall. A counter card listed a 50 percent off special on all fish flavored varieties. Pixies zipped and zagged approaching them to take their orders.

"I'll take a chicken and waffle donut and chocolate soda pop, "Aubrey said showing off her donut patterned bow hair clips. A pixie zoomed up into the air, no longer in sight. She sprinted back with Aubrey's donut leaving a trail of magic in the air. The donut was a yellow cake with a waffle iron texture, a maple icing that held in place fried chicken nuggets that were drizzled in a maple syrup sauce. The large mug of chocolate soda pop bubbled a froth foam tower at least five inches above the rim of the glass. She took a large gulp that left a chocolatey, foamy mustache on her face.

"I'll have a seven-flavor donut and a vanilla soda pop?" Dara asked. The pixie took off in haste, still visible but very high up. She removed the large donut from the wooden peg and instantly the peg refilled itself. The donut was seven times the size of a regular donut, each layer a different color and flavor. Seeing that Ezekiel was staring at it she answered, "Chocolate, vanilla, strawberry, pistachio, lemon, blueberry and smoky barbecue."

"Barbecue?" Ezekiel asked with a surprised tone.

"Mr. Dulcebus is a genius. Trust me. It's amazing," she replied taking her order and stepping aside. Ezekiel stared at the tiny print menu with thousands of flavors listed.

"Um, I'll take Several Times Chocolate Dipped donut and fizzy honey mead," Ezekiel said in an asking tone. The pixie nodded and pointed for Ezekiel to proceed to a table because it needed to be prepared. She flew up just a few pegs up to grab what seemed like a plain chocolate donut. She flew to a pink metal pot, removed its lid and with golden tongs she dipped the donut inside the pot filled with melted chocolate. She shook off the drips of chocolate which seemed to rapidly harden. She then placed the donut into another pot filled with warm donut batter, then in a fryer. She lifted the donut, which was now three times the size it was prior to her dipping. She repeated the process four times then plopped the donut onto a white gold trimmed porcelain plate. She tapped the donut with her tongs and it shrunk in size. She was easily able to lift the plate and deliver to Ezekiel's table. Once the plate hit the table it grew to the size of a birthday cake. The pixie left and returned with what looked like a pink and gold steak knife and fork.

"Whoa dude. You're going to need help with that!" Miles said.

"I had no idea it could feed a village. I thought it was going to be a simple, chocolate dipped donut," Ezekiel couldn't take his eyes off the chocolate monstrosity. He used his utensils to cut into the donut exposing its chocolate and fried donut insides. It was mouth-watering and each bite melted in his mouth.

After their morning snack was done, the group left the bakery thanking Genery for the delectable delights. It was now time to part ways to complete his community service.

"Well, looks like I'll be off to Green Pastures now," he said.

"We're going to the Book Chamber, then window shopping for Summer Solstice Bash dresses, right Dara?" Aubrey asked with a sly grin.

"Yeah, that's the agreement," Dara replied.

"We're off to the Bazaar. There are so many cool toys and collectible things to see there," Kalos said with enthusiasm. "We will get you something. I owe you for kind of saving my life last week."

"Yeah. Okay. I'll take a, thanks–for–saving–my–life present," Ezekiel joked.

"We can meet up in an hour over there near the front of the Bazaar sign," Ethan said pointing to the large tent banner entrance that led to rows and rows of multi-color canopies.

The friends separated ways. Ezekiel was just a short walk from the Green Pastures Retirement Village. He could see the colorful landscape from afar. The entrance gate was white rod iron with an intricate floral pattern woven throughout. A security booth was cornered off to the side. A very tall red-headed and mustached man sat in the booth. He wore a grey uniform with a silver badge that said *Kevin*. When he noticed Ezekiel, he swiveled his chair revealing his red wings.

"Hello. Who are you visiting today?"

"I'm here to do some, um, community service from the camp," he stammered.

"Ah, yes I see your name on here," Kevin said as he reviewed his floating clipboard. "You will report to Cottage 11. You'll be helping Ms. Iva Rose. Follow the path to the right."

"Thanks."

Kevin opened the white iron gate just enough for Ezekiel to enter shutting it behind him. He proceeded down the concrete path that trailed with festive flowers and shrubs. He passed by two ladies with large grey bouffant hair-do's who were hand in hand.

"Look Jeanne! Is that Madge's grandson? Hello sweetie!"

"No I don't think that is him Lisa. Looks a lot like him but Madge's grandson is taller and sprouted white remember? That's all she can go on and on about is her grandson with the white wings."

Ezekiel gave a nod to the ladies in an attempt to not be rude. He found his way in front of a lavender colored cottage. It had white wooden shutters and was surrounded by white roses. The path that led to the front door were giant tiles of tree trunk. He knocked on her door.

Very quickly it opened as if Iva had been waiting behind the door the entire time for his knock. She had a kind round face, curly perfectly placed white hair, large green-eyes with deep dimples on her rosy cheeks. She was the cutest old lady he'd ever seen. She reminded him of a doll.

"Well hello there! You must be Ezekiel. I am Iva Rose. Please, come in."

"Yes, hi, thank you," Ezekiel replied. She was so proper in her mannerisms he felt he had to reciprocate.

Her cottage walls were lavender and covered in small porcelain decorative plates of roses. She had a pink rose patterned couch with green throw pillows that matched the leaves of the rose print. The coffee table had a small white porcelain vase filled with white roses likely plucked from her garden outside.

"Please have a seat dear. Honey mead?" she asked him as she proceeded to fill his cup with it. She placed a scoop of whipped cream on top. "It's homemade. I whipped it by hand with no charms all by myself. He was still very full from his visit to Dulcebus' but he did not want to make Iva feel bad so he took a sip. It was warm, sweet and tasted ten times better than the honey mead he had at camp and in town.

"Hmmm," he said out loud. He didn't mean to be so loud with his satisfaction.

"Oh, you love it! "I'm so glad!" she said clapping her hands together. "Well there is plenty more here for you dear."

"Is there anything I can help you with?" Ezekiel asked hoping that it wouldn't be anything too labor intensive. He was a bit worn out from practicing flight for his test.

"Oh, no dear. I don't get too many outside visitors, especially a Fledgling like yourself. I'm around these old fogies all day and they have me feeling like an old fogie too. I thought if I asked for some help I'd be more likely to get a young person who can make me feel more, hip. Do kids still say *hip*? *Fresh*?" She laughed and her laughing made Ezekiel laugh. He liked her immediately.

"Both work. We can work on bringing them both back," he said causing her to laugh more.

The two spent the hour chatting about his family and camp. He felt so comfortable with her as she seemed to enjoy listening to him and asking for more details of his experiences. He shared with her the strange things that happened to him at home, how his mom did not tell him he was Faerman, and how he didn't know his father.

"Everything happens for a reason sweetie. I am sure your mother had good reason. If it is meant for you to know your father, one day you will. Who knew that you and I would ever meet and hit it off like we have? This is one of the best afternoons I've ever had. Well look at the time. It's been well over an hour. I'm sure if you're not back in time Nelson will not be pleased. Same day and time next week dear?" she smiled at him as she stood up.

"Yes! For sure! Is there anything I could bring you before I come? He asked.

"No, no. Perhaps next time I'll get out the cards and we can have some fun playing some Hold Em."

"You mean like poker?" he asked stunned she knew what that was.

"You bet. For cookies that is. I'll bake before you arrive. Now don't let my sweet ladylike manners fool you. I can play a strong game." She winked at him teasingly.

"Okay! Sounds like a plan. See you then," he replied as he walked out the door. Iva stood in the doorway watching him walk all the way through the path and out the white iron gate.

Ezekiel walked swiftly. He didn't realize how long he had been visiting with Iva. She was the coolest old lady he ever met.

"Dude! What took you so long?" Kalos groaned. "You're missing the awesomeness inside the Bazaar!"

"Yeah, there is a special on magic carpets. Got one for my mom. She's going to love it and I'll be back on top as her favorite kid," Ethan joked.

Dara shot him a look. "You do need all the help you can get."

"Nice," Aubrey said laughing. I found the cutest bow! It has a temporary charm on it. It changes color based on my mood!"

"I got this cool action figure," Miles said as he held up a small plastic figurine. The figure had no face or color to it. It was a white silhouette.

"What does it do?" Ezekiel asked assuming it had to do more than what they were seeing.

"It's a Mimic! Here hold it," he handed it to Ezekiel. Once in Ezekiel's hands, the Mimic's face filled in a caramel brown, brown hair and a face they all recognized. The clothing on the body of it also filled in matching Ezekiel's exact camp uniform.

"Crazy weird!" Ezekiel said.

"Crazy weird!" the Mimic replied.

"Oh, my gosh! It's copying me!"

"Oh, my gosh! It's copying me!"

Ezekiel handed it back to Miles. He was not going to let the weird little toy win. Sitting in Miles' hand, it still appeared that he was holding a little

Ezekiel.

"When does it go back to being white?" asked Kalos.

"That's the cool thing! Once it mimics you once, it always remembers you, even if you have it mimic someone else," Miles explained.

The children groaned.

A very thin dark man with circular purple-tinted spectacles and a turban came running up to Miles.

"You ran off so fast, you forgot your gold pieces my friend!"

"Thanks, Ansh. This toy is really cool. I got distracted by its coolness," he said as he tucked the Mimic back into his bag.

"Hello there, friends! I'm Ansh Veer. I run the Bazaar. Please come by again to see all the enchanted goodies. We've got genie lamps, flying mozzards, hard to find gemstones and elements, dragon's teeth, flying magic carpets that seat up to six! Kelpie repellant, wands, pre-made dust, forever flavor gumballs, charmed candles of every scent that never burn out!"

Ansh's enthusiasm halted when around the corner flew in a dozen Guards.

Chapter Nineteen
Agamemnon's Ride

"It was very nice meeting you kids. You should make your way back to camp," Ansh said scurrying off into the Bazaar tent.

The children couldn't take their eyes off the landing Guard. Their dark green uniforms popped vibrantly in the solid bright blue sky. As they landed they kept their hands on their daggers taking place on various corners on Murlock's main street. Faerman walking by on the street seemed alarmed but went about their way. The children walked briskly to the nearest patch of earth they could find to dagger back to the gate at the camp entrance.

"I wonder what that was about," Dara said.

"I'll write my mom. I'm sure if it's anything to worry about my grandfather would know," Kalos said.

The children had a few hours until dinner time to enjoy the campgrounds. The group decided to give riding a try. The walk to the stables was a bit of a walk. To pass the time, Ezekiel thought he'd inquire more about the Guard.

"Have any of you seen the Guard come out like that?" he asked.

"It's protocol for them if there is an increased threat," Kalos replied.

"A threat? Are we talking about Hematite stuff again?" Ezekiel asked.

"Yeah. The local paper, The Faerman Chronicle have been reporting a rising threat. Guard intel has reported that double agents uncovered a plot for their return. They have been finding the Black Stain painted on Council walls," Dara said.

"It could be the Chronicle trying to sell papers you know," Kalos said with skepticism. "To keep everyone at ease, the Guard could be just making a presence."

"The Black Stain?" Ezekiel asked.

"It's a sign of support for the Hematites," Dara said. "They use black paint and wipe it like this." She motioned her hands like she dipped her hands into paint, placing them side by side on a wall and wiping them both out. "It leaves what looks like black wings." She made the motion again. It gave Ezekiel the creeps.

The friends arrived at the stables. Some of the Pegasus laid in the grass amongst each other for a late noon nap. There was a mint colored one that trotted across the field making eye contact with the children as if showing off his mane, wings then tail.

"Ooh. I want to ride him!" Aubrey said.

Mateo Conti approached the children. "Are we riding today? We have just enough peggie's saddled up." He led the children into the wooden barn.

Each of the friends checked their Murlock goodies into the stable cubbies. Mateo led each camper to their assigned peggie.

Ezekiel was escorted to the gate of a large steel grey steed named Agamemnon. His mane, was a perfectly coiffed silver as was his long tail. Agamemnon seemed indifferent towards him but went with him willingly out onto the stable pasture. All the peggie's had brown leather saddles with the camp emblem pressed along the leather detail.

"Pet your peggie so he trusts you. Once he gives you the okay, step high using the stirrup and fling your other leg over," Mateo demonstrated on his own steed. The children followed his steps perfectly.

"Now you may trot on the field here, enjoy the hurdle jumping or you may take your peggie out onto the trail. The peggies are trained to not fly outside the field. Any questions?" Mateo asked.

"No, thanks," Ezekiel replied on behalf of the group.

"Follow me!" Aubrey cheered as she trotted her mint peggie along the pasture. The others followed. Aubrey seemed naturally gifted at riding as she led her peggie up into flight. The other peggie's followed suit and the group took off into a circular flight over the stable grounds.

"I can see our compound from here!" yelled Kalos.

"I can see the tree of the Feasting Hall!" yelled Miles.

Ezekiel and Agamemnon pulled near Dara and her blue peggie. He could see that she was clinging on to him with a face of apprehension. It made him like her a bit more seeing her out of her comfort zone trying to have fun.

"Having the time of your life?" he shouted to her.

Not taking her eyes off of her direction she replied, "Oh yeah, can't you tell?"

"Let's do the trail then guys?" he shouted to the others to land.

The kids landed their peggies and trotted them out the stable ground gate. The trail was familiar to the peggies so they didn't need much direction for their riders. Side by side they trotted giving Ezekiel the chance to pull alongside Dara. She looked at him and grinned. "Thanks. I'm still not a huge fan of things I can't control."

The trail had them trot past the Observatory, Seers Lake, the Granters compound which was a bit marshy and Aubrey's peggie walked through as if repulsed by the marshland. They were led past the Flames compound then alongside the Pond where they paused to break.

"Which path of the trail should we take now?" Ethan asked.

"Maybe we go back? That way we have enough time to get ready for dinner?" Dara asked unusually nice.

"That sounds good! I wonder what Sweet Sally has for us for dinner?" Miles asked.

"Ugh, you guys are boring," Ethan replied. "Okay, let's go back, but let's race there to make it more fun!" He pulled out his map which illuminated the steps back to the stable.

"You don't need that. Your peggie knows the trail," Aubrey reminded him.

The children positioned their peggie's side by side so they were all getting a fair start in the race. Dara didn't care about winning, she just wanted to stop riding.

"Ready, set, go!" Ethan yelled.

The children gave their peggie's a kick of encouragement to trot faster. Aubrey's peggie was determined to not be beaten and had a strong lead on the others while Dara's trailed far behind. Ezekiel turned back to keep his eye on her while Agamemnon pulled his speed faster and faster, so fast that he lifted himself off the ground and took off into flight.

"Oh, my gosh!" Ezekiel cried.

Agamemnon pulled up so high he completely abandoned the trail. Ezekiel could see his friends who were now just small colored dots below. He held onto Agamemnon's reins tightly. The silver steed flew off beyond the campgrounds and over what seemed like miles of green trees. The camp was now miles away.

"Where are we going?" Ezekiel asked him.

Agamemnon kept flying on. His pulse was so smooth as he soared amongst the clouds. Had Ezekiel not known the rules, he would have been enjoying himself. He felt the air brush his face. It was so refreshing that the possibility of receiving another demerit seemed worth it.

They lowered and approached an area of rock and water. Large powerful rock cliffs framed an intense waterfall. The sound of the water crashed, pushing the crystal, clear water into a small pool. It seemed odd to Ezekiel that the waterfall was so powerful for such a tiny area of water. He had seen waterfalls many times and this one was not like any he had ever seen. Agamemnon lowered even more circling the fall and rocks. From above the rocks seemed dark and spotted. Now up close, he could see the rocks more clearly.

Hundreds of boulders, stacked on top of each other, born a wash of grey were all covered with the stain of the black painted wings. The sight caused Ezekiel's heart to jump. Sensing his fear, Agamemnon circled around and took off into a powerful flight heading back to the camp. Ezekiel felt a sense of relief.

Of course, I got the strange *peggie*, he thought to himself.

Ezekiel could see Seers Lake in view. Wondering why Agamemnon wasn't taking him to the east side of the campground where his stable was. The large blue body of water grew closer and closer.

"Where are you going!?" yelled Ezekiel. Agamemnon ignored him and flew on. He pulled down, plummeting into what seemed to be a landing into the lake. They flew just inches above water heading closer to shore. Agamemnon stopped and pulsed over the same spot of the lake where he had his Dagger Bonding. He lifted his front legs, dropping his hind down as to flip Ezekiel off his back. Ezekiel clung on. Agamemnon bucked up and down, then to the side. Ezekiel lost his grip and fell plummeting into the lake. He could feel the freshwater ivy around his legs. As he sank he could see Agamemnon's silver tail flip then disappear. Quickly thinking, he swam toward the bottom placing his hand on his dagger.

He was surrounded by darkness. He could see the cold dark moist walls of a long corridor. A black hooded figure walked briskly. The palms of the hands were black. It entered a large chamber where the walls displayed skulls and wings. A single black velvet plush throne perched in the center of the room. It walked in and the others revered as it took its seat. It raised its hands making a gesture swooping its hands outward. The figure was blocked from his view once the other black figures rose from kneeling to standing also doing the same hand gesture. Their black wings spread wide. A large dark crown of darkened rose thorns embedded with black diamonds was placed on its' head.

Ezekiel wanted to run but he was stuck. He could hear the chanting, "Take the fall. Take the fall. Take the fall."

A white figure approached him. It had clouded pinched eyes framed with a red lid and a mouth that covered more than half its face. The mouth was wide open exposing its pink gums and rows of jagged teeth. Its body almost looked human but had skin so white and transparent you could see its bones. As it swam closer Ezekiel could see it had four legs that reminded him of a spider. Quickly it was accompanied by a dozen more.

Ezekiel couldn't react fast enough. There was no way he was going to outswim these water creatures. He instantly thought of Furwat and called for him in his mind. Before he could complete his thought one of the creatures from behind came forward metamorphosing into a friendly dolphin face.

Ezekiel, we have got to stop running into each other like this. Furwat thought had a light tone. Ezekiel swore he was smiling.

I was peggie riding and my peggie dumped me here!

Ah, I see. Pardon the appearance of my friends. Our kind is in a state of defensiveness per the Magnus' request. There are dark forces out there that would like access throughout Murlock.

Ezekiel instantly remembered the story of the kidnappings the Magnus told him. He connected it to what the lake just shared with him. Furwat read his thoughts.

Your insight is good little Fledgling. For unknown reasons the lake has blessed you with warning. Now you see the darkness we fear. We must go now to guard the lake. Stay safe.

He and the other tandos swam off. Ezekiel plunged down to the lake floor daggering back to the stable dry.

Ezekiel appeared at the stable. It was now night. The stables were quiet and illuminated by the light of the moon and the slight glimmer of stars. He pulled his camp map from his pocket. The footsteps led him to the Fledgling compound to retire for the night. Rather than dagger there, he used the short walk to think of what he was going to say if the Magnus was there waiting for him or how he would respond to his friends when they freaked out on him. When he approached the staircase he hesitated. He was glad the Magnus wasn't present but still carried a huge level of guilt on his shoulders.

He tiptoed into the room. The Enchandrapes were closed and the boys were in their hammocks. He opened his trunk to get his pajamas.

"Looking for these?"

He whipped around to see Dara sitting in the corner chair, now illuminated by a sunflower charm.

"Uh, yes," he replied casually.

Dara approached him and slugged him in the arm.

"Ouch!"

Whispering fiercely, "Do you have any idea how much trouble you would be in if the Magnus found out that you took your peggie flying? We had to cover for you when Agamemnon showed up to the stable without you. I wanted to go to him but these guys insisted that you were fine. Well? What do you have to say for yourself? Where have you been?"

"I'm fine. There was something wrong with that stupid peggie. He took off in flight way off grounds and way beyond town near some waterfall. Then he dumped me into the lake."

"What?! Beyond town! That isn't safe! Were you in the woods?"

"We stayed in the air over the woods," he replied.

"You said there was a waterfall? Are you sure? I'm not aware of any waterfall in that direction. Are you sure that is what you saw?"

"I'm positive. The only time we swooped down was to get close to it. It was like the peggie wanted me to see it. It has large grey boulder rocks. That handprint painting you were talking about earlier was all over them."

"The Black Stain? Like this?" she demonstrated the two-handed wipe.

"Yes. Just like that but all over the rocks."

"We need to tell the Magnus, the Guard! The Praeses needs to know!"

"Dara, I think you are overreacting. I'm sure it was just an area where a bunch of thugs got together to vandalize," he responded.

"We have a duty to report all possible Hematite activity. Wait – you said the peggie dropped you into the lake. Why would he do that?"

"Cause he's broken. I don't know!"

Dara paused for a moment to think. "What did you see down there. I know the lake showed you something."

"Ugh! Can we just let this be until tomorrow?" Ezekiel could tell immediately she wasn't going to leave his room. He told her all he saw in the vision and what Furwat told him about guarding the lake.

"Everything you saw sounds like what the Guard fears the most. If the Hematite has crowned a Malum Coacter, then they will fight to rise again. If the tandos are guarding the entrance into the lake from the outside of the campgrounds then what exactly is the Magnus trying to keep out?" Ezekiel could see the wheels turning in her eyes.

"The kidnappings, I guess?"

"Exactly. Where else is there a large group of Faerman? Snatch them while they are young and -"

"Force them to do their dirty work."

They were both surprised he was on point.

"Yes. Exactly. Now how do we stop this?" Dara asked bravely.

"We? Isn't this one of those things where we don't get involved, leave it up to the adults and we go about our day? We're just kids, what can we do?"

"If everyone said that, nothing would get better! Just because we're kids, doesn't mean we can't help make a difference! It has to start with us!" Dara grabbed his arm pleading with him.

"Okay. I will tell the Magnus first thing after our Flight Tests. I promise." Her hand was still on his arm.

"Good. Then we'll come up with a plan to help." She looked pleased that she was able to persuade him. She handed him back his pajamas.

"Yep. A super plan," he said smiling.

"Well good then. Good night," she turned to step out. Ezekiel wasn't sure what came over him, but a surge of bravery filled his chest forcing his arm out to grab her hand.

"Dara?"

"Huh?" She turned, warm and pink in the face. Her heart fluttered.

"Will you go with me to the Summer Solstice Bash?" As the words flowed from his mouth, so did the courage that got him here in the first place as he gazed at her big brown eyes.

She smiled the largest smile he'd ever seen from her.

"Of course, good night!" She ran out in a flash before he could see her flushed cheeks.

Ezekiel changed into his camp pajamas. He slid into his hammock with a giant smile on his face.

Chapter Twenty
Flight Test

Flight Test day had approached. The Flag Ceremony seemed to take a million times longer than usual as everyone had their minds on their test. They had been practicing the flight patterns daily. The course had them targeting, push off, pulsing, hovering, flight, wing speed, descending and landing. Ezekiel was fairly confident he would pass. He and his friends had no trouble with the course. Just a handful of campers had difficulty with controlling their landing.

The children approached the field early after breakfast keeping it light even though Sweet Sally tried her best to fill them with strawberry filled puff pastries with creamed cheese. The campers assembled on the cloudless field to stretch their wings and warm up before the test.

Trav arrived with high energy and excitement for the day.

"Goooood Morning campers! Take a few moments to stretch and we will get started." He walked around assisting with wing stretching.

"You guys ready?" Ezekiel asked his friends.

"Oh yeah, let's do this!" Ethan said enthusiastically.

Trav called the children over to assemble near the flag pillars.

"Okay kiddos. Just like we've been practicing. You will fly up, pause and then come down to show your hover skills. Then you will fly to the top of the pillar you are lined up with. Take a breath, then you will fly straight out, then around back to the pillar so I can observe your wing technique. From the pillar, you will descend then land back where we started. We've practiced this every day so I'm confident we've got it but does anyone have any questions?"

The children formed five lines waiting for Trav to blow his whistle to send them off. He stood on the sideline with an enchanted clipboard to track the results. Group by group Fledglings pushed forward successfully completing the course. It was now time for Ezekiel, Ethan, Miles, Kalos and Lucas to go.

Pew!

The group successfully demonstrated their hover and take off to the pillar. Flight made Ezekiel feel free of worry or stress. It reminded him of his gift making him less frustrated that his mom kept this world a secret. He felt more appreciative that he now knew, and enjoyed each day that much more. He hit his landing with ease wishing it could have lasted just a moment longer but he knew that once he passed he would be able to fly everywhere, even into town like the color unit campers. He looked around and saw how pleased Trav was with him. He then looked up. The other boys were still just pushing off the pillar platform into the wing test of the course. He observed his friends land back onto the platform, then go into descending. Lucas landed a bit hard, pulling his wings in quickly and straightening up to prevent a fall. He had such effort on his face.

"Nice job man," Ezekiel offered a high five to Lucas.

"Thanks. I tried really hard. Practiced for an hour before the morning trumpets, after lunch during break and after dinner before campfire," he was heaving for breath but maintained a smile throughout.

"That was amazing!" Trav said to Ezekiel patting him on the back. I wish I had been timing that.

"I think it was just nerves that got me all wound up. I hope my technique was okay?" he said.

"Flawless. You, hands down have a spot on the Fledgling Unit Flight Championship," he replied excitedly.

Ezekiel could see that Ethan was a bit crestfallen. Lucas looked rejuvenated and started to clap with enthusiasm with Miles and Kalos.

"Luck I think. Ethan wipes the field with me every day," he replied nudging Ethan. Ethan gave a sheepish grin.

"Well of course, I think he's a fine candidate for the championship too!" Trav cheered. Ethan was beaming.

"Wonderful job Fledglings! I am so proud of your work over the past weeks. I am very excited to say that each of you have successfully passed your Flight Test! You are the toughest most determined group of fliers I have seen in my days here. Now I'd like to personally hand each of you your flight card. Our friend Sam here will be taking a picture memento for you to send to your parents."

The campers went line by line to shake Trav's hand and receive their card.

A blonde-haired boy walked up first, stuck out his hand to shake Trav's, and the other to grab his card. He turned to smile toward Sam and as Trav squeezed his hand it sent a full body buzz through his hand causing him to leap and spread his wings.

Laughter exploded. The blonde boy was laughing hysterically. Each camper received the same congratulatory reverie. So much so, they began to use the force of the buzz to make fun poses for the photo. When it was Ezekiel's turn, he tilted his head, widened his eyes and opened his mouth wide and gave the handshake a bit of a jump lifting his legs in the air. This made both Sam and Trav laugh.

Once the friends all had their official flight cards, they made their way to the Feasting Hall to celebrate over lunch. Sweet Sally was prepared for the festivities as the entire hall was decorated with tissue paper wings hovering above each table. A large banner hovered in the center of the room that read:

Congratulations on your Flight Cards!

The children enjoyed a heavy lunch. Ezekiel went for a third serving of Sweet Sally's cornbread when she came around. The sweet butter she spread on top melted softening the texture of the bread to a cake-like consistency.

"Will we be going to chat with the Magnus after lunch?" Dara asked him casually.

"Oh, yeah. Coming with me?" Ezekiel asked.

"Where you going? What?" Ethan asked leaning over.

"You didn't tell them?" Dara asked with surprise.

"It didn't come up since then," Ezekiel replied.

"Are we going to get filled in?" Aubrey asked snobbishly as she tossed her hair to the side showing her bow shift color from blue to grey.

Ezekiel went into detail about his short adventure with Agamemnon and his chat with Furwat.

"Seriously are we even at the same camp?" Ethan joked.

"This is not funny. This isn't one of those things you shove off as a joke. The lake keeps showing him visions. He is shown for a reason. We're going to the Magnus to tell him what happened," she said looking at Ezekiel for support.

"Yeah, it's best. If it's nothing, then it's nothing, right?" he replied trying his hardest to support her.

"Well what if when you say something, my grandfather sends us all home? Cancels camp?" Kalos asked.

That possibility had not crossed their minds.

"I don't think they will cancel camp if they are telling the tandos to guard the lake. Nothing has been in the Chronicle about the camp being threatened." Miles chimed in.

"That's a good point," Aubrey agreed.

Ezekiel and his friends finished their meal and made way to the Magnus' quarters. As they approached they could see through a small tear in the Enchandrapes that were closed. All the unit leaders were inside as were several navy suited Faerman. A stern looking man with black and white hair with a highly-decorated uniform seemed to lead the conversation. At the door stood a single Guard.

"Looks like they are having a meeting," Ezekiel whispered. He stepped aside so the others could take a peak.

"Crap. My grandfather is in there!" Kalos said.

"He is?!" Dara asked jumping forward to peak. "Shhh! Let's listen to what they're talking about!"

"The threat is greater. The Praeses is aware and doesn't want to create a panic. If we let the Chronicle know, Faerman will flee, crossover and not return. Our Council will collapse. All what the sludge mongers are hoping for," said Diego.

"My concern is for the large population here Diego. If they continue their old plan, pick up from where they left off, they have a camp full of children to do so. There are not enough fully trained Faerman here to ward them off if our protections in place do not hold them back," replied the Magnus.

"I propose we continue to cover the streets and the town. I can have my troops dispersed throughout the campgrounds. We have communicated with the tandos to keep the lake safe. The mountain nymphs, woodland fauns, griffins, dessert cyclops', grassland trolls and uvams are all alert. We have seen the Black Stain, but there hasn't been an abduction or C.O.M. reported in years. I am confident once they make a move, we will find them and end them for good," Diego said.

"C.O.M?" asked Ezekiel.

"Crime of Malevolence. That's what they call the wing theft," Kalos whispered back.

"Are there any leads to their palace?" asked one of the navy-suited council members.

"I'm afraid not. They must be using some sort of camouflaging charm. We have combed every inch of Faera casting out every revealing charm we know. Our best Granters have sacrificed their lives to have their palace revealed. They are working with ancient dark magic," Diego replied.

"Very well then. Please be subtle and remind your troops that we have children here. I will send notice to the parents that this is the case as a precaution. I can't assure you that the press will not find out once we issue our notices," the Magnus summoned for some post pixies to get the notices out. They quickly agreed and set forth to the post.

"Let's go! They are coming out. We can't be caught snooping here!" Dara said.

"Wait, you said to tell him what I saw," Ezekiel stammered.

"Go! Go!" Dara said. The others listened and plunged their daggers into the ground and vanished.

Ezekiel and Dara stood firm.

"You ready to tell him?" Dara asked.

"Wait, I thought–", Ezekiel started.

"I didn't want the others to have to get involved. Especially my brother," she replied.

The group inside the Magnus' office trailed out eying Ezekiel and Dara. As the Magnus walked them out he noticed his campers there waiting for him.

"Well what do I owe for this visit?" he said.

"I have something I need to tell you. I think it can help all of you," he replied speaking outwardly to the group.

The Magnus led them all back into his quarters. He poured warm honey mead for everyone.

"Yesterday we went riding on the peggies. I rode Agamemnon," Ezekiel started.

"Yes, I recall that," Mateo Conti confirmed.

"On the trail, he just seemed to go crazy. He took off in flight and carried me off of the grounds. We flew and flew over the forest way out of camp."

"That's impossible. The peggies are trained to not fly outside the stable gates," Mateo shot back.

"We saw it happen," Dara chimed in. "The entire group who rode yesterday saw the peggie lift off and head into the northeast."

"It was like Agamemnon wanted to show me something. After flying for at least a half hour we flew down to a waterfall surrounded by a lot of rock boulders," Ezekiel continued.

"Son, there are no waterfalls north east of town. It's complete forest, which the Guard has combed many times I can assure you," said one of the navy suits.

"I'm telling you what I saw," he started to feel defensive. They looked at him with skepticism. "The boulders had big black smears painted like wings on them."

One of the suits dropped his cup of honey mead. Mouths all dropped open in terror.

The Guard in the corner placed his hand on his dust pouch in defense.

"Stand down," Diego said raising his hand to the Guard. Can you retrace your flight to this area? I'm assuming you have your flight card now. You can show us the way?"

"I can try," Ezekiel stammered.

"I am not sending my camper out there. I don't think his family would appreciate him getting involved Diego," the Magnus said sternly.

"I know all too well about *his* family," Diego said with an irritable tone.

"Look, I am sure we can come up with a better solution than sending a child into the woods," Dr. Walker said.

Ezekiel felt irritated. His gut had told him not to bother the Magnus with this information.

"We need to have the boy help us Nelson," Diego said. "We're running out of leads here."

"Let me think about it for the night," the Magnus replied. "I agree to all the other protective actions. We can also start protection charms within our Fledgling Faerman Craft courses. This would be two years earlier than we typically do. You two are dismissed while us grownups finish up here."

Ezekiel and Dara took the queue. They walked off together. Once out of earshot Ezekiel asked, "Want to dagger back?" She nodded.

The pair appeared in front of their compound. Neither felt like participating in any recreation. Ezekiel definitely was not looking forward to riding a peggie ever again.

"What should I do?" Ezekiel asked Dara.

"I honestly don't know," she replied. "If that was the Hematite palace then it couldn't be safe, but I think something should be done about it! We can't just sit here and do nothing."

"What's on the schedule for the rest of the day?" he asked as he pulled out his map. They were currently missing archery with Mateo Conti. The next course would be Faerman Craft in a short time.

"We can get a super head start on to Faerman Craft? It's in fifteen minutes," Ezekiel offered. "We even have time to fly there."

"Okay," she said.

Both pushed off flying into the air. They soared passing over the Pond where they could see the Granters running a practice. Nearby the amphitheater was filled with campers practicing their skits for the weekend jamboree. Within their sights, Ezekiel could see Agamemnon trotting along the stable. He turned sharply to descend onto the ground, landing at the Craft Hut. The pair took their usual seats.

"Want to practice our binding charm?" Dara asked.

"Sure!"

They both exchanged turns practiced the shoe-tying charm. They worked their way up to removing the laces completely and twisting them to make shapes and short words in cursive. Ezekiel formed his into a word. "Guess what it says!"

"Poop?" Dara cracked up laughing.

"Yes! You go!"

Dara cast her charm on the laces. They danced around a moment as she formed her word.

Ezekiel started laughing immediately. "Fart?"

"Yes!" Dara was kneeled over laughing so hard her eyes were closed.

"Okay, you go!" she said.

Ezekiel focused on the form of the letters and the force of the shoelace. He lost his focus as Ethan, Miles, Kalos and Aubrey arrived.

"Hi! Whatcha doin'!?" Aubrey said

"Nothing," they said in unison.

"So, what happened after we left the Magnus' quarters?" Kalos asked.

"I spoke with the Magnus. Told him everything," Ezekiel replied.

"Wait! I thought you weren't gonna," Ethan said.

"I thought it best he go alone at it. No offense," Dara said turning especially to Aubrey. "He needed to focus on what he was going to say. I think we got the job done."

"Well I don't think they believe me," Ezekiel replied.

Kunal led the class to the side of the Craft Hut. Demonstrating a new spell, he called for their attention.

"Today we will work on a beckoning spell. This will be most helpful to collect reeds, pull them along this short path, onto your work area to weave into a basket for you to take to your room. You will use just a pinch of dust as you let it release, make sure you use your elbow – really put your arm into it. Then you will tell the earth what you need. The simpler you say it, the better. You must also visualize what you want done. Once you have successfully moved your reeds, go ahead and start to weave a basket using your binding charm. I will demonstrate.

"Reeds come to me!" Kunal said firmly. A perfect bundle of reeds plucked themselves from the ground hovering neatly to him. Moving his hand from his initial command he shifted the pile to the Craft Hut work area onto a table.

"Now you all spread out. There is a lot of field here. Please be careful to not bump each other."

Ezekiel took a pinch of his dust from his pouch and flung it out over the field of reed. His dust flew in the air, glittering as it fell into the earth and cast a warm glow smoothly removing the bundle of reed from the land. The bold scent of magic filled the air. Holding his focus on the bundle, he rotated his hand, pushing the bundle to his workstation. As he plopped onto his stool, Dara did too. They grinned at each other competitively and went to work.

Weaving and binding each strand of reed was easy for Ezekiel. He looked over and could see that Dara was well on her way with the base complete. As he turned to look at her he could see in the horizon troops of Guard descend into landing.

Chapter Twenty-One
The Night of the Stars

Dear Mom,

Tell everyone thanks for all the goodies, especially the hat! I plan to wear it to keep the sun out of my eyes when I'm on the Flight Field practicing for the Summer Solstice Games! I was selected to represent the Fledglings with my friend Ethan. We practice every day at least twice, even three times sometimes! It was so awesome getting my Flight Card. I've included a picture so you can see me getting it.

I like my Faerman Craft course. I'm learning a lot and have made you a few baskets for the house. I tried riding a Pegasus, wasn't really a fan of it, especially since I can fly on my own now. I think I got a crazy one. It made me fall into the lake!

My friends took me to Dulcebus' Bakery. It was my favorite! I had the most gigantic chocolate donut. While in town I did my community service for my demerit. I was assigned to help this really cool old lady named Iva. She made me homemade whipped cream and next time we're going to play poker for cookies!

Anyway, I got to go to the flag ceremony. Today should be great – it's Night of the Stars. We get to spend the night at the Astro-Observatory.

Love,

Ezie

P.S. Can you send me my red bow tie? I got a dance to go to.

P.P.S. Yes, I asked a girl!

The morning flag ceremony was more delightful than usual despite the presence of the Guard. When each unit arrived at the flagpole, the entire area was decorated with colorful streamers, banners and enchanted confetti that floated along above head suspended in the sky. Each color unit had taken a space to show their team spirit and competitive stakes for the Padsphere Tournament. Only two teams would be left standing for the championship. Between more advanced craft lessons, Flight Field time to practice for the

Games, kayaking in the lake, archery and doing everything to avoid the stable time, camp was flying by.

The Magnus entered and did not look happy. The unit leaders had solemn faces as well.

"Campers, it is with great sadness I announce that our prized, silver steed Agamemnon is missing from his stables."

There were shock and awe amongst the campers.

"We're hoping his disappearance was accidental – gate left unlatched and perhaps he wandered out. We are hopeful, but recognize that the reality could be that he was taken."

More chatter erupted among the worried faces. Ezekiel looked at his friends to find they were already looking at him. He nodded giving them the acknowledgment they were looking for. He knew in his gut Agamemnon was taken.

The friends gathered after breakfast. Ezekiel was ready to take more action. He felt guilty. If something had happened to that wonderful creature he wouldn't be able to forgive himself. Someone did not want Agamemnon taking Ezekiel back to the waterfall.

"We've got to do something. There has to be a way for us to help the Guard find the waterfall," Ezekiel said.

"But if you can't remember, then we're going in blind," Dara said.

"Are we sure we want to find the waterfall. I mean, I feel bad for the peggie and all but say we find it. The Hematite will likely not mind. They kidnap kids and brainwash them. We would be walking into a trap," Kalos said.

"He has a point," Aubrey agreed. "Plus, my mom would kill me. If I got caught on some crazy adventure outside the camp being kidnapped might not be so bad."

"I have an idea. I'm not sure it will work but it's worth a try," Ezekiel said. "Let's go take a kayak ride."

Dara raised her eyebrows with a grin.

The kids pulled out two kayaks from the dock. Dara waved at a very pretty lady in a sky-blue camp vest who was handing out inner tubes to swimmers. Bianca Pulham was the unit leader of the Granters who ran all the water activities. Ezekiel, Ethan and Kalos in one and Dara, Miles and Aubrey in the other. Both kayaks pushed off into the glistening lake.

"So, are you just going to jump in?" Dara asked.

"Well, yeah." Ezekiel replied as he stood up balancing a foot on the edge of the kayak. "Wish me luck!" He dived in.

He swam down being careful of the freshwater ivy with each stroke. The kayaks were out of view and the water was now dark.

Show me.

Nothing happened in the darkness. He felt like someone was watching him from behind. He whipped around. Nothing. Perhaps he was not focused enough on what he needed. He concentrated hard on the flight he had with Agamemnon retracing in his mind everything he had done the minute he pulled him out of his gate. The feeling he had trotting along, soaring in the stable and heading on the trail.

Nothing.

Show me the waterfall!

He recalled how he clenched the reins tight to not fall when Agamemnon took off into flight off the trail leaving his friends behind. The flight soaring over the never, ending trees and the liberating breeze on his face. Camp was no longer in view. All that remained was the horizon and the sun sitting perfectly round, golden and at a forty-five, degree angle from the acres of green trees when Agamemnon started to descend to the waterfall. The perfect circle was the last thing he noticed until he was stunned by the Black Stains on the boulders and how tiny the pool of water was collecting the intense flow of water. He tightened on the peggie's reins and could see the sun perfectly in place.

That was it.

Ezekiel swam up as fast as he could. The bottom of the kayaks came into view. When he hit the surface of the water he felt the warm air hit his lungs. He flew up and hovered between his friends.

"Anything?" Dara asked eagerly.

"I think so. I could be wrong, but the memory, I mean the vision – I'm not sure if it was a memory or an actual vision. It was there I could see it. It was more like it happened again."

"Did you notice anything different? Anything that said 'Hematite here'?" asked Ethan.

Ezekiel plopped into the kayak.

"We need to go back to the stables after lunch but between dinner just like we did the other day. What time would you say we were at the stables?"

"It was around 3 o'clock. We rode for about a half hour before the peggie took you off," Dara said.

"I'm sure I was up there for at least thirty minutes before we found the waterfall. That means it would have been around 4 o'clock. The sun was so clear. I'm sure I'd recognize its placement in the sky!" Ezekiel said with excitement.

"We'll have to retrace your steps then. Tomorrow. You took too much time down there we missed lunch. We haven't the time today with the Night of the Stars on the map," Dara said.

"Tomorrow then. You all in?" Ezekiel asked the group.

They all nodded. Kalos looked unsure.

After a full dinner of pot roast stew and cheddar biscuits the friends made their way to the Observatory. The large purple building stood tall. The top of the building had a large dome of black glass. A large telescope shot into the sky. The sky was black yet speckled with thousands of tiny sparkling lights.

The children entered the building. The walls were covered with the mappings of the sky with brief explanations on each constellation, star and celestial body. It was all unfamiliar to Ezekiel, nothing like he had studied in school. Bianca entered the room and the children swiftly took their seats. She was soon followed by the Magnus and Dux Diego who took seats in the corner.

"Good evening campers. My name is Bianca Pulham, unit leader of the Granters. I welcome you all to our annual Night of the Stars. We will cover some fun information about the magical night skyline you see above." She raised her hand and snapped. The glass above turned from black to the open sky sprinkled with the twinkles of stars. The campers 'oohs' and 'aahs' were in unison.

"Every star you see above has been mapped out for each and every Faerman life that has come to an end. Those that study faeric astronomics have designed this facility for us as well the star charts you see before our walls."

Ezekiel looked hard at the walls. There were a lot of names.

My dad. I wonder...

"Now you may ask yourself, 'how do I find someone specific amongst all these stars?' Well that has been solved with a simple enchantment within the map! Let me demonstrate for you all." She walked to the center of the map, dipping her finger into her dust. She placed that finger onto the map. "Muriel Pulham, best grandma in the universe." A red dot illuminated on the wall on the opposite side she stood. She walked to the other side of the room. She magnified the spot on the map along with the text.

Muriel Pulham
1780 - 2016

Ezekiel was shocked about how old she was when she passed. He caught himself with his mouth dropped open.

"You may notice that her star illuminated red. She was a wonderful Flame and very gifted with fire." She smiled at the campers to show that she was okay and just being nostalgic.

"Now this also works if you are less specific," she added more dust to her finger and touched the map. "Praeses," she said. The map illuminated a dozen star points. She turned to the campers. "This is great for historical purposes. You can see when each of our Praeses moved on to the stars."

A hushed chatter overcame the room. Bianca was delighted she was still able to impress young Fledglings.

"Now why don't you all give it a try before we move on to constellations."

The children spread out quickly engaging in her request. Most researched family members or famous Faerman – actors, musicians and Padsphere stars. There was only one person Ezekiel cared to look up. He nervously placed his finger in his dust pouch. He trembled with anticipation and the hair on his arm began to stand. He wanted to know if his dad was alive. If he was not he would finally have a name his mom couldn't hide. He placed his finger on the map.

"My dad," he said barely able to keep his finger on the map.

He scanned around. His dust did not illuminate a spot for him to retrieve. His heart dropped.

He's alive. He's alive! Is he here in Faera?

Ezekiel's friends approached him. They loved the course, especially Ethan who found every star Padsphere player. He collected Padsphere cards and used this experience to cross-reference his memorization of their details.

"Dude! I found so many of my favorite players! Ken Onishi, Noe Jerkens and my all-time favorite, Viramontes Harris. He broke the all-time record for most points scored during a single season, like, *ever!*"

"Who did you look up?" Dara asked Ezekiel.

"Just family," he replied. He didn't want to get into the story of his dad again.

"Us too. Well, me and Aubrey took a glance at some of our favorite old singers," she smiled at Aubrey. She was enjoying finding more things in common with her. She didn't understand her infatuation with bows, but truly enjoyed her friendship.

"Now campers, please group together and look above at our stars. The observatory orb will map out each constellation we will be discussing today."

The children all looked to the skies.

"There are many to gaze upon," she began to illuminate the outlines of the constellations in the giant orb. The Great Big Dust Pouch, The Quo and Faun – note the distinct connecting lines of the quo's sword and the lines of the Faun's pipes. Remarkable. You can see the battle about to occur. A story for another time. The Nymph, The Scroll and The Urn. Fascinating, aren't they?"

She scanned the open-mouthed children who were squinting to make out the star formations above.

"Yeah, I don't see a dust pouch. It looks like a crooked ball," Ethan said.

"Yep. I don't see it. That is not a scroll. I just see a bunch of squiggles," Ezekiel laughed. He was never able to see the Big Dipper when the camp instructor at his old camp would point it out. He was starting to think it was like going on a snipe hunt – something the adults gave you to do to pass time before lights out.

"My favorite constellation would be the Royal Infinity." As Bianca spoke, the squiggly line that connected each royal Faerman filled in forming a perfect infinity shape.

"What makes this very interesting are the royals that are missing," she said mysteriously. "Many generations ago, during the last and final reign of King Aoberon and Queen Navi, the queen went missing. The Council declared her to be deceased, however her star has yet to show up on the star chart. The King is here as is her children who all lived to be a few hundred years old."

Reaction from the children amused her. She loved when they enjoyed her tales.

"There are theories on why her star is not there. One being that she is still alive!" Chuckles came from the audience in response to her enthusiasm. "That would be quite remarkable as she would be well over five-hundred years old today, so I'm sure that is not it." More giggles from the crowd. "The other is that she publically gave up her crown making her non-royal restoring her to her original name, not the royal name bestowed upon her. This being such a long time ago, and the process of star-mapping being so new, there are no records of her original name prior to the marriage. Such a disappointing end for our last sacrificial queen."

Ezekiel's eyes were glazing over. He was thinking about how he was going to go about finding Agamemnon. He enjoyed camp but the one thing he found common to the real world outside of Faera, was the tall tales meant to give kids the feeling of magic, triumph and everlasting friendship. His real world taught him that family is not perfect, people lie, people like Bradley the bully exist. His guilt for the peggie was making him anxious for the morning.

"Now another favorite, and the last I have to share above our view tonight is the Golden Wings. Legend has it that the stars of all golden Faerman land within this constellation. The last known golden Faerman was Jareth Oscuridad. His goodness is known throughout Faera but he has not been seen since the death of his sister Naya. Many believe that he is in hiding, aging in his final days. The years of keeping the Hematite activity down has worn him."

Gasps from the campers arose. The realization that not having an active gold Faerman was the likely reason for the increase of Guard presence. It was clear that the children were very familiar with the Hematite objectives and now were cast with fear. Bianca sensed this and looked at the Magnus for help.

"Campers. This is not time for alarm. As Faerman we have to evolve and be willing to change. The Guard is doing everything they can to keep us safe. The time of the gold Faerman may end as the monarchy did. That is okay. We will be resilient and aware."

"But what about Agamemnon? Someone took him from the camp. What if they start taking kids again?"

The crowd whipped around to look at which camper spoke. The Dux raised his head with a scowl on his face.

Ezekiel didn't know what came over him. It was as if he was having an out of body experience watching himself speak these challenging words to the Magnus. He wasn't trying to be disrespectful, just inquisitive.

The Magnus grinned a reaction Ezekiel would not have expected. His boldness seemed to please him.

"Well yes. That is what we are worried about too. It is natural to worry but we will not let it overcome us. We have sent letters to your parents letting them know about the disappearance of Agamemnon and the additional precautions we are taking." He turned to Bianca, "Thank you for walking our friends through that delightful review of faeric astrometrics. Let us prepare to retire for the night under the stars."

With dust in hand, he scattered the shimmer above their heads and the illumination parted multiple ways forming into several stacks of floating hammocks. The campers took to their assigned hammocks.

Ezekiel laid in his hammock gazing up at the starry night sky tracing the outline of the constellation of the Golden Wings.

Chapter Twenty-Two
Hold Em'

The next morning most campers head into Murlock early. Ezekiel and his friends gathered at the steps of the Fledgling compound.

"So, what's the plan?" Kalos asked. Ethan looked at him with surprise for his eagerness was not typical.

"Look, I'm not excited to go looking for the Hematite trap but I'd feel rotten if he got killed trying," Kalos jested.

"It's town travel day so most of the campers will be off campgrounds," Dara replied. "If we're going to do something, it needs to be timed at the exact time you saw the position of the sun. That will lead you to the area of the waterfall. We have to be prepared to handle any enchantments that may make it invisible to us. Any ideas for that?"

"I think I may know someone who could help us without me having to tell them everything," Ezekiel said. "We have a lot of time until our adventure so I'm going to stop by Iva's to log in some service time. I'm going to ask her for help."

"What if she tells someone? That will ruin our chances of doing this," Aubrey said. Her comment surprised Dara as it was usually her place to be the overly analytical one.

The group flew off to Murlock. As they landed they could see a festive commotion on the street. Small furry green creatures with large blue eyes were running amok, pushing feverishly to get into Dulcebus'. The pixies had the door barricaded. Several of them were making their way to the Gorging Gargoyle. Those that reached the front entrance met Gorgie's displeasure and were already pink and vomit covered. They seemed to cry and tantrum like a toddler who was not getting their way.

"What the heck are those?" Ezekiel asked.

"Awesome! The uvams are flying south for the winter!" Dara said. "They're pesky little creatures that crave sugar, candy and treats. Once you appease them they turn back to their normal brown color. These are quite hungry."

Ezekiel could see she was delighted to see them in action. Children on the street were tossing them sticks of gum, peppermints and taffy's watching them chomp the sticky confections and transform back into what seemed like reasonable, tame beings.

"Let's grab some food at the Gorge," Miles said. "I'm starving."

The group approached a satisfied Gorgie. He clearly was happy that he bested the uvams from entering the restaurant. The friends were greeted by Everett the Great.

"Well hello there, little Fledglings! I have a table for you right here," he led them to a table covered in brightly colored Easter eggs. He handed them menus and went over the specials. "I highly recommend the eurp eggs and hash. They come with a side of jelly root."

All the friends agreed to the special. A pixie flew overfilling their steins with warm honey mead. Ezekiel heard some familiar voices around the corner. There was a table of the unit leaders enjoying their breakfast. Trav caught Ezekiel's glance.

"Well hello there, campers!" he said. "You won't regret the eurp eggs, they're very fresh today. You two should eat up so you have a lot of energy for today's Flight Championship practice."

Ezekiel shot Ethan a look. They both completely forgot that open camp days were flight field days until the Games. Not wanting to act like they didn't know, Ezekiel pulled out his map, unfolded it to see when they were meeting. Trav had them scheduled to meet at 3 o'clock.

"Shoot!" Ezekiel whispered to Ethan. Our practice is at the same time I should be heading out to find the waterfall."

"Well we will go tomorrow," Ethan said. "There is no way I'm missing a practice for the Games."

Ezekiel looked at Dara to read her face.

"Well you will be expected to show up to practice. If you don't, they'll worry and it will cause more trouble than it's worth," she said.

"Plus, it gives us another day to plan out what we are going to do when we actually find the waterfall," Aubrey said adjusting her giant bow that held together her ponytail.

The friends were startled when a cluster of pixies flew in their direction toting tiny platters they shoot onto the table. The warm smell of the breakfast filled their noses.

"These are good!" Miles said. He was definitely a food connoisseur.

The kids finished their breakfast, thanked the pixies and Everett as they head out the door with caution to avoid the tricky antics of Gorgie.

"Well there is plenty of time in the afternoon now that we aren't going to save the world today. Can we go to the Bazaar?" asked Ezekiel who missed out on the last visit.

The friends approached the vibrantly colored mismatched tents. Upon pulling back the first curtain to walk in, they ran right into Ansh trying to sell Chinese finger traps to a group of Healers.

"I'll give you a great deal! Buy three, get one free," Ansh said as he held three traps in his left hand and conjured one to float in overhead. The kids waved at him and he offered them a wink behind his purple-hued spectacles.

The children wandering into a wine-colored tent that had a ceiling that was as high as a skyscraper. Faerman on stilts walked by, enchanted toy cars raced by as children ran by enchanting them to make them beat out each other. Talking baby dolls sitting in high chairs winked at them with long life-like eyelashes. There were those annoying little mimics, multi-colored dragons that sprouted fire, toy dust making kits, toy daggers, and mustache elixir.

"Why would this be in a toy store?" asked Ezekiel picking up a bottle.

"So, you can have a stache when you're playing!" Ethan ran over hoping for a sample then getting blocked by Dara and a sassy glance.

"I'm getting a mimic to take to my cousin as a souvenir. I am sure she's going to love it," Ezekiel said laughing to himself as he handed the pixie gold. "Can you put it in a bag? I'd hate for anyone to get their hands on it before she does." The pixie handed Ezekiel his bag and fluttered off.

There was a giant display of magic balls that needed enchantment to stop bouncing. The balls bounced and bounced never ceasing in energy. This caught Ezekiel's eye drawing him to the enchanted card sets. He picked up a pack and pulled the cards out. He started to shuffle through them. The red cards featured all of the familiar kings, queens, jacks he was accustomed to, but instead of hearts, spades, clubs and diamonds there were daggers, flames, trees and crowns.

"Hey! Watch your stubby fingers bubb!" said the Jack of Flames.

"Oh, sorry. I didn't realize you could talk, er feel. I'll be more careful," Ezekiel stammered at the grouchy card placing him and the others back in the box. He bought them thinking Iva would enjoy using them for their poker game.

Ethan and Kalos purchased fire-breathing dragon toys. Ethan was prepared to enchant his to torment Dara. Miles found a box set of little green Guards. Once enchanted they could fly around and battle. Aubrey and Dara wanted to look at the book and jewelry tents and were starting to pressure the boys to hurry. Ezekiel was running out of time. He needed to get to Iva's to log in his hour.

"Hey guys, I gotta go. Want to meet up back here or should I just meet you all back at camp?

"We can wait for you," Ethan said. We can dagger back so we get there faster."

"Okay, thanks. See you soon," Ezekiel said walking out of the tent and plunging his dagger focused on the white iron gate of the Green Pastures Retirement Home. There he could see that Kevin the security guard was sitting at his post.

"Hi. I'm here to see Iva Rose," Ezekiel said.

"Go on in," Kevin said not taking his eyes off his Padsphere Weekly magazine.

Ezekiel arrived at the cute lavender cottage. Before he could take a step on the tile logs, Iva opened her door.

"Hello sweetie! I've been looking forward to your visit! Come on in. Cookies are ready to go!"

Ezekiel followed her in. "Hi! I brought us some playing cards I found at the Bazaar," he said as he set his bags on the entry table. He pulled out the box of cards and sat on the flower couch.

"Very, rad," Iva said. Ezekiel giggled. His mom said that. She returned with a tray of freshly baked cookies and set them on the coffee table.

"I'm not sure how to play with these though. I figured you could help me?" Ezekiel asked.

"Of course. They work similar to those quo ones." She said carefully opening the box and sliding the cards out. "You have to pull each by the center of the card, otherwise they get quite fussy if you touch their faces."

She proceeded to shuffle the deck and although done smoothly, they could hear the muffles of the royals as they folded into each other. She distributed two cards to him and placed two in front of herself, then placed three on the table.

"Now this works just like quo poker. All the same type like all daggers is a flush. Any type but in numerical order is still a straight. What is really fun is when you get a pair or more of different royal cards – that's a royal rumble! It's one of the strongest hands you can have. Pick up your cards."

Ezekiel picked up his cards. He had a crown of five and two. Iva flipped the three cards up that they had to play off of. There was an urn of three, dagger king and crown king.

"How dare you enter my realm!" said the dagger king.

"You scum! Your dagger is nothing to my crown!" said the crown king.

"Oh, my gosh! They're fighting!" Ezekiel exclaimed.

"Oh yes, they have quite the rivalry, don't they?" She chuckled. "Will you be placing a wager?"

"Oh yes!" he tossed in two cookies.

"Wow. Two cookies huh. I call your two cookies," she challenged back. "Let's see what you have."

They both flipped their cards over. In her hand, she had the urn queen and crown nine.

"Well you are both nothing compared to my King Urn. If he was here he'd wipe the floor with you!" the urn queen said.

"Oh, my!" Iva said laughing and scooping up the cards. "Looks like I beat you that time. Let's go again."

They continued to play Hold 'Em, Ezekiel loving the reaction of the royal cards as they came out to play. He enjoyed telling her about his successful flight test and being selected for the Flight Championship Game along with Ethan and how brave he felt when he asked Dara to the dance.

"A dance you say? Well I assume you will need a suit from Gastelum's then?" she asked as she poured him some honey mead.

"Oh, I hadn't thought about it. I guess I should get fancy."

"Oh yes, and you must order your date a corsage from Feldman's. He has the best, most beautiful florals."

Ezekiel blushed and the reality of having to dance with Dara set in with the thought that he would be putting a corsage on her hand. Iva sensed this by his pink face.

"You know, I'd be happy to go to town with you to get a fitting and pick out the best corsage for her."

"Yes! I could use the help. I mean, I thought about asking Aubrey, but she's kind of a blabbermouth so this is so much better," he exclaimed.

"Sounds wonderful. As for dancing, you know what you're doing?" she asked with a smile.

"Yeah, about that, um–"

"I have you covered on that too. Thanks for giving an old gal some purpose. Well look at the time! I've done it again – kept you longer than an hour, almost two! Please, let me sign your sheet and get back to camp. We can meet at Gastalum's next week, same time?"

She boxed him up some cookies in haste. Cookies in hand he ran out the door thanking her.

"See you next week Iva!"

Her smile was so large showing off her dimples and perfect smile.

"Bye sweetie! See you then!"

Ezekiel shot up into flight. He hoped his friends wouldn't be too angry with him because he was so late. He landed at the Bazaar entrance and his friends weren't there. He raised the fabric to enter and began to scan around the shops to see if he could spot them.

"Back already?" Ansh asked him. "Can I interest you in some dried swurt? You shred some into your fae dust and you'll be able to move rocks, boulders and small mountains even!"

"Uh, no thanks. Just looking for my friends," Ezekiel replied still scanning around.

"Take some as a sample. You'll be back. It's a great thing to have, especially in the next years at camp when you color sprout and do more advanced craft. It's real, good stuff."

"Thanks," he said apprehensively. He felt like a kid who took candy from a stranger.

"Your friends left here about a half hour ago. The little one with the glasses was saying something about shooting arrows?"

"Thanks, Ansh. See you later!"

Ezekiel stepped out of the tent and daggered back to camp.

He landed at the Fledgling compound and quickly ran up the stairs. The boys were not in their room. He dashed back down passing by several Fledglings. He could feel their eyes avert toward him, staring. He knew what they were thinking. *There's that weird kid who the lake talks to, ruins our Flight Field and scares the crap out of us before we camp out in the dark at the Observatory.*

He didn't care. He had bigger more important things to do. He flew off to the Flight Field. As he passed he could see Kalos near the stables with a bow in hand. He looked very satisfied.

"Hey," Ezekiel said. "Sorry I took so long. Everyone come back?"

"I think the girls were still shopping after we waited a bit for you. It's cool, we figured the old lady needed some help or something," Kalos said.

"What's going on here? I wasn't expecting this many people to be into archery," Ezekiel said looking around at all the campers of every unit waiting their turn to be called to shoot.

"Well, since I didn't make the Flight Games, I thought I'd give shooting a shot. Turns out, I'm not half bad," he said with a smile.

"Teardhmen. You're up," said Mateo.

Kalos raised his bow and pulled an arrow from his quiver. The bow rested so still on his arm he looked like a statue. His aiming eye was strong and focused as he released the arrow. The arrow hit the bullseye right in the center. He pulled another arrow, aimed and released it, splicing the bullseye arrow in half.

"Whoa man! Awesome!" Ezekiel cheered.

Kalos looked around and was basking in the glory of the other unit color campers who were impressed by his performance.

Mateo assembled all the campers and thanked them for a great shoot.

"Results are on this clipboard that I will leave here," he said, enchanting it to a stationary hover so the campers could find their results.

"They only take five and it seems like everyone from our unit showed up today," he said.

"Did you see your shot? I don't think you have anything to worry about," Ezekiel assured him.

"Yeah, but did you see anyone else's?"

Ezekiel and Kalos pushed their way forward to see the results.

"I made it!"

"That's awesome! We're both in the games!" Ezekiel was stoked for his friend.

"I have to get over to the Flight Field for practice but I'll see you in a bit! Congrats!" Ezekiel flew off and landed just in time for stretches.

"Line up!" Trav said.

Each flight champion athlete lined up by unit, spread out opening and revealing their wings in a full stretch.

"Now up and downs," Trav said.

The kids leapt up, paused and landed down in a push-up position. They repeated three sets of twenty-five.

"Now laps on my whistle. Last one in from each unit has to do more up and downs."

Pew!

Ezekiel pushed off hard toward the pillars. The air hit his face, it was cool and liberating. He could feel the presence of the others gaining on him. He pulsed his wings a bit harder swaying easily in and out of the pillars descending smoothly to the finish line. Trav had a huge smile on his face as he recorded the time Ezekiel landed. The next camper to land was a tall fifteen-year-old Flame who looked at Ezekiel with astonishment. Several other teens landed shocked they were beat out by a Fledgling. The response was much different than what he saw Kalos receive.

"Well looks like we have a new record to beat this summer. And from a Fledgling!" Trav was cracking up. Ezekiel could feel the heat on him from the stare of the other flight champions.

Trav pulled aside the fliers who came in last to do their up and downs.

"So, you think your special hmm?" asked the Flame.

"I think he does Fabian," said another.

They closed in closer to him.

"No. I don't think I'm special," Ezekiel said nervously.

"Good. Remember that," he responded turning away as he noticed Trav coming back.

Chapter Twenty-Three
Camp Rally

The next days were filled with so many activities, Ezekiel and his friends were not able to coordinate a plan to get away to look for the waterfall. The demands of the map were greater each day. Faerman Craft was becoming more advanced as the group was well on their way to mixing dust to compound it with sunflower petals to cast light and his favorite charm so far was taking a tin stein of water and heating it to a boil using bits of charcoal. Ezekiel had to also coordinate himself away from Fabian and his cronies, especially at the Flight Field. The entire camp was preparing for the Summer Solstice Camp Rally and all extra time was spent on rehearsing their unit skits. The presence of the Guard during each course was starting to seem normal.

The Flag Ceremony to kick off the Summer Solstice was festive as it was completely decorated in Granters and Flames colors. One side was completely blue with streamers, floating blue confetti and bubbles that would pop leaving behind a fun message, "Go Granters! Put those Flames Out!" The red side was decorated in streamers, confetti and letters of fire flashing their spirit, "Go Flames! Burn those Granters!"

The campers were led to the amphitheater and were greeted by the musical harmony of the camp band.

"Look! It's Miles!" Aubrey said waving to Miles up on stage.

"Awesome for him! He's killing that pipe horn," Ezekiel said.

The Fledglings took their seats. It had been a while since they assembled in these very same seats. All but two units also took their seats.

"Oh boo. No chant off?" Aubrey said.

"I know. Not during the Summer Solstice week. It's all about the two Padsphere teams that are going to face off," Dara said.

The amphitheater started to mist. Rainbow colors refracted off the misted air. Thousands of blue bubbles filled the theater with a strong scent of magic that choked Ezekiel a bit. The blue campers entered in all angles releasing sprays of water onto the crowd. Then, a large water formation raised high, then crashed down like a tidal wave just over the heads of the campers as if a force field was preventing the water from hitting them.

Everywhere we go, people want to know,
Who are we are,
So, we tell them!
We're the mighty, mighty Granters!
The mighty, mighty Granters!
If they can't hear us, we'll shout a little louder!
Go Granters! We're going to put those Flames Out!

They all sat celebrating their entrance.

A cluster of red campers hovered in with their red hood over their faces. From the center of their cluster each camper raised their hand creating a flame in their palm. They brought the flame together forming a large ball of fire. They quickly separated circulating the area, flames in hand chanting repetitively.

We're fired up!
We're sizzling!
We're turning up the heat!
When it comes to everything, the Flames can't be beat!
We're going to burn those Granters!

The Flames threw their fire in hand up in the air creating a giant wall of fire above the campers. The Flames flew through it and it evaporated in the air.

The theater exploded with cheers and applause. The Magnus took the stage.

"Good evening campers! Welcome to the Summer Solstice Camp Rally. This celebration is to kick off the fun for the last week of camp. I would like to congratulate our Game Champions who have been selected to represent their units in Shooting, Flight and Padsphere."

More thunderous applause filled the room.

The Magnus raised his hand to silence the campers.

"Yes, I am very excited too. Before we start our theatrical delights, I will remind you all that our Games begin on Monday. Seating will be available for those that would like to root for their favorite unit. Shooting and Flight will be completed in a sudden death tournament fashion. The Padsphere championship game between the Granters-" he was interrupted by more applause, chants and hoots, "and the Flames," he was interrupted again. The crowd went crazy.

He raised his hand again.

"Our game will have the honor of having the Praeses in attendance." There was a hush of silent whispers of excitement. "At the end of the week we will hold our formal event, at the lake shore under the moonlight. Don't worry, we will have a dance floor so no one has to worry about ruined shoes." He chuckled at his own joke.

Ezekiel thought that was strange. Couldn't he just fly so he wasn't in the sand?

"The next morning will be your last until next summer. Our closing camp ceremony will take place here after breakfast where we will give our final words and special honors."

"We will begin our skits. Campers from each unit volunteered to create a skit on their most memorable camp experience. Now let me welcome the Fledgling unit to the stage to present their skit they call, 'The Lake'."

A group of Fledglings took the stage with mischievous grins on their faces. They held a large blue camp blanket as a prop to represent the lake. A few campers hid beneath it. A brown-haired boy named Gilligan walked on stage exaggerating his hand through his hair to make it stick up in the front. Another camper wearing a fake beard pretending to be the Magnus approached Gilligan.

"It's your turn to go bond with your dagger."

"But I am sooooo scared," said Gilligan as a very recognizable camper.

"Let me help you then!" said the pretend Magnus as he shoved Gilligan into the 'lake'. Gilligan disappeared under the blue blanket and in a whiny voice said, "Oh no. my dagger isn't working." A boy ran by with a sign that read '3 hours later'. As he ran off stage, a girl dressed as a dolphin popped up out of the blanket lake waving her flipper. "Bye Ezekiel! Nice to meet you!" Gilligan/Ezekiel leapt out of the blanket lake with an exaggerated, terrified look on his face. The audience was laughing hysterically.

He cuddled himself as he rocked back and forth. Then five more Fledglings joined the stage. A boy had woven straw together to make a blonde colored wig where he used fabric to tie an extra-large green bow in his straw hair. The others on stage were poor replicas of Ethan, Dara, Kalos and Miles. The kid playing Kalos was taller than everyone but was on his knees crawling around the stage with glasses pretending to be short.

"Is that supposed to be me?" Aubrey scowled, standing with her hand on her dust pouch ready to cast a fart enchantment on him. Dara grabbed her hand, shaking her head, "We can't afford the demerit." Kalos sunk in his chair. Ethan laughed. Ezekiel swore he saw one of the Guards crack a slight grin.

Aubrey reluctantly sat down. Ezekiel looked at her and said, "Well at least you aren't a crybaby that is scared of dolphins." His face burned with irritation. How could the Magnus let this go on? He looked around and saw that the Magnus wasn't in his usual seat with the staff. He was in the very back row in what seemed like a heated conversation with the Dux. Ezekiel was so fixed on them that he missed the ending of the Fledgling skit. He took notice when the Magnus separated himself to take the stage to introduce the next unit. For just one moment, the fact that he didn't feel bothered by the petty display sent a wave of satisfaction through him.

The next skit was presented by the Arbors and was less eventful and centered around tree hopping. They always tended to be airy, dreamers who spent a lot of time hlyking in the woods. The Elements were slightly more amusing as they shared their affinity for tossing boulder like rocks to each other using their skillful inclination for the earthen craft. Ezekiel could see the look of discomfort on Dr. Walker's face. He imagined that she must be mentally preparing herself for a night of a full infirmary. Her unit, all in white, gracefully showcased their favorite infirmary heals which included a split shin bone and partially severed ear. Predictably, both the Granters and Flames focused their skits on beating out every other team for a place in the Games. Both ended with a strong implication they were the true champion and winner of the Games. Ezekiel loved watching Dara roll her eyes at the terrible acting and absurdity of their athletic prowess.

The Magnus seemed distracted as he approached the stage. "Well campers, that concludes our rally. You may all return to your unit compounds for the night. Best of luck to all of our Game Champions as you prepare for competition." He sped off the stage to join the Dux and his Guards. They flew off heading toward his quarters.

"Did you guys notice that the Magnus seemed distracted tonight?" Ezekiel said.

"Not really, but then again, I was distracted by the hilarious skit of you," Ethan joked.

Dara shot him a look. "That was not funny and Ezie is right. The Magnus normally would not have let that stupid skit carry on had he been paying attention. Something is going on."

Ezekiel's cheeks got warm. She called him by his nickname. He had to fight a megawatt grin that wanted to explode from his face.

Miles approached the group holding the case of his large windpipe. It seemed awkward for him to carry as it was as large as him. "Hi! How'd I do?" he asked.

"You were wonderful!" Dara exclaimed sticking out her hand for a high-five.

"I think it's awesome you learned to play that well just over a month. You sure you haven't played before?" Aubrey asked with a smile.

"Nope, just started here. I practice a lot while these guys are practicing for the Games. I'm really excited because we're going to play during the tournaments for the Praeses as she enters and during breaks in the Games," Miles was beaming.

"That could be why the Magnus is acting weird. The Praeses coming means security being even tighter than usual," Kalos pointed out.

"Yeah, well more security means it's going to be even harder to find that waterfall. How will we get off the campgrounds without being seen?" Ethan said.

"We have to go during recreation time. We say we're going off to Murlock. That's a bit out of the way but we can take off and fly from the backside of the Bazaar. It is far away enough from the backside of the camp so there shouldn't be too much Guard presence," Dara said.

Ezekiel remembered he had told Iva that he would meet her at Gastelum's.

They had quite the afternoon planned. "I have to meet Iva for my service time. Plus, afterward we have practice for the Games. Let's do it on Sunday. Everyone will be distracted with the Summer Solstice set up, they won't even notice if we don't show up for dinner."

The friends all agreed, half mostly because Saturday was a day to be spent at Murlock having fun and not going on a potentially dangerous mission. The other half knew it was what needed to be done to save Agamemnon.

Ezekiel laid in his hammock. Miles was asleep snoring loudly. He wasn't sure about Kalos and Ethan but they were so quiet he was sure they were asleep but figured he'd try them anyway.

"Are you guys still awake?" he whispered.

"Yeah. This guy over here is like having growling bear in the room," Ethan replied from beneath Miles.

Ezekiel had to hold in his laugh by covering his mouth. "Did you ask anyone to the dance?"

"Naw. I'm going to keep my options open. I figure that there may be more guys out there too scared to ask a girl to the dance so most of the ladies will be going solo. That's where I come in," he replied. Ezekiel could feel his Cheshire grin from his bunk above.

"Nice plan. I don't know how to dance. I've never done it seriously. I've done it making fun of my cousin and her dancing but that's about it. I'm going to have Iva show me how. Is that lame?" he asked instantly regretting the question.

"Naw, it's not lame. If you don't want to look like a fool, you practice. Makes sense to me. I don't think my sister knows how to dance. I wasn't even sure she could run until we came to camp since she's always reading," Ethan said.

"Do you think we'll find Agamemnon?" Ezekiel asked.

"I don't know man. It's kind of a crazy thing to be worried about. I mean, we're kids and we're at camp. Shouldn't we be doing craft, sports and hanging out at the lake?" Ethan replied.

"I don't think this camp is meant for just that. There is a reason they want us at this age, at this time," Ezekiel said seriously trying to get Ethan to listen.

"Why can't it be? After a week, we'll all be back to our quo friends, then school and this won't be our problem." Ethan paused for a moment. "I mean, I'll write you and maybe ma will let you come visit if yours will bring you."

"Of course. Sounds good," Ezekiel said trying to hide his disappointment. "Good night."

"Night," Ethan replied realizing his friend was disappointed. He felt bad that he couldn't laugh his way out of the situation but he genuinely didn't feel that they could do anything to make a difference.

●   ●   ●   ●   ●

He was there again. The air was cold and uninviting. The sky was dark and there wasn't a single light on the street turned on. He ran a short while forgetting he had wings he could control. He pushed off the pavement and took off into flight toward the yellow, white fenced house. The single window had a hazy, sheen of light trying to escape the shade that concealed it. He approached the gate and pushed it open, walked up the steps of the patio to the door that had been left ajar.

The room was so long he couldn't make out the end. Just his shadow spread along the wall. He squinted, straining his eyes to make out the figure at the end of the room. He realized it was the dream again. He focused on not waking but running toward the figure in the shadow. The figure ran from him. He pushed off the floor to fly after it. It looked back at him and flew off even faster disappearing into darkness.

He was surrounded by a familiar darkness he had seen before. The air smelled moist and he couldn't see in front of him. He slowed down to land. Each step echoed as though down a long stone corridor. He reached out and the stone walls were wet. He wiped his hand on his vest, feeling his dagger and keeping his hand there just in case. He could hear a rhythmic noise. He walked toward it. There was a faint crack of light. He walked forward cautiously filled with curiosity.

The crack of light was a flaw in the black curtain that hung from the ceiling. He stuck his head up to the break in the fabric and peered inside. It was something he had seen before.

There were hundreds of dark-clothed Faerman standing. He could see the black, sparkling crown of thorns as it towered above the crowd. He could only see the pale hands of its wearer remove the crown seeming to disappear below the crowd. The crowd seemed focused on the floor, then they cheered,

"Coacter!" motioning their hands outward, with their hands webbed out strong. He stood on his toes trying to see, careful to not bump the curtain or fall through. He felt a hot breath on his neck. Immediately panic set in and his throat fell into his stomach.

He turned around and was face to face with Agamemnon.

Chapter Twenty-Four
Learning to Dance

Ezekiel awoke in a deep sweat with a feeling over his body as though he had not slept. He knew he was dreaming but his mind wanted answers so he let his dream control him. A feeling of wanting to return to the dream cast over him as the morning trumpets played. He wanted to find Agamemnon so badly that it was now haunting his dreams.

The boys quickly dressed and flew down the staircase to meet with Dara and Aubrey. It was obvious they had a plan to visit Dulcebus' as Aubrey had on a large white bow speckled with colorful donut delights. Dara had a matching bow that was much smaller clipped into her hair. Ezekiel felt bummed he couldn't go with them.

"So, I know you'll helping Iva today, but can we pick you up anything at Duclebus'? Dara asked. "The inside-out custard balls are so good! I can bring you one for later."

"Sure. That sounds great," Ezekiel replied trying to not show his giddiness.

"Can we dagger there? I don't feel like getting all sweaty from the flight. It's hot," Aubrey complained.

Dara nodded and the girls plunged their daggers into the ground waving off. Aubrey was right, the summer heat was in full force.

"I think I'll do the same. See you guys later," he said plunging his dagger into the ground heading off the storefront of Gastelum's. The bold emerald green storefront canopy was a refreshing retreat from the sun. He could see through the glass that Iva was inside engaged in a friendly chat with Richard Gastelum, shop owner and Pop Pop to Dara and Ethan.

Ezekiel pushed the door open and as he walked in a little charming harp jingle played and a group of pixies hovered around him donning long strings of measuring tape and pins. The walls were filled with suit jackets of all colors and patterns. A tweed plaid, seersucker, polka dot, striped, elbow-patched, red leather, with penguin tails, blue velvet crushed, fur covered, feather detailed, star patterned, ruffled, rubber, neon with puffed shoulders and of course, all the traditional colors he's seen in department store catalogs. He laughed to himself considering the rubber as he imagined himself in it, flying up and launching himself onto the ground so he could be a ball. The look he imagined on Ethan's face made it worth it. The look on Dara's changed his mind.

"Hello there, sweetie!" Iva called to him with an enormous smile framed with her doll dimples. She was wearing a lavender cardigan sweater over her lavender flowery dress. It reminded him of her cottage.

"Hi. Am I late?" he asked.

"Oh no, I was just catching up with Richie here. Richie dear, this handsome Fledgling, needs something to impress a young lady next week at the Summer Solstice Dance," she said as she pointed to the suits and tuxedos shifting through them in the air.

"Size 16 I see," said Richard as he sized Ezekiel up and down. "Do you know what color your date will be wearing? So, we can coordinate?

"Um, no. I forgot to ask," Ezekiel replied.

"Well then we go with something safe – Patterns away!" he shouted sending the patterned jackets away to the back. They flew off as if sad not be chosen. All that remained were variations of black and navy.

"Let's have you stand here," he said placing Ezekiel on top of a wooden box in front of a three-paneled mirror. Each suit flew hovering in front of him just for a moment to allow Iva and Richard to assess which was best. This was making Ezekiel dizzy.

"I think I like the black one," he said. "Plus, I have a red bow tie I'd like to wear with it that my mom sent me."

"How sharp you will look! It's double breasted with satin collared trim and buttons. What a gentleman!" Iva said with cheery excitement. She stopped reflecting about what she said, "I mean you'll be the dopest guy there." Ezekiel and Richard roared with laughter. Iva let out a spirited chuckle. "We'll take this one," she said still giggling.

Richard called the pixies over with a wave of his hand. "Please take this to be pressed in the back. Let's package this up nicely. This, young Fledge is taking my Dara to the dance!" Ezekiel's eyes grew as his cheeks flushed. It had just occurred to him that was Ethan's Pop Pop. Ethan and Dara are actually related twins despite being complete total opposite. That makes him Dara's Pop Pop.

Luckily for Ezekiel the pixies returned quickly with his tuxedo pressed and packaged in an emerald colored garment bag on a gold hanger. Ezekiel was ready to escape. He wasn't sure why he felt so shy all of a sudden. He just realized that he didn't have enough Faerons to cover the cost of the suit. Iva read his face immediately. "I invited you here today. I hope you'll make an old gal happy by accepting this gift. I never had a son so please let me be a part of this for you." He couldn't say no to her dimpled smile.

"Maybe I can pay you back? Do some chores?" Ezekiel asked.

"Oh no. You know how tidy I am. I don't need much help. How about this. Get all spiffed up and stop by my cottage so I can get a photo of you for my album. Then we will call it even," she offered.

"Of course! I'd do that anyway," he said with a smile of promise.

"Thanks Richie. We have to jet off to Feldman's to order the most beautiful corsage for the stunning Miss Dara. Obviously only the best will do," she said with a flattering tone.

"Yes of course," he replied with a wink, "Have fun."

•   •   •   •   •

Ezekiel and Iva exited to the chime of the harp. He noticed her raised eyebrow as she noticed the group of Guards on the street. She seemed to purse her lip. She noticed Ezekiel look at her. "It's a shame our beautiful streets have to be filled with the Guard. The idea our home isn't safe is absurd. I don't know what they're afraid of. Waste of Faerman tax dollars out here and I'm sure they scare you kids."

Ezekiel had got used to seeing them everywhere in town and at camp he did not notice them. She was right. Aside from Agamemnon, there wasn't much reported in the Chronicle.

"Here we are!" she exclaimed stopping in front of a shop covered in green. The entire exterior looked like bold green English Ivy. The window was an arched piece of glass framed by blossoms of flowers that cascaded around it. The door to enter was arched as well, wooden and painted yellow. Vines of violet morning glories turned their heads watching them enter the shop.

Rows and rows of buckets were filled with every floral in every color you could imagine. Daisies, magnolias, roses, irises, poppies, carnations, tulips and an interesting flower that seemed to come in various bold colors, moving vines and squirt what looked like a wad of spit into the air and then would catch it in its blossom. He was definitely not choosing that one.

There were refrigerators filled with exotic, out of this world pre-made floral wreaths, arrangements and bouquets. Ezekiel could see a large arrangement that included several of the weird spitting flower in teals and oranges. The counter was empty with the exception of what looked like hundreds of notes tacked to the wall. Being nosy, he leaned to see what was written on them. They seemed to just be handwritten orders. It didn't seem like a very organized method for a Faerman.

Iva tapped on the silver bell with a sign that read, 'Please Ring'.

"Just a minute!" yelled a voice from the back. Behind the counter there was a doorway with no door, just a yellow curtain hiding the mysteries of the flower shop behind it. He could hear rustling of a sort. Then a bang.

"Are you okay?" she asked, raising her eyes and hands at Ezekiel. He shrugged in agreeance.

"Just fine! Be right there!" shouted the voice over what sounded like more wrestling, banging and an, "Ouch!" Out from behind the curtain came a blonde-haired man who was very short with pointed ears. He was completely proportioned in size but seemed to be the size of an average six-year-old.

"Sorry to keep you folks waiting. How can I help you?" he asked wiping his brow and removing his brown leather gloves. He had scratches on his face.

"Yes. Are you sure you're alright?" Iva asked as she saw he looked a bit beat up.

"Oh yes. I just received a Spindelous Petrium that is quite wild, needs training. I have a dozen of them in the back, but this one in particular is quite rowdy," he replied. Ezekiel could see on his yellow apron the name Caleb.

"I need to order a corsage for, um, for my uh –" Iva helped him out, "For his date. He has the Summer Solstice Bash." She smiled at them both.

"How exciting. Fledgling I see. Now us Elfins don't do camp but we do attend a boarding school where we learn our craft. Summers were spent traveling the land in large packs. Such fun memories. Anyway, anything in particular you'd like in it?" he asked as a small motion with his hand raised a small piece of paper in the air.

"I don't know. I know she likes gardenias," Ezekiel said. Iva smiled. "That's wonderful that you know that! See what a gent this boy is!"

"Okay, I see what we can do. How is this?" he asked as he charmed the paper wider and with the movement of his hand he cast lines of a perfect gardenia framed by curled greenery and tiny baby's breath. Ezekiel could smell the fragrance of the flower with a tinge of magic all around the shop.

"I think that looks lovely!" Iva said excitedly. "What do you think?"

This was where a flower looked like a flower to him. Ezekiel could see they came in different colors and had a bit of a different look but he wasn't really interested in them. Since Iva looked happy and seemed to always be classy he assumed this would be a good choice.

"Looks great!" he said pulling out his gold. Caleb listed the price of ten Faerons which is exactly what Ezekiel had on him. He didn't want Iva to step in. Caleb shrank his paper down and cast it to the wall with the others.

"It will be ready for pick up on Saturday by 5 o'clock so it will be fresh for the dance," Caleb said, turning to an order that jumped off the wall and began to follow him around as though annoyed.

"Yes, yes. I know. I'm getting it started right now," he said to the paper annoyed as he went to the flower buckets to retrieve some stems. "These pesky things won't leave me be until I fill the order. Interested, Ezekiel stood and watched him assemble a bouquet into a jeweled vase. Satisfied with his completed order the paper laid itself onto the counter as if to rest.

"Thanks! See you next week!" Ezekiel said as he flung his emerald garment bag over his shoulder and walked out the door with Iva.

"Looks like we have everything covered," Iva said.

"Yes, well except the dancing part," Ezekiel said.

"Ah, yes. To my cottage then?" she asked as she pulled out her dagger. It was the first time he had seen it. It was tiny, feminine with a white jeweled handle. They plunged their daggers into the ground and landed on her porch steps.

With a pinch of dust, she illuminated her den and turned on her radio.

"Now you have to be able to dance to the fast upbeat songs like this," she said as she started to move and groove to what sounded like 70's funk. Ezekiel lost it when she started to pump her hands in the air. "You gotta feel it. You try," she pulled him in. He felt silly but obliged.

"There you go. Now side to side," she said, snapping her fingers letting the music get louder. Ezekiel started to pump his arms in the air mimicking her. He laughed thinking of his Nan since this was her type of jam. If she could see him. He'd have to remember these moves to show her.

"Okay, so from what I hear you kids are into this hippity hop. That is what will likely be at your dance. I started you with the classics because that's where the hippity hop gets its beat from. Let me find a channel," she said flipping through to find something she deemed 'hippity hop'. He couldn't find it in him to correct her.

"Ah! Here we go!" she said when she found a station with the upbeat sounds of rhythmic lyricist. He was surprised that she knew what style of music this was. Iva pumped and moved on beat with such a zest of life. So, carefree. He joined her trying to keep up with the beat of the music.

"You're not so bad for a first-time dancer!" she shouted over the music. Ezekiel was starting to think this was the craziest thing he'd seen since arriving at Faera. He'd never asked Iva how old she is, even for Quotidian women he knew that was rude and they didn't live for half as long as Faerman did.

The song ended and both were winded. "Thirsty?" she asked as she headed into the kitchen to pull a pitcher of cold honey mead out. With a wave of her hand she plucked ice cubes from the icebox into the glasses and filled their glasses handing over Ezekiel his glass. He took a long gulp that cooled him instantly. Dancing was much more tiring than he anticipated.

"You'll likely get tired so be sure to offer her a drink so you can take a break and chat just like you did today," Iva said. "I bet you're hungry! We've had quite the afternoon hmm?"

Ezekiel nodded eagerly. He was hungry now that she mentioned it. "Yes. Something to eat sounds great!"

They both entered her kitchen. It was the first time he got to see how a home in Faera worked. There were no pixies here to whip things out as there were in other places he'd seen so he was curious.

Iva moved quick. With a small pinch of dust, she summoned an entire chicken from the fridge, charmed rosemary, broth and butter into a casserole dish. A wooden pepper grinder was in the air shifting and twisting on the bird. From a pantry flew out tiny purple potatoes, plopping into the dish, rolling themselves into the olive oil that splattered all over. All in one swoop the dish went into the oven. The door clicked and the timer went on with a beep.

"More honey mead dear?" she asked. He wasn't going to pass up on it. It was beginning to be his new favorite drink. "Yes please."

While waiting for dinner he told her all about Flight Field practice and his trouble with Fabian and his posse. He also re-enacted the terrible acting from the Fledglings who mocked him in their lake production. She laughed and clapped when he used the bottom of her mop to describe to her Aubrey and her reaction.

"Yes, kids can be cruel. It's a shame though. It goes by so fast, youth that is," she said with a look of nostalgia or reflection on a past she could not change. "We learn from ourselves. You wonder if your choices are the right ones and then you have to live with them as you grow." The oven beeped alerting that their feast was now ready.

Iva showed Ezekiel how to do the dining room table set up. She showed him just the right amount of dust to use, how to aim it and flow the fine china onto the table softly placing each piece of silver into the linen napkin. He was a bit rough on his first try as he rattled the crystal goblet as it set down.

"It's okay dear. Wonderful first go. I'm sure your mom will be thrilled you can do it when you get back home," she said.

The meal was delicious and by far the best chicken, purple potato meal he had ever eaten. Iva summoned a banana caramel, toffee cream pie from the fridge. He thought he was going to explode but once he saw it his stomach made room for it.

"That may have been the best meal I've ever had in my entire life," Ezekiel said.

"Oh stop, you little charmer!" Iva giggled. "I do hope that you will write me during your quo school year. I'd be most interested in how you're doing until you come back for camp next year and visit me." Her eyes twinkled.

"Of course. Quo life is definitely not as exciting as it is here but I will," he said.

"So, you're ready. For your big week, hmm?"

"I think so. I mean, I worry if I go too fast in the Flight Games and beat out the times of the other units I'll get the crap kicked out of me so I might have to just be fast enough to win my unit but not too fast to beat everyone."

"That is disappointing. Never let anyone hold you back from your potential," she said with the most serious face he had ever seen from her.

"You're right," he succumbed. "I'll let you know how it goes."

"Well then, back to our lesson. We have to cover my favorite style of dance. The waltz!" She stood up enthusiastically holding out her hand. He took it and she led him to the open space in the den. Flicking on the radio a ballad filled the room. She placed his hand on her waist and her hand on his shoulder. She swayed him into a perfect box step repetitively to the melody of the song. She paused a step outward into a pivoted turn back into him.

"Make sure you're leading her. If she follows your steps the tricks should be easy," she said as they swayed in perfect unison. He was surprised how easy this seemed to come to him.

"I think you got the hang of it. You should practice those steps every day just humming to yourself and you'll do fine," she said with a smile.

"Thanks so much. I had so much fun today. I'll let you know how the games go when I come by on Saturday," he said cheerfully.

"I'm looking forward to it," she said with her wholesome smile waving him off out the door.

$$\bullet \quad \bullet \quad \bullet \quad \bullet \quad \bullet$$

Garment bag in hand, Ezekiel opted to dagger back to camp since it was a bit heavy to carry for the flight back. Walking up the winding staircase he ran into Miles.

"Hi! How'd it, go? Oooh. What'd you get?" he asked pointing to the garment bag."

"It's my suit for the dance. Are you going?" Ezekiel asked.

"Oh yeah. I asked Aubrey and we're going as friends," he replied. "Kalos is supposed to ask her bunkmate Pippa today. We'll see if he gets the nerve to."

This made Ezekiel laugh. He didn't see Miles as the Casanova any more than he saw it in Kalos.

"I gotta run off to the Field for practice. See you later," Ezekiel darted off into the powdered blue sky. The gush of the hot air hit his face as he flew onward to the Flight Field. Excitement filled him as he imagined himself all dapper in his suit, escorting Dara by the gloved fingertips like a lady. He had seen this in Nan's old movie's where the guys had cool handlebar mustaches.

He landed on the field aside Ethan who was already stretching.

"Hey," Ezekiel said as he took a lunge to the ground to stretch his legs.

"Hey," Ethan replied with a groan as he arched his back and wings. "Dude, I'm feeling kind of sore from yesterday's flight."

"Tell me about it."

"Tell you about what? How you think you're something but you're not?" Fabian hissed tussling his brown-blonde hair underneath a Padsphere hat as he and his clan took their place on the field.

"Ignore him," Ethan said. Ezekiel already had his eyes fixed on him.

Fabian came over to Ezekiel and stood over him. Ezekiel didn't flinch. He slowly placed his hand on his dust pouch. Just in case.

"So, you're deaf now?" he jeered.

Ezekiel switched his position and stretched arching over to face Fabian. "No. Not deaf. Just don't see anyone worth responding to."

Fabian's buddies burst out into laughter. He looked heated and shot them a look that shut them up immediately. He seized Ezekiel by the wing and pulled him up to his face with other, fist clenched tight.

"Well hey there you two. Were you about to give Mr. Raroso a congratulatory kiss?" Trav stepped to the field seizing Fabian by the wing, pulling him from Ezekiel.

Ethan felt brave. "Yes. That's exactly what was going on." Fabian's buddies had to stifle their laughter.

"Laps campers. Ten in and outs, then return here and five sets of up and downs. While I have a chat with Mr. Dartmouth." He blew his whistle and they were off.

Fabian scowled.

Chapter Twenty-Five
Missing and Still Missing

After the fire tale, Ezekiel was glad to get to his hammock. He was exhausted from the long day. Murmurs and whispers within the compound were gushes on how Ezekiel stood up to Fabian, the Flames star flier and strongest Sphereguard on the Padsphere team. He was too tired to engage so he quickly shuffled off to bed.

Sitting on his hammock was a package. Guilt hit him as he knew he should have written his mom a bit more but he was busy. She would understand. At this point he only had about a week left at camp anyway. He ripped open the box and inside was his beloved red-bow tie. He picked it up and a pang of reverence hit his heart. A giant five-pound bag of gummy bears was beneath a plastic baggie of a large square of Nan's homemade fudge. He picked up the fudge and sniffed it. Although the aroma filled his nose of sweetness, there was a touch of his kitchen in the scent. He opened the letter.

Dear Ezie,

I hope you are having fun! Sorry I did not write sooner. I've been quite busy in the office. The Department of Health & Wellness has sure been flooded with inquiries lately!

It is such great news to hear about your Flight Card. I loved the photo as I am sure Mr. Iocus loved taking it. He has always been very silly. I wish I could make it to see you during the Games. Seats are hard to come by because the Praeses will be there but I will try. Best of luck to you!

I also heard about the peggie. Don't feel like it is your fault. Nelson told me everything and I am sure he will be found. You just never know with animals.

I'm so excited for your first dance. Please take pictures. There's nothing like your first one.

I love you. Uncle Mark and Nan send their love and goodies. Uncle Mark found those gummy bears on sale. He insisted I send the entire bag even though I insisted there was no way you were going to eat all those in one week.

See you soon!

Mom

Ezekiel was happy to get a letter from his mom but he was too tired for gummies and fudge. He settled his goodies into the box and stashed it away in his trunk. Miles was already dozing off eying the gummies, Ethan went to bed an hour ago and Kalos fell asleep reading a comic book. Ezekiel snuggled into his hammock with his soft, cozy blanket and fell asleep.

•   •   •   •   •

The morning trumpets sounded. This particular morning Ezekiel felt like he had the best sleep he'd had since camp started. He knew that today was the day they would venture out into the woods to find the waterfall and with luck his dream would come true. He didn't have a plan on how to get him out. He could jump on his back and ride him out. He wasn't sure if he would know how to even get out of there if he made it that far.

The boys got dressed and met the girl's downstairs. They all assembled downstairs amongst what seemed like frenzied chaos. Ezekiel had to take a moment to think about what day it was. Typically, weekend days were not this frantic.

"Did you hear? We're not allowed off the grounds today," Dara said with panic in her voice.

"What?! Why?" Ezekiel said. He felt his heart drop.

"I don't know. Everyone who went to leave grounds to have breakfast at the Gorge were denied pass."

The campers all sat around the stumps and mushroom stools around their fire pit. The embers of burnt wood logs filled the area. Everyone whispered but overall was mostly quietly awaiting the news.

"Could there have been some sort of attack in town?" Ethan asked after a long pause of quiet.

"Maybe. We're not that far from town though. I'd think we could see or hear something," Kalos said.

"I'm hungry. Can we assume the worst and still go eat?" Miles asked whining.

He was right. It made no sense sitting there starving and upset. At least one need could be met. The friends walked to the Feasting Hall. Sweet Sally was ready for the disappointed campers. She had sweet cream-cheese stuffed, sugar-powdered French toast, eurp omelets and hash. The food was delicious but there as a somber undertone amongst the campers.

As breakfast wrapped up, the group started to head back to the compound when a loud announcement boomed overhead.

"Attention all campers. Please report to the amphitheater now. Thank you."

It was the Magnus. It was hard to read his voice as it was flat with no excitement or energy. At a glance, it was obvious they were going to rush there by dagger. They weren't going to waste time flying.

The group entered the amphitheater. There were at least five times as many Guards surrounding the theater on the outside and inside. The Dux was there onstage with the Magnus. The staff was onstage and Mateo Conti looked as though he hadn't slept all night. His eyes were swollen as though he had been crying.

There were no chant offs or jeers to the other units. The only sound was from the whispers amongst the campers and the sounds of the stragglers taking their seats. It felt like a million years until the someone approached the podium. The Dux took the center of the stage. He took a pinch of the amp dust from a small gold bowl fixed on the podium and cast it from the front of his mouth. The campers had seen the Magnus do this many, times, but the way the Dux did this was stiff and pompous.

"Campers. We appreciate your cooperation during this confusing time. There is no gentle way to announce this. I am afraid to say a camper has gone missing." Loud chatter and shock waved through the theater. "Flame camper Fabian Dartmouth was last seen at campfire walking back to his compound. He was not present in his room during the morning trumpets. We have several Guard on search on the grounds, the woods and the town. We have not ruled out the possibility of a Summer Solstice week prank," he said looking over to the Granters seating area. "We have the situation under control and will be on site monitoring for any suspicious activity. We have contacted the Dartmouth family who will be on site shortly."

A cry soon muffled was heard from the Arbors side. Ezekiel glanced and could see a girl just older than him with the same brown-blonde hair as Fabian sniffing a strong cry into the arm of her friend.

"His sister," Dara whispered. Ezekiel nodded with sympathy for her.

"However, if anyone is discovered to be involved with the plot of disappearance – joke or not, will experience serious consequences including expulsion from the camp upward to a sentence in the Caves with the Manticores."

Hushed whispers spread amongst the campers.

"What are the Caves?" Ezekiel asked Kalos.

"It's like jail here. They are overseen by the Manticores," he replied with a clear look of terror on his face. "I didn't think they could send kids there with *them*."

The way he said *them*, made Ezekiel uncomfortable. There was still so much he needed to learn about this world.

"It's supposed to be bad. The Manticores are your worst nightmare. They have a normal face like you and I with body of a lion and the tail of a scorpion. You may look at them and think, 'Oh just a big prison guard guy' but you'd be wrong. They control their prisoners with the fear of their poisonous tails," Ethan said.

Ezekiel laughed but saw his friends faces didn't change, except Ethan. He seemed a bit amused. "I'm sorry to laugh but are you serious? That sounds fake, even for here."

"Look around. Do you see anyone laughing," Dara said seriously.

That was enough for him.

The Magnus took the podium. "We will continue business as usual after today. Let us allow the Guard to assess to our grounds. After today we will resume the scheduled Summer Solstice activities. You may all return to your compounds for the remainder of the day as all courses and the lake are closed. Please be orderly. This is not the time to panic but a time for cooperation. You are all dismissed." He turned and patted Mateo on the shoulder.

Ezekiel studied Mateo's face. He didn't look as tough and creepy as he had once thought. He felt sorry for him. The guilt of having a camper taken under his watch wretched on him. Ezekiel could not stand Fabian and was glad he was gone.

He then felt guilty for thinking that.

•   •   •   •   •

The friends made their way back to the Fledgling compound. The boys retreated to their room to trade and barter the goodies sent from home. Ezekiel felt good about his power position with a five-pound bag of gummy bears and a large chunk of fudge. He also found the pink and white striped box from Duclebus' with the inside out custard ball sitting on his hammock. He wasn't willing to part with it, but he'd share a piece for a sliver of the lemon tart Miles swiped from the Feasting Hall.

"Kinda weird about Fabian huh," Ethan said stuffing a handful of gummy bears in his mouth.

"Yeah, but I'm sure he's just messing around. He seems like the type to try and cause trouble when everyone is already upset about Agamemnon's disappearance," Ezekiel replied.

"I mean it's weird he's gone after he tried to practically rip your wing off."

Ezekiel paused. He wasn't sure if he should be offended. What was he implying?

"Well I didn't make that happen. If anything, I try and stay away from the creep," he replied coolly.

"He tried to rip your wing off?" Kalos nearly choked on his butter muffin. "When did that happen?"

"Yesterday on the field. Fabian, has it for him bad," Ethan instigated.

"I know what you guys are leaning at and it wasn't me. I don't even know what charms or spells to use to make someone vanish." He was starting to get upset. He could feel the blood in his face begin to boil. He stood up dropping candies and confections onto the floor.

"I was with at least one of you since he was last seen at the field until now. Wouldn't I have needed to get near him to do it?" The blank expressions on his friends faces made him more, angry. "I didn't ask to come to Camp Strange and have wings. I just wish I was normal!"

In the reflection of Ethan's light green eyes, he could see light. His friends were fixed on him. The same light was in all three of them and they were frozen in terror. Seeing their faces so afraid of what he was saying or worse, of *him*, settled his facial expression.

"What is it? Say something." Ezekiel stammered.

Slowly backing away from him, Miles mouth dropped open. Kalos' glasses melted down his nose. Ethan stood.

"Dude. You're on fire."

"No, I'm-"

Oh crap. He was.

He touched his back and didn't feel heat. He touched his hair carefully and it wasn't burning. He passed his hand through the flame beneath his neck just above his wing lines on his back. He tried to grab at it. Now his palm was on fire just like the Flames did at the rallies.

"What should I do?"

"Um, stay still and try to be calm. We don't want to set the place on fire even though I'm certain there is an enchantment to protect it from harm," Kalos said.

"I'm afraid to move."

"I can go dagger to get help," Ethan said.

"No, no. I don't want any attention from the Guard, the Dux or the Magnus. There has to be something we can do!"

"You can go for a flight," Miles said opening the Enchandrapes with a wave of his hand.

Ezekiel carefully walked to the edge of room, stepped to the ledge and took a giant leap. He pulsed his wings hard, soaring through the air. He flew overhead a group of Fledglings sitting at the fire pit. Mouths dropped seeing a flying ball of fire in the air.

He made his way to the lake. He knew the lake was off limits but figured that there could be exceptions considering he was on fire and all. From afar he could see Guards on the opposite side of the lake near the hillside.

He built up his speed and plunged into the water. The coolness of the water felt amazing, easing the burning he had felt in his face. He worried that his plunge caused a commotion that could alert the Guard. He sank to the bottom with a plan to dagger back to his room.

As he went deeper and deeper into the darkness of the lake he could see an empty chair approached by two dark figures. One forced the other into the chair, casting a reddish dust over the hooded cloak of the other. The figure walked out leaving the chair bound figure to fall over. Once the chair hit the ground, his hood fell off exposing his brown-blonde hair.

Ezekiel panicked and gasped for air. His instinct had him wanting to go back to the surface of the water but he remembered he had to dagger back, not get caught. He plunged his dagger in the lake floor. The force of magic yanked his body hard taking his breath away. Before he could gasp, he was back in his room, panting and out of breath.

"Cool you're not on fire anymore," Ethan cheered.

Ezekiel looked at him defeated. He knew where Fabian was and he needed help *now*.

Chapter Twenty-Six
The Solstice Games

The morning of the Games was not as jovial as intended. The staff attempted to put personality and life into the unit décor around the Game sights. Unit banners hovered with enchantments all throughout the Flight Field and shooting range. Large stands of bleachers were brought in to accommodate the seating of spectators from the Council, dignitaries, the elite and the Praeses. The pomp and circumstance despite the dark looming feeling made Ezekiel feel sick.

Ezekiel and Ethan stood on the side of the shooting range to get a peak of Kalos take his shots. Dara and Aubrey were seated in the stands in the camper section. He could see Aubrey's giant navy bow with the golden crest for their unit from where he stood. Both girls were in the spirit with navy and gold pom poms. Ezekiel found it hard to be so spirited. He couldn't figure out why he carried such responsibility for the disappearances. He couldn't shake the feeling and was still cooking up a plan in his mind.

On the grass, lines of chairs started to fill out with the band. Miles walked in with his colossal pipe awkwardly as he plopped in his chair to review his sheet music. Crowds of Faerman began to enter donning colorful garb of support for their unit. A group of girls shot out a streamer charm that sent white bits of sparkle into the air that seemed to dance. Spectators had their faces painted in complete sky blue, red and green. A large group of Granters entered with their bellies painted with large letters spelling out G-O G-R-A-N-T-E-R-S! Their hair was colored sky blue as well. All the fandom did well to distract from the dark blue-black outline of Guards that surrounded every inch of the field.

A large crowd that seemed like a flying block of people entered. In the center of the block, Ezekiel could see a woman, who in quo years would have been in her sixties, walking dressed sharply in an emerald green suit jacket with matching skirt, shoes and box pill hat. Her white gloved hand reached into the sky as she waved to the cheering crowd. A large group of Guard and fancy dressed Faerman escorted her by hand up the bleachers to take her seat.

"It's Praeses Amare!" Ethan said as he poked Ezekiel in the ribs.

The Magnus stepped out. The stands went crazy with applause and cheer. He flung the amp dust perfectly in line with his mouth and addressed the excited crowd.

"Welcome to the Games!" he said as the band kicked off an upbeat tune. As the music played the athletes walked in by color unit, five by five taking their place on the field. Ezekiel could spot Kalos immediately because of his glasses and lack of boastfulness compared to his competitors. He followed the trail of Kalos' focus and could see the Dux in his field of vision.

The Fledgling shooters all took to their line. Trav was monitoring the shot. He raised his hand which had a red flag, then quickly waved it down alerting the shooters to take their shot. Kalos took his time. He raised his bow and pulled his first arrow from his quiver. He could hear the hits of the other arrows against the haystacks. Once silent he aimed, pulling his bowstring back so still and solid. He let go.

Cheers exploded from the stands. Trav sent the red flag back up to alert the shooters that their shot was over. The Fledgling banners that hovered over each of the five haystacks was reduced to four. The shooter, second from the far right was eliminated. Kalos had a perfectly centered bullseye.

Ezekiel and Ethan ran out to the field and lifted their friend. The Fledgling stands were going wild. The Dux was standing and clapping with enthusiasm receiving congratulatory pats on the back from fellow dignitaries.

"We'd love to stay and celebrate but we have to get to the Flight Field. You should go up with your grandfather. He looks awfully proud of you. I thought he was going to fall over when you hit the eye!" Ezekiel said.

"I doubt that," Kalos replied slyly, looking over at his grandfather. "I'll be out there in just a sec to see you guys."

The Flight Field was just as spectacular if not more so. The fans created a rainbow of colors in the stands. The chants were so loud you couldn't make out any specific one. Charmed banners flew overhead. The band started to march in playing another energetic melody to appease the crowd with their whistles, horns and cowbells of unit color.

Ezekiel and Ethan made it a habit to allow themselves a good wing stretch and warm up. They enjoyed working together and pumping each other up before a flight. As they arched their wings into a stretch, Ezekiel's heart fell a bit seeing that the Flames were down one flier. Fabian's cronies didn't look so tough now. They looked down trodden and sad.

He tried to focus. The crowd was wild but not as crazy as it would be tomorrow when the Praeses would be watching the Flight Games. He used this time to focus on the flight track. He'd done it a million times, just not with an audience. He started his up and downs to warm up his back and legs. As he leapt up he spotted a familiar pouf of white hair wearing a bright pink cardigan. He waved. Iva made it to see him. Having someone there to support him lifted his spirits. He scanned the stands to see if he could see his mom. He spotted Aubrey, Dara, and her Pop-Pop Richard joyously waving pom poms. Trav stepped onto the field giving a high-five to each flier. He approached Ezekiel last giving him a nod and wink. He raised a yellow flag giving the fliers warning that they were to take their place at the race line. Each flier stepped to their assigned spot.

Trav lifted the green flag and held it high. Ezekiel nodded to Ethan mentally telling him good luck. His eyes were focused on the first turning point just around the Healers banner and first pillar. The flag zipped down and Ezekiel pushed off hard toward the white banner. He rapidly hit the first target, then the second. The sound of the wind passing through him was consuming him with a faint flicker of the cheers from the stands. The thought of stupid Bradley the bully, being picked last at virtually all playground sports and being ridiculed at this school crossed his mind. He wasn't exactly popular here either, but he had friends and was good at something. He was great at something. The satisfaction of it gave him more energy, sending more strength to pulse his wings faster and faster.

He hit the final platform. He stood for a moment seeing the specs of color from the other fliers rounding the third pillar while he stood the clear champion at the fifth. He raised his hands and waved to the crowd. They went nuts at his showmanship. He plunged into a swim-like dive soaring gracefully fierce into the air, plunging toward the finish line.

He crossed and rather than land on his feet he soared across the crowd as he had saw Trav do his very first day at the Flight Field. The Fledglings all stood up waving their pom poms, shaking their cowbells in the air. He rounded his landing at the finish to see the fliers coming in. One by one the older fliers made their way. Ethan rounded out with intensity on his way in coming in second to Ezekiel for their unit while it was clear a boy named Gregory was going to be last of all the fliers. He gave Ethan a giant hug and they laughed at Ezekiel's display that almost distracted Ethan from his last turn.

What caught his eye was the solid wall of red that flew in firm. The four Flames came in with linked arms exactly at the same time. This set the crowd into a frenzy. A large fireball shot into the air from the stands. After the Flames waved at their fans they walked past Ezekiel. One stopped slightly turning his head.

"We flew for our unit brother today. I know he's missing because of you." He took a step as to walk away, then spun back around.

"You have guilt you can't control. That's why you caught on fire the other day. I saw you go into the lake even though it was forbidden. You make weird things happen cause you're a freak. I know it's because of you the peggie was snatched and I'm certain that you had something to do with Fab. If I can prove it, I'm going to Conti who will have the Dux throw you into the Caves."

He walked off to join his team.

Ezekiel looked at Ethan who hung his head and eyes low.

I hadn't made this happen, did I?

* * * * *

The next few days of the Games were just as exciting as the first. Kalos couldn't miss a shot. Each time Trav went out to measure the target he walked away satisfied. Ezekiel and Ethan proved themselves worthy each race and were the final racers left in their unit. In the next flights the Flames competed against each other as they typically did still scowling at Ezekiel's general direction. On the final day when the boys took the field they were delighted that in the stands the fans all wore large, black-rimmed glasses just like Kalos with their unit garb.

"Wow! Looks like the entire camp is rooting for you dude!" Ethan said giving Kalos a slight shove.

Kalos turned to look at his friends and burst out laughing. Both Ezekiel and Ethan had the same glasses. It was even better when the band walked in wearing glasses as well. Miles spotted them trying to balance his colossal pipe, while waving, then pointing at his glasses and giving an enthusiastic thumbs up.

Kalos took his place at the shooting line. He held up a bow and pulled an arrow from his quiver. He could feel the intensity of his competitor. There seemed to be a long pause. He didn't need more time. He had this. He pulled his bow back and let go. The arrow hit the bullseye. The crowd went crazy. Kalos looked back and could see his grandfather smiling and clapping. He looked to his right, eyes fixed on his competitor, Teresa. Her long brown hair was pulled back into a ponytail that reached her waist. She was focused as she pulled her bowstring back.

The crowd cheered. She hit the bullseye. Trav measured both lines to make sure it was a draw. Kalos was up again. One had to be off for the game to end. He took his line.

Steadily holding his bow, he pulled his arrow and aimed with such focused concentration. The red dot on the mark seemed too easy for him. This part of the game was mental. His competitor also had her bow drawn but had a patience about her that bugged him as it was one he typically had. He let go hitting his target but not quite splicing the perfectly centered shot he had made. Teresa landed her shot splicing her previous shot in half. The crowd went crazy. Kalos could see her cheeks turn pink. She gave the crowd a wave.

He was disappointed at his loss. He didn't want to look up at the stands and see his grandfather's face. It would likely be just as let down. He bent down to tie his shoe to avoid them. When he looked up, Teresa approached him and stuck out her hand. "Awesome shooting Kalos." She had thick black rimmed glasses on too. He shook her hand and said, "Thanks. You were better."

"I was, wasn't I," she joked.

He felt awkward but forced a laugh and nod.

"So, I know this may not be the best timing but was wondering if you had a date for the dance yet. I mean, I get that you probably have a date already and all, a fan maybe you're going with," she rambled nervously.

"Uh, nope. I'd love to go. I mean, will you go with me? Am I supposed to ask you?" Kalos was nervous. A girl never showed any interest in him. "I don't know what I'm doing."

They both burst out laughing. They both felt relief the games were over and agreed to meet up at the Padsphere game tomorrow night.

Ezekiel didn't want to approach Kalos as he seemed to be making a new friend. Ethan was laughing on the floor overly amused at Kalos' lack of smoothness with Teresa and they both pondered whatever happened to him getting the nerve to ask Pippa.

•   •   •   •   •

The boys arrived at the Flight Field friendly but focused, they both wanted to win but were well aware there could be only one winner for their unit. They did their ritual stretch side by side quietly as did the other fliers. Each unit had two fliers left standing.

The stands filled as spectators emerged. Dara and Aubrey waved dressed head to toe in Fledgling gear but seemed to drown in a wave of Fledgling mania. Ezekiel could see Iva in the crowd as she was the only person wearing a bright yellow cardigan. She caught his eye waving excitedly.

Trav walked in at the same time as the usual pomp and circumstance that followed the Praeses and her Council. Today she had a bold purple pantsuit with matching shoes. As she entered the band played her Faera anthem concluding as she took her seat.

The Magnus walked in and faced the Flight Field. With dust flung into the air a large Faera flag waved in the center of the field. The camp flag drawn next to it. Each athlete stood beneath.

"Please stand as we recite our pledge."

"Wings out!" shouted the color guard.

"Ready, begin."

I pledge to try my best,
In all the camp tests.
Enchantments and charms,
To protect, not harm,
To create Faera peace,
I will never cease.

"Please be seated."

The Magnus took a seat amongst the staff. Trav flew out to the field yellow flag on hand. The fliers took to their lines in a lunged starting position. Trav raised his green flag. Roars of thunderous cheer and applause from the crowd in suspense filled the field. He whipped his flag down and the fliers were off.

Ezekiel pushed off as hard as he ever had. Each muscle was doing its part to pulse his wings. He approached the first pillar rounding it with ease. He was tempted to look back but didn't.

As he rounded the bright, red banner, emblazoned with the Flames crest the vision he had in the lake replayed. Could that have been Fabian? He looked like he was there against his will, but how would Ezekiel be certain. The guy was a bit of a jerk and it wouldn't be a surprise to him if he decided to join the Hematite.

He plopped hard on the platform of the final pillar. His lead was not a long as it was prior and several fliers were coming up quickly with no indication of slowing down. He leapt down hard, nose diving to the ground. Twisting and turning, spinning fast he landed on his feet at the finish line. Although his feet were on the ground and he could hear the roars of cheers and applause he still felt like he was spinning. He took two steps, bumping into an orange blob then puked, finally collapsing on the ground.

Turns out the orange blob was Trav.

"You okay? You went into a bit of a tailspin there, kiddo!" Trav said excitedly.

Ezekiel groaned. The smell of his barf made him want to barf more.

"Give him some room to breathe. He's going to be fine," Trav shouted to onlookers. He escorted him to the nearest bench and gave him some Ginger-Aid. Ezekiel had seen other fliers drink it before and after flying to ease their stomachs.

"Guess we can't showboat every time we win huh. I bet the folks weren't expecting a big finish like that huh?" Trav gave his shoulder a tug and a hearty laugh.

"Right."

Ethan sat next to him. "You smell gross man but congrats. From my view, it looked like you took the whole race."

"How'd you do?" Ezekiel asked hoping the best.

"Fourth. I'll take it. I hear they medal the top five." He had a huge grin.

"I'm happy for you. On another note. I need your help tomorrow. I have a *plan*."

Chapter Twenty-Seven
Game Day

Excitement was in the air and the anticipation of the Padsphere Championship had the campers electrified. The courses for the day had been canceled to allow for ample time to decorate the Pond with the effervescent colors of sky blue and red. The two colors side by side were such natural enemies – cool versus hot, ice versus fire, and Granters versus Flames. One side of the Pond was overloaded with the Granters crest, a multi-blue series of waves under a dark navy sky full of stars. The other side was an abundance of red insignia featuring the crest of the Flames, a flame of fire surrounded by a thick layer of smoke. Campers assembled Spirit Squads for both teams to lead chants and novelty charms to entertain the audience during game breaks.

Spectators started to line up at the camp gates early. Ezekiel swore he heard the noises of game horns and cowbells before the morning trumpets. He still didn't really get what was the big hype over Padsphere. The Guard was prepared early too. They stationed themselves at the entrance gate blocking off access to paths to the unit compounds. A wall of Guards set a path directly to the Pond, surrounding the Pond and were stationed all throughout the air above the Pond. It was rumored that there were undercover Guards seated amongst the fans.

"You got everything you need?" Ezekiel asked Ethan.

"Yes, for the gazillionth time," Ethan said with an eye roll.

"You know what to say? You won't forget?"

"Nooooooooo."

"Sure, we don't have to go over it again?"

"Come on man! I got this!" Ethan said filled with confidence.

"You ready to go then?"

"Seriously? Yes! Let's get it over with!" Ethan said. He was ready to get out to the game. He committed to helping Ezekiel but was not going to miss the

Padsphere game for anything.

"You didn't tell anyone. Kalos. Miles. Especially not Dara."

"NO! Sheesh! Hey. You didn't ask about Aubrey." Ethan said laughing.

"Okay, did you tell Aubrey?" Ezekiel was getting impatient.

"Are you serious? NO! Let's go. I'm leaving to meet them down there." Ethan began to walk out of the room. Ezekiel grabbed on his arm.

"Hey. If I don't get a chance to tell you. Thank you for helping me," Ezekiel said

"You'll get a chance. Come on," Ethan led Ezekiel out the door.

•   •   •   •   •

The crowd was massive entering the Pond. Kunal Veer and Bianca Pulcham had to quadruple the bleacher seating of the Pond using the basic multiplying charm he taught the campers just the day prior. Tickets were selling out faster than they could set up the seating. The Guard stood firm prepared for any potential rule breaker or unlawfulness despite very little actual Hematite activity known to the public.

Ezekiel had yet to see an actual Hematite and wasn't sure he'd recognize one if he saw one anyway. He assumed the high levels of security were precautionary, just in case the disappearances were tied to them. He had to keep shaking the thought that the disappearances were somehow tied to *him*.

Over campfire the campers would tell scary stories about them. That they had black wings once fully exposed. They might try and enchant him if he was caught. He wasn't worried that they would take his wings as he hadn't colored yet. He was most worried he wouldn't remember his mom.

The boys walked along the barricade of Guard. They stood at the farthest northwest point or the Pond exterior. This happened to be the closest they could get to camp entrance.

"Ugh. I don't feel too good," Ethan said exaggerating a stumbled walk clutching his stomach. He peaked up to see if the Guards had flinched.

"Are you okay buddy?" Ezekiel said loudly, patting Ethan on the back also peaking up. Ethan keeled over, then went to his knees dramatically heaving.

"Ughhhhh," Ethan groaned. A couple Guards started to come over.

"Ughhhhh," he groaned even louder, now on all fours looking really pathetic.

"Hey kid. You alright?" a Guard asked with a look of concern.

"I think I'm going to ba-ba-bahh—"

Ethan didn't finish his sentence. He appeared to hurl up what looked like an ocean of colorful, chewed up gummy bears. Fans making their way to the Pond walked away in disgust. More Guards came over to observe what was going on.

Ethan kept spewing and spewing thick rainbow gel mush. Hacking and heaving until a group of Guards left their post to check on him.

"Looks like we may need a medic. Isn't there a doctor on site?" a Guard asked patting Ethan on the back.

Ethan's eyes were focused. Once Ezekiel vanished down the path, he stopped puking.

"Oh. My stomach. I think I had too much candy," he said rubbing his belly.

"You think?" joked a Guard as he summoned some pixies to enchant the mess away.

"I think I'm just so excited to see the game. I'm sorry for the mess," Ethan said making his eyes big and doe-like.

"It's alright little buddy. Why don't you head in and get yourself a Ginger-Aid for that tummy, eh," said the Guard waving him off.

Flight wasn't permitted due to the game and it was impossible to dagger in and out of the grounds. Ezekiel literally had to make a run for it. Thank goodness for Kunal teaching them that multiplying charm. Ethan was more than willing to cast it onto a couple half chewed up gummy bears he stuffed in his cheeks.

Ezekiel passed the camp entrance and was able to make way through a large crowd of spectators still trying to come into the camp. He continued to walk looking around to ensure no one was watching him. As soon as he had the chance he plunged his dagger into the ground to make his way to the backside of the Bazaar. He needed somewhere to hide out for a short while until the sun took the spot he needed.

He found a small wooden crate to sit on. He could see shadows of shoppers walking around just behind the tent wall. He began to ponder about the type of vendor it was. Exotic produce? Books on charms and spells? Taffies the flavor of meats and veggies? He wished he had visited the Bazaar more. His few visits were short and he only bought a strange deck of cards and the mimic. It had just dawned on him he left both items at Iva's house. Luckily, he would visit her tomorrow before the dance and be able to retrieve them.

He began to fidget with his dagger pulling it from its leather sheath. He swirled the amber beads on the leather straps. It crossed his mind that if they really protected the possessor, this was the time they needed to kick into action. He used the blade to draw a smiley face in the dirt. This made his dagger dirty so he wiped it off on his shorts and put it away.

He felt his dust pouch and wondered if he'd be allowed to carry it once he went home. He would miss not being able to practice his charms openly. The pouch was full. Kunal was very good about making sure the campers had an ample supply. The pocket of his pouch felt crunchy. He stuck his finger in it and remembered the dried up swurt that Ansh gave him. It had the texture of dried up boogers.

The sun seemed about right. Ezekiel pulled his map from his pocket and unfolded it to see the time. 3:07 PM. It was time.

He folded the map and jammed it back into his pocket. He scanned around to see if any Guard was around. He pushed off the ground and flew hard and fast toward the woods.

It was a beautiful day. The sky was clear with just small smears of white clouds speckled through the sky. The bright sun and daylight provided him a feeling of security. Beneath him was the earth covered by towering, thick trees. The green, fullness of their branches left no gap making the ground inexistent. He looked back and Murlock was no longer in sight.

He wasn't sure what his plan was. What would he do once he found the spot? If he found the waterfall covered in hand-painted rocks, how could he be sure that was an entrance into a hidden lair? All he knew was what the lake was willing to show him. Was it going to be enough?

There it was. The perfect glowing, yellow specimen showing off in the sky. The sun sat at a forty-five, degree angle from the green horizon just like they did on his math worksheet when Ms. Flagrin had the class working on angles. It was super boring to him then, but he was super thankful for learning it now. He pulsed in place above mounds and mounds of trees.

Where's the waterfall?

He looked around. Everything was green. He kept his mark of the sun and flew lower toward the trees. They seemed to carpet the land.

His heart started to race.

"Waterfall show yourself!" he shouted throwing dust hoping he would say the magic word that would reveal what he wanted. Nothing happened.

I wish I could find you, creepy Hematite hideout. I wish I could find you and save Agamemnon.

His thoughts were getting testy and aggravated. He was getting tired of flying and decided on taking a break down below.

That was it. Agamemnon had flung him down from the air and he fell through the trees to the waterfall. The words of the lake vision came to him.

Take the fall.

He closed his eyes, held his breath and allowed himself to fall into the woods. As he dropped he could see the sun disappear as he fell between the trees hitting branches. He landed awkwardly on his feet.

There it was. It was silent as it streamed into the tiny reservoir. The solid rock boulders with black smudged wings were just as he had remembered them. The water flow was fierce. He was afraid if he flew through it he would crash into the boulders behind it. From his view, there was no door. The floor of the pool of water catching the waterfall just hit his knees so there was no going underneath it. If he could just turn off the flow of water.

Wait. He had done that before. He hadn't even tried the last time he did it. He just, *wished* for it to happen. He walked up to the stream of water, grounding his feet into the floor to not be knocked over. He reached his hand out and let the water hit his hand. He closed his eyes and focused on turning it off. The flow weakened and reduced to just drips of water off the glistening boulders. Carefully he stepped up on the boulders holding on to the wall of rock usually hidden by the fall.

He pushed. He pulled on the rock using a cracked space he could wedge his hand in. It did nothing. This wasn't like the waterfall. He opened it in his mind, told it to open with his mind and still nothing made it budge. He reached into his dust pouch to grab a pinch. He wasn't sure which enchantment he would use but he knew he had to use something to help him.

If only I could move this rock.

It hit him hard in the face. The dried swurt! He pulled a flake of the swurt and crushed it with his dust. He rubbed the palms of his hands in it resulting in a burnt sienna hue. He placed his hands on the rock, focused on moving it. He pushed and it slid open effortlessly like a sliding glass door.

There it was, the long black corridor. His first steps inside were timid and long. He had no light, except for the light that crept in behind him. He used his hands to feel along the wet stone walls. A small cut of light appeared in front of him. He walked faster. It was the black curtain with a small flaw in the lining that let light escape. He peeked through the tear. The room was empty yet illuminated. Slowly he pushed the curtain aside.

He stepped in. The tall walls were dark wine just lit by wall sconces. The black velvet thorn throne sat above a platform. Without the black-robed crowd, he was accustomed to seeing there, the large room would have made nice for a ball or fancy wedding.

The room had a few doors that led out. The first was locked. The next-door handle turned easily. Slowly he opened it keeping one hand on his dagger. It too was empty. It was a small room, about the size of his bedroom and empty with the exception of a single chair and remnants of a red scatter on the floor. The walls were more decorative than he recalled in his vision. A dark brown-black thorn mural surrounded the walls. A single stained glass window of multi-colored wings surrounding a black hand cast a rainbow light across the room. Above this window was a dark wood plaque that read *In virtute manus.*

He walked back through the large ceremony room to the final door anticipating to have more difficulty. He turned the knob and it opened easily. Light hit his face blinding him as though he had just taken a picture. Shaking it off it appeared that he was outside under a bright summer sun. He strained his eyes. Faintly he could see the bends in the wall. There was some sort of enchantment on this room making it look like the outdoors. The green plains ahead of him had eurps running through and a small squirrel looking animal that had the face of a dissatisfied giraffe. A peaceful stream of water ran through leading into a sight beyond.

In the sky, he saw a glimmer that reflected into his face. It was coming closer at a rapid speed. Ezekiel took a step back. It wasn't slowing. He turned and ran for the door. Once he was through he turned to pull it shut. He raised his face and saw him.

Agamemnon was standing before him.

"You're here!" Ezekiel exclaimed. He was thrilled as he wanted to find him but had extreme doubts he would.

Agamemnon seemed happy, not hurt and hesitant to leave as Ezekiel pulled his reins.

"Come on peggie! We have to get out of here before someone comes," he plead.

Agamemnon neighed at him but trotted along down the corridor. He didn't like the darkness. Ezekiel stroked his mane.

"It's okay. I don't like the dark either. Let's run a bit so we can get out of here." He pulled on his reins and broke into a run out of the darkness.

This made Agamemnon thirsty. Surrounded by a pool of water he lapped some up. Ezekiel was growing impatient with him.

"Come on! Let's go!" he shouted.

Agamemnon gave him a dirty look and trotted around so his rear was facing him. He proceeded to drink.

Standing center framed by the dark corridor stood a black cloaked figure. Ezekiel froze. A million thoughts raced through his mind. Should he fly off? Cast a charm? Fight?

He ran into the pool, jumped on top of Agamemnon, seized his reins, pulling him away as to steer him off.

"Let's go! Come one!"

At a snail's pace Agamemnon turned taking steps out of the pool. Ezekiel kept his eyes fixed on the figure. The figure raised its hand closing the rock wall. The waterfall gushed ferociously.

Ezekiel and Agamemnon flew off. Ezekiel held on tight looking back every few moments to make sure he was not being followed. The flight back to camp seemed to take much longer than it had been going there. As the warm air hit his face, combing his hair he felt like a champion. He was successful in finding the peggie. It was almost too easy.

It was odd that Agamemnon seemed like he did not want to be saved. He was not afraid of the black cloaked figure.

Ezekiel was now faced with what to do with this knowledge. If he put the peggie back into the stable, everyone would assume he just wandered off and found his way back. If he led the Guard to this spot tomorrow he would miss the dance. The Guard didn't believe him when he told them about the waterfall before so who was to say they'd believe him now?

Chapter Twenty-Eight
From Anonymous

Ezekiel steered Agamemnon into Murlock. They landed next to the wooden crate behind the Bazaar. The streets were pretty empty as everyone was either at the Padsphere game or at home watching it on T.V. He trotted Agamemnon down the path up to the camp entrance. Ezekiel felt nostalgic as he passed beneath the Camp Faera banner reflecting on the first time he laid eyes on it. So much has happened since then. He wasn't the same boy who passed through that day.

As he trotted past the Feasting Hall tree he could hear the crowds boo and cheer from the distance. He could see what looked like a black ring above the Pond walls. The Guard had left the entrance and compound trails to place all their focus on the Pond.

"Thank goodness," Ezekiel said to himself under his breath. He really didn't feel like being questioned. He knew he would be detained in a long series of questions if seen with the missing peggie and not at the game.

He hopped off of Agamemnon as they approached the stable gate. He walked him into his stable. Agamemnon seemed to look at him sadly. Ezekiel pet him which he seemed to like. He closed the latch tightly pulling on it to make sure it was closed.

"See you. Be a good peggie and stay here."

Agamemnon neighed at him.

Ezekiel hurried to the Pond. The good thing was there wasn't a line or crowd to fight through. The pixie taking tickets didn't even notice him walk in as she was fixed on the game. He punched his ticket and walked in.

There were only three minutes left in the game. The Granters were up 8 to 4. There was no way the Flames would catch up. Going into the game they were the underdog as they were missing a key player. Ezekiel looked around. The crowd was much too large. There was no unit seating so finding his friends was nearly impossible.

The Granters Sphereguards protected their ball pile fiercely. The Flames Retrievers could not advance. On the other side of the Pond, #15 burst from the pool clenching tightly to the ball. His sky-blue suit gleaming in the light as he ventured across the defensive line. Once crossing he threw it to #8, the Celerpoint. She caught it. The crowd was rowdy cheering for a point.

The Celerpoint was guarded by the Retrievers who swam beneath her to ward off the Flames Sphereguards. Twenty seconds left on the clock. Once she crossed the centerline her Sphereguards trailed her defending her pass. She now faced the Padguard who looked a bit unsure of herself. Ten seconds. In a brief standoff, #8 plunged forward slamming the ball onto the Pad. The clock buzzed ending the game 9 to 4.

Ezekiel had to admit. He was enthralled by the brief glimpse of the actual gameplay he was able to see. He now understood the hype. Sky-blue streamers shot into the sky dancing to the beat of the band's spirit tunes. The Granters Spirit Squad, spun and twirled in sync toting signs of victory. Spectators began to leave the stands so Ezekiel made his way out daggering back to the Fledgling compound to wait for his friends.

·　　·　　·　　·　　·

He sat on a wooden stump at the fire pit. Fledglings started to arrive, some exhilarated others crestfallen from the game's result. He noticed his friends approaching because he could see Aubrey's gigantic sky-blue bow from the top of the crowd.

"That was such a good game!" Ethan cheered. "Did you catch any of it?"

"Why would he have missed it?" Dara inquired with a tone of suspiciousness.

Ezekiel shot Ethan a hard look. There was no way out of it.

"I found the peggie," Ezekiel whispered.

"You found Agamemnon!?" Dara whispered back as loud as a whisper could be.

"Shhh! Yes. It was actually easy. Too easy. The enchantments were all basic Granters, Elements kind of stuff. I literally just walked in, got the peggie and walked out. I would have got him faster but it didn't seem like he wanted to come with me. It was weird," he said. "I even saw one and it just let me leave." He could see the wheels turning in Dara's head.

"Are you going to tell the Magnus?" she asked. He was surprised this was a question from her and not an expectation.

"I'm not sure," Ezekiel replied. "The last time I mentioned the waterfall no one believed me. It was like they didn't want to believe me. Also, if I tell them and take them there, I will miss the dance." Dara's face fell.

"Am I missing the obvious here?" Kalos said. "If that was the Hematite palace then you have to tell the Guard."

"I'm still wondering why we have to be involved? We're freaking kids! We're supposed to be enjoying camp, not going on death missions!" Ethan argued. "I mean, he found the darn peggie. End of mission."

"They'll wonder how the peggie got back too," Miles added.

"What about Fabian? He wasn't there?" Kalos asked.

"No. However…"

"However, what?" they all said.

Ezekiel proceeded to tell them about the vision he had at the lake the day he set himself on fire. He was sure it was Fabian he saw bound by some enchantment in that chair. The red dust remnants the dark figure tossed on him was still on the floor. The friends were quiet in thought and shock.

"Couldn't you just write an anonymous note?" Aubrey said.

They all stared at her.

"Aubrey, you are brilliant," Dara said with a giant smile.

The friends grouped around the floor of the boy's room. They drew the Enchandrapes closed. Ezekiel had paper out ready to write his note.

"Should we do those cut out magazine letters? That way no one recognizes your handwriting?" Ethan said. It was hard to tell if he was joking or being serious.

"Where are we going to get magazines blockhead?" Dara snapped.

"It's fine. I'll write it," Ezekiel said.

Dear Dux Diego,

I found the entrance to the Hematite palace. Travel north into the woods at 3 o'clock in the afternoon. A good starting point is behind the Bazaar.

When you reach a point where the sun is at a forty-five-degree angle you are just above the waterfall hidden beneath the woods. You have to have a Granter wish the waterfall into sight. You have to plunge down and fall into the trees.

Landing on your feet you should see a small pool of water and the waterfall. There are rocks painted with the black wings all over. Approach the waterfall with a Granter to turn the water off.

Use dried swurt dust or an Element to slide open the rock wall. There should be a long creepy corridor that is dark that leads you to a giant room.

I found Agamemnon and put him in his stable when everyone was at the Padsphere game. Don't think your Guards were doing a bad job. I just hid from them really well.

From, Anonymous

He re-read the letter multiple times. All the instructions were there. He had his friends read it too.

"I'm going to the Pixie Post to send it to the Council Office. If they take the time to try and tie it to me, I'll already be back at home," Ezekiel said smiling. "I'll be right back."

He flew down the staircase and daggered his way to the Pixie Post. The pixies on shift weren't as bustling busy as they usually were with camp winding down to its final days. Ezekiel pulled an envelope addressing it to the Council Office leaving the Dux off of it to avoid attention from the pixie who was rolling mounds of stamps. He pressed the blue wax seal and put it into the slot. He quickly walked off daggering back to the compound.

He shot up the stairs where the boys sat waiting for him.

"I'm starving? Anyone else?" Ezekiel asked.

Miles shot up. "Yes!" The others nodded. The friends made their way down to meet up with the girls for their last dinner in the Feasting Hall.

Chapter Twenty-Nine
The Missing is Found

After a fun-filled day of Faerman Craft tests that were so easy they were enjoyable the friends were eager to receive their 'passes' on dust-making, simple compounding, binding, basket weaving, illumination and multiplying simple small objects. Dara had to beg Ethan to not replicate the gummy bear charm although he was insistent to do so.

The boys spent the afternoon half seriously talking about dance steps and coordinating timed breaks so they wouldn't be alone with their dates to avoid awkward moments. They had a hand signal gesture that looked like a talking hand to alert one another. Their dapper threads were suspended in the air by a floating charm.

"Did you guys get your dates corsages?" Ezekiel asked.

"No date, no corsage," Ethan said proudly as he put on his ivory suit jacket over his sky-blue button down. He tucked in a matching blue handkerchief into his pocket.

"Yes. We picked them up this morning," Kalos said holding up a clear box with a large yellow flower. He pulled on his navy-blue suit over a bright white shirt. He added personality with a yellow bow tie.

Miles held up his flower box showing off his pink mix of orchids and roses for Aubrey. He wore a dark green plaid suit.

"Thanks for telling me. I made my pick up for 5 o'clock. I was worried it wouldn't keep if I got it too early," Ezekiel said.

"Sucks you gotta go into town all spiffed up," Ethan said. "Want me to come with you?"

"Yeah I kind of told Iva I'd stop by to show her my suit and so I could say bye," he said.

"That's cool of you," Kalos said. "You'd better get going so you're back in time."

Ezekiel buttoned the cuffs of his black shirt. He just needed his final touch. He reached into his trunk and pulled out his red bow tie. Miles pulled out his camera and they snapped a few silly photos before Ezekiel had to run off.

●   ●   ●   ●   ●

The streets of Murlock were bustling with shoppers and full shops. Ezekiel enjoyed the delightful grins he received from ladies passing him by on the street. He knew he looked adorable. The bow tie always brought that look from the ladies. He made his way to Feldman's and could see him running around the shop being chased by tiny pieces of angry paper. There was other fancy dressed campers standing waiting amongst the weird spitting flowers. The purple heads of the morning glories seemed to cover their faces with their leaves out of disgrace for the disorganization of their shop. This made Ezekiel laugh.

Ezekiel patiently waiting for his turn. Caleb was frantically running into his refrigerators, to the counter and to his flower buckets to assemble last minute requests for bouquets. The phone would ring and he'd have to answer it or it too followed him around the shop.

"Hello there little Fledgling! You're looking dapper today," he said cheerily as he led his little piece of paper to the refrigerator. The little paper was so angry and trembling he thought it would combust. Caleb handed Ezekiel the clear flower box. It was just as he had designed it. He knew Dara was going to love it. The little bit of paper laid down happily.

"Thanks Caleb! Hang in there!" Ezekiel said walking out the door.

●   ●   ●   ●   ●

Meanwhile back at camp the girls finished the touches on their hair and lip gloss that Aubrey insisted on. Dara agreed only because it was a fancy occasion.

"I love your dress!" Aubrey said to Dara admiring her white halter dress full of silk flower embellishments and sparkle. She had her hair pulled up decorated with a sparkly ribbon woven between her kinky curls. "Thanks, I like yours too."

Aubrey was wearing her trademark color in a neon variety. The sheer pink sleeves were embellished with floral vines that led to her neckline. The dress was more fitted and fashion forward in typical Aubrey style. Her hair was curled, twisted up like a princess.

"Wait, no bow today?" Dara asked.

"Nope. I'm going with this pink rose hair clip," she said adjusting it in the mirror into her hair. "Should we go now?"

"Okay." Dara was nervous. She wasn't sure if things would be weird now. She enjoyed the simplicities of being a kid but knew this is what kids did. They went to dances, felt shy, would drink punch and dance. Everyone felt a bit shy, well maybe not Ethan, but all normal kids did.

The lake scene was beautiful. The setting sun cast a pinkish rainbow hue into a purple sky. The lake sparkled from the last rays of the sun that fought through the hills. A white acrylic floor was set onto the sand that had so many round linen tables the girls couldn't count. Tall floral arrangements with cascading orchids decorated each table illuminated by floating buds of enchanted white roses.

"Hello ladies!" Ethan said cheerily, strutting his stuff.

"Hi," Miles said approaching Aubrey. He was stunned at how pretty she looked. She looked like a princess from his fantasy books. He handed her the flower box, opening it.

"Oh, my gosh Miles! I love it! It's my favorite color!" She pulled the corsage from the box revealing the bright pink ribbon bows that cascade down her wrist. She gave him a big bear hug. He turned as pink as her dress.

"I'm going to look for Teresa. I'll see you guys in a bit," Kalos said starting to get a shade of pink himself.

"Where's Ezie?" Dara asked.

"The dope had to pick up your flower thingy and he was stopping by the old lady's house to say bye. It's been a while though. He should have been back by now," Ethan said.

Dara raised her eyebrows.

•　　•　　•　　•　　•

Ezekiel approached the front gate of the Green Pastures Retirement Village. As usual Kevin, the security guard was enthralled with the latest Padsphere

Weekly magazine and just lazily waved him in.

Ezekiel approached the door and raised his hand to knock anticipating that Iva would open before his hand touched the door as she always did. This time she didn't. He knocked loudly. He waited a beat and she didn't come. He leaned over to peak in the open window. All her lights were on. He could clearly see her floral couch and porcelain plates on the wall.

He reached to ring her doorbell. *Bing!*

"Ezie? Is that you? I'll be right there!" Iva called from another room. He was glad to hear her voice. He was starting to feel worried.

"Hello there! Why don't you look like a movie star?!" She said guiding him in. "That tux fits you perfectly! And that bow tie!" she said giving it a little tug. Being gushed over never got old for him. She gave him a hug.

"Oh honey, you shouldn't wear that dagger with that tux. It just takes away from it all."

"Thanks Iva. I just wanted to come by and show you my threads," he joked making a little spin to show himself off. He took his holster off and set it on the coffee table. He was so used to wearing it to easily carry his dust and be able to travel he just wore it under his jacket. Now that he thought about it, he was sure Dara wouldn't have her holster on with a dress.

She laughed. "Well thanks. I'm so excited for you. The flower looks great too. Caleb always does great work."

"Yeah he does but he was going crazy today with all the orders for the dance. Those little bits of paper were chasing after him like crazy," they both laughed.

"Well I know you've got to go. I let the day get ahead of me and I didn't pull my camera from the attic. Do you mind giving me a few minutes to go look for it? I'll turn on the T.V. for you," she said clicking the T.V. on. She walked through the kitchen past the den.

He picked up the remote. It had a million buttons. He hated that and was afraid to mess something up so he left it on the local news. It was a boring news anchor spewing news about an anonymous letter received by the Council about the Hematite palace.

Wait, what?

The storyline changed to highlights from the Padsphere game from the day before.

"Ugh. I missed it," he muttered to himself plopping himself onto the rose couch. He sat there staring at the T.V. Each story after the next bored him. A tiny little figurine on top of her console table caught his eye.

It's my mimic!

He got up and approached the table reaching out for it. He stopped to look at it. It looked as though it had been used as it wasn't white anymore. He avoided touching it so it would not mimic him. He kneeled down setting the corsage box onto the table.

He knocked over a few books on the floor that made him jump. He stood up quick picking up his flower box and the books. He realized that they were photo albums just like his Nan's at home. They were leather bound on the outside with those sticky pages with clear film on the inside. He rested the albums onto the table and opened one.

There were a lot of very old photos that seemed like they were from a lifetime before. The clothing looked medieval. The men had tights and the women wore long fancy dresses with corsets. The young woman with strong dimpled cheeks had long flowing ginger hair and familiar sparkling green eyes. The photo that caught his attention was one of a younger Iva in an all, white gown standing with a man dressed in a fur-lined robe, golden crown and jeweled scepter. She was beautiful. A small weave of lettering read, *King Aoberon & Queen Navi.*

Ezekiel felt confused. He backed the pages up to get a better look at the face of the girl in the photos. Although faded and a bit worn he could clearly see they were a much younger Iva riding a silver peggie who looked like Agamemnon. He lifted the film off the first photo, carefully pulling the photo off the sticky paper to see if there was anything written on the back.

Navi 1814

It couldn't be?

He looked up to check to see if Iva was coming back. She wasn't so he flipped through the next pages. There were more photos of her adorned with crowns in a throne, at galas and parades. He set that album down and pulled out the next. He could see the King and babies with her who through page flips grew to be beautiful princesses.

The next pages were of newspaper clippings from the Chronicle featuring headlines of terror of the Hematites. Photos of the black stain, reports of stolen children and the Council response all documented.

The final page had white piece of parchment that seemed ages old. The writing looked like it was in Latin. *In virtute manus.*

There were two black charcoal smudges in the center.

It was the black stain.

He dropped the album to the floor. Out flew a large black and white photo, landing at his tip of his shiny black shoes. He quickly kneeled to the floor to retrieve it. He could see it was a group photo of many fancy dressed grownups standing in front of banners displaying the black stain. Fighting back a tear of disappointment and fear he spotted Iva in a long black gown.

He clamped the album shut and carefully set it back in place. He shifted his glance at the mimic.

"Who is this?" he whispered to the mimic being very careful to not touch him.

"What does the Coacter know! If it wasn't for me he would have never got him back. I returned him under the eyes of the Guard. It should have been me! You should have picked me!" shouted the angry little brown-blonde haired mimic.

Ezekiel stared closer. It had a red camp issue vest and khaki colored pants.

•　　•　　•　　•　　•

Dara thought it was odd that Ezekiel was now over an hour late. It just didn't seem like him. The moment did cross her mind that he chickened out, but as she looked out at Kalos dancing offbeat with Teresa, smiling happy she knew this was not the case.

She waved down Ethan who was in the middle of a group of girls dancing. He was annoyed she was ruining his fun but could see that Ezekiel still had not arrived. He pulled himself away.

"He's still not here?"

"No. I'm worried. I'm going to see if he got stuck in town."

"What! And leave this party. No way," he said waving at the girls on the dance floor.

"You don't have to come. I'll go by myself," she said walking away and pushing off into flight.

"Ugh!" he stammered looking at her go, then looking at the fun on the dance floor.

Ethan pushed off after her.

"Wait up! I'm coming!" he shouted.

Once out of the camp gate they daggered to the entrance of the Green Pastures Retirement Village. They could see that there was a security guard at his post who seemed uninterested at their presence.

"Who are you here to see?" the guard asked.

"Iva Rose. We're volunteers from Camp Faera," Dara said with a big smile.

"Yeah okay," he said waving them in.

"That was a lot easier than I expected," Ethan said.

"You ready dear?"

.   .   .   .   .

Ezekiel's heart jumped out of his chest. Iva was standing there with her camera, large dimpled smile and twinkling green eyes.

"Uh, yes," he sputtered.

"You okay honey? You look like you saw a ghost," she said taking a step toward him.

He stepped back placing his hand where his dagger would normally be. Then his other for his dust. Neither were on him.

"Smile!" she said snapping a photo of him.

He backed away. He scanned the room. She was standing too close to his dagger making it pointless to run out the door.

He ran into the kitchen, then through her den almost falling over a dining room chair.

"Ezekiel. There is no point in running my dear," she said sweetly.

Through the back of the den there was the back door. He ran to it and pushed it open running through. He toppled down a long staircase into darkness just pulsing his wings enough to break a fall to the head.

He looked up. The corner of the room was lit by a table lamp. The walls were covered in Hematite insignia, photos and clipping from the Chronicle.

The brown-blonde hair he'd grown to loathe back facing him sitting at a desk writing. He turned around with an annoyed look on his face.

"Surprised to see me?" Fabian asked with a smirk on his face.

Ezekiel pushed off the floor harder than he ever had in any flight race slamming the door behind him.

Stay shut door.

He breezed past Iva who for the first time exposed her wings bursting the jet-black monstrosities from her lavender cashmere sweater. He was faster than her but she more skilled in craft. From the kitchen, she ensnared him in an enchantment that bound him to the chair. Floating red lingered in the air.

"I told you there was no point in running. I'd hate for you to ruin that tux," she said with a smile. "And I'd hate for you to leave before I got a photo for your father."

Ezekiel couldn't answer. She did something to him that rendered him completely frozen.

"Now I know you have a lot of questions. That is understandable. I will start by saying that I will not hurt you. Fabian won't either. He's just a bit jealous right now. He's a bit spoiled being the son of a princess and all."

Ezekiel scowled. She lied to him about having kids.

"Now don't look at me like that. I said I didn't have a son. I never said anything about daughters. As I see you've seen my photos, I had three who were all very disappointing. Bless their hearts." She sighed.

"See I am very old. I knew I couldn't do it forever. Leading and running the group takes a lot out of you but when you've got the whole Hand of Power you live much longer." She looked at Ezekiel's expression of terror and confusion. "The Hand of Power is the possession of all color powers sweetie. I'm sure you've learned a bit about us during those Fire Tales. Nelson's sole purpose to keep the camp going is for fear of our activities, right? Having Fabian there has tremendously helped me understand what goes on over there."

"I'm sure you're wondering why? Why did she do this? Well I was tired of the inequality of the Faerman. After seeing how disappointing my own children were with their natural abilities I naturally sought ways to help them enhance their capabilities. Joining the Hematite was the best way to move our people to a closer natural selection of how we were intended to be."

"With Deuce out of the way, very old or dead, I am sure our new leader – your father - will find it much easier to pick up where I left off. If you joined us, you could stay here. We can make Faera harmonious and equal. You could have your father again and learn the truth.

Iva pulled the group photo from her album and held it to Ezekiel's face. "Look here. This was the night he was chosen." Her wrinkled finger pointed to the handsomely familiar face.

Hot tears streamed down Ezekiel's cheeks. He did not believe it. This must be some sort of enchantment she used to trick him.

But why did mom keep Faera from me?

•　　•　　•　　•　　•

There were dozens of little cottages spread amongst the village. They walked along the main path searching for any sign of Ezekiel.

"It's a lavender cottage," Dara said picking up speed. Her shoes had a bit of a heel and it was making it hard for her to run so she kicked them off abandoning them onto the grass.

"Really?" Ethan asked.

"Uh, yeah. I need to go quick. I'll get them later," she snapped.

There it was. The lavender cottage with the white shutters. They could see Ezekiel sitting in a chair so still he looked like a statue. There was Iva standing there with giant black wings.

"Get down!" She whispered aggressively pulling Ethan down. "Did you see her wings?"

Ethan took another peak. "Oh crap! She's a freakin' Hematite!" He plunged himself down holding onto his sister. She shook him off.

"This is not the time to panic!" She thought for a moment then pulled the long white ribbon from hair. From the pocket of her dress she grabbed a heap of dust and rubbed it along the ribbon, "Multiply, multiply, multiply."

The white ribbon began to grow and grow and grow. She grabbed more dust, flung it up with the ribbon in the open window, "Bind her!" Dara focused on the speed of her ribbon winding Iva from around all directions. In her mind, she told the ribbon to make the largest, tight basket she'd ever made.

"What's this?" Iva said trying to wave off the white ribbon fiercely attacking her. The ribbons went for her face covering her eyes. The ribbon wove around her arms, torso, legs and wings, pulling her down, to the side knocking her off her feet to the floor. All that remained on the floor was a large satin ribbon mummy.

Ezekiel was now able to move. He jumped up, grabbed his belt and the flower box scooping up the mimic running to the door. He pulled at the door handle and was unable to open it. She had enchanted it. He made way for the window.

"Ezie!" Dara shouted running to help him escape.

Ezekiel kicked the screen and leapt out the window, toppling on the ground. He grabbed Dara's hand and seized Ethan's arm. "Let's go!" All three pushed off as hard as they could and flew away.

"Oh, my gosh! Are you okay? What was she trying to do to you?" Dara cried.

"I don't know. She didn't get that far thanks to you," Ezekiel said.

"Yeah, hey guys, I was there too," Ethan said jokingly with a nervous tone trying to lighten the mood.

The three landed at the camp entrance running inside to the Magnus' quarters. They pounded on his door.

"Well hello there, oh my," he said looking at how disheveled Dara's hair was and the once gleaming white gown was covered in dirt, grass and torn. The boys who were once dapper looked like they were cleaning chimneys.

"We need your help!" Ezekiel said shoving his way in. The Magnus stepped aside letting the others in.

"We know who the leader of the Hematite is, or was. I know where the palace is," Ezekiel started. "You need to tell the Guard where to get her and Fabian."

"Fabian Dartmouth?" The Magnus asked. "Her?"

Ezekiel explained everything. He confessed to sending the letter to lead the Guard to the waterfall after saving Agamemnon. He told him about what he saw in the photo albums and what Iva did. His heart couldn't bring him to repeat what she said about his dad. That empty piece of him still held out hope that he would have him back some day. He could not do anything to ruin that.

He handed him the flower box with the mimic of Fabian inside.

The Magnus opened it and it shouted at him as it shouted at Ezekiel earlier. His face fell.

"That is terrible news," he said lifting his phone to make a call. He gave all the details to the Dux who quickly arrived by dagger.

"I have sent the Guard to this Iva Rose's cottage. They should be reporting back on what they find shortly," the Dux said. He turned to Ezekiel, "Thank you for the letter."

"Wait, how did you know I sent it? "Did you find the waterfall?" Ezekiel began to stammer.

"I didn't until you just told me now," he replied. "We found the site you reported. The waterfall was not there, however there were boulders left with the black stain. Our analysts found strong evidence to support your claim that there was a body of water there recently. They moved."

"How can you move an entire waterfall?" Ezekiel asked in disbelief.

"Have you not learned anything while you've been here?" the Dux jested. "You're talking about a waterfall that could appear and disappear."

The phone rang. The Dux answered.

Waiting for him to hear what the Guard found at Iva's felt like a lifetime. Ezekiel felt like his heart was suspended in his stomach.

The Dux hung up the phone.

"They have Iva in custody and are transporting her to the Caves. They searched the entire cottage and there was no sign of Fabian," he said.

"What!? How can that be!" Dara shouted.

"Hematite magic has the darkness of the full Hand of Power. We don't know enough about it," the Magnus said.

"That's it? They found nothing? What about the pictures?" Ezekiel shouted.

"Yes, we recovered the photos and a lot of evidence to support everything you have told us. Fabian has been the eyes for the Hematite inside the camp. He stole Agamemnon which was easy as the peggie is trained to go easily with campers. Agamemnon was desired because he used to belong to the Royal Family of Aoberon. If Iva is Queen Navi, it answers a lot of questions the Faerman people have had about her disappearance decades ago," the Dux explained.

"If you kids remember, her husband gave up the monarchy for her. She orchestrated everything to take down Faera for the Hematites," the Magnus said. "Lucky for us, we had the Gold Faerman, the power of the people – Guard included to organize and fight back."

The friends stood exhausted and in shock. The Magnus poured them each a mug of warm, creamy honey mead. Ezekiel knew Iva was bad news, but the warm drink down his throat made him melancholy as he thought of her. Her laugh and dimples. She was his friend.

Chapter Thirty
A Champion's Farewell

The morning trumpets sounded awakening and singing a tune that sounded different to Ezekiel. He jumped up to watch them blow and sway for the last time. As they floated down to the ground shifting into little furry balls he was panged with the feeling of missing them already.

The boys got dressed in their navy hooded camp vests. There was a clear sadness in the air as they stuffed their trunks packing for their travel home.

"Do we get to dagger home?" Ezekiel asked his friends.

"Yes. Our trunks are size charmed by the pixie's and are sent home while we get to dagger back," Kalos said.

"Okay, not to be a cheeseball but you guys will write? I can give you my email address too. I don't have a cell phone but I'm trying to work my ma into getting me one so we can text," Ethan said.

"Of course! I thought I was invited to come over?" Ezekiel said laughing.

"Let's promise to call or write at least once a week," Miles said pulling out his camera. The boys snapped a few silly photos. Ezekiel went with his go-to silly face where he exaggerated his jawline to show off his bottom teeth, making one eye sleepy and the other wide open.

The friends agreed. Ezekiel already worried that regular life would get in the way from this commitment. He already missed them.

The friends walked down the winded staircase for the last time this summer. The girls joined them as they walked to the amphitheater for the final camp rally. Seeing both wrenched Ezekiel's heart. He was going to miss Dara's witty banter and even Aubrey's bows. Miles assembled them all at the steps for another photo op. He focused his camera and with a tiny pinch of dust enchanted it in place as he ran into the picture.

"Ready? One, two, three, cheese!" Miles shouted at the camera charming it to click a series of photos.

I want that in my first letter," Ezekiel said to him with a smile.

"Of course!"

The group walked in to take their seats in the amphitheater. Many eyes were on them followed by unclear whispers Ezekiel ignored. He knew that the events of the day before were buzzing all through the camp. He had preferred to pretend it was just another bad dream.

There was no chanting, showboating or cat calls. Just crowds of friends exchanging addresses with promises to call and write. Unit banners hovered proudly over each color unit section. The stage was unusually blank and empty.

The Magnus followed by the staff took the stage. Their colored camp wear formed a rainbow Ezekiel took for granted and would miss.

"Welcome campers! I am excited to conclude another wonderful camp session with all of you. Now I know that the jubilance of the dance did not overshadow the events you may discuss in your whispers. However, I would like to present our Game Champions with their recognition before we address those matters."

The two Padsphere teams were called up and with the wave of his hand the Magnus lit the stage with the sky-blue and red banners of the Granters and Flames. The Flames were given silver medallions which none seemed particularly thrilled with. The Granters each received gold medallions and a gigantic, gold Championship Chalice. Once in their possession, the stage décor filled with Granters blue, streamers, confetti, blue tinted bubbles and streams of enchanted water that shot throughout the theater. The campers applauded their success.

The archery finalists were called to the stage and were all given silver medallions. When the Magnus placed the navy-blue ribbon around Kalos' head he was smiling so big his glasses fell off his face. He looked over at Teresa who stepped up onto the champion platform and was awarded the Golden Arrow as the Fledgling Champion.

The Magnus proceeded to call each flight team to the stage by color unit to present their silver medallions. Ezekiel and Ethan both made their way to the stage beaming. When the Magnus placed the navy-blue ribbon around Ezekiel's neck an overwhelming sense of emotion hit him. He had never won anything. As he looked at all the athletes on stage with him, he was in disbelief that he was amongst them.

"And now for the Fledgling Flight Champion, I award this gold medallion to Mr. Ethan LaVie," the Magnus announced placed the prize onto Ethan.

Wait? I thought I won? Was it because I barfed? Did I not cross the line?

Ezekiel plastered a smiled on his face for his friend because he had manners but he was confused. He knew he completed the race before Ethan had.

"And lastly, I would like to award the Golden Wings to our Grand Flight Champion - who from what Mr. Iocus tells me now holds the camp record for fastest flight, and is the youngest camper to ever hold that title. Mr. Ezekiel Raroso."

Ezekiel was stunned. It was like someone punched him in the throat. The Magnus handed him a magnificent, golden-winged trophy. The heavy wings glistened in the light, fully spread and proud. He looked at the engraving on the shiny plate.

Grand Flight Champion
Ezekiel Raroso

The campers stood in applause. His friends were going nuts with cheers and catcalls. He smiled at them with a big cheesy grin allowing Miles to snap his photo. He went back to his seat lugging his new prized possession with him.

"Yes, very wonderful performances to each of you," the Magnus said. "Now I will address the draphcus in the room."

The campers giggled. "What is a draphcus?" he asked Ethan.

"It's a gigantic, furry animal with tall ears and pink eyes. Quo's call them bunnies but they're more the size of an elephant," he explained. Ezekiel had to fight back the laughter of the thought of it.

"Now as many of you have heard, the Guard received a reliable tip that led them to the home of a Hematite leader as well as their palace."

The campers gasped. It was as though all of the night time scary stories they have heard were actually true.

"The ancient Queen Navi was discovered as the prime organizer of the fall of our old, world monarchy and at one time Malum Coacter. She is in custody of the Guard and will be sentenced to the Caves. She was not alone as she had inside help from one of our campers to obtain information on our courses, security and how to access the grounds. The disappearance of the peggie was by the said camper as well." He paused to sigh. "Unfortunately, the Guard was not able to apprehend him."

The campers broke out into chatters of questions. The Magnus raised his hand to quiet them down.

"Do not fear our failures. Applaud our successes," he started. "This leads me to my last and final award for a camper who has demonstrated an all-around skill for craft, loyalty, bravery and friendship – all attributes of what we strive to teach here at camp."

He held up a cherry wood plaque with a gold detailed Faera crest. Ezekiel's friends looked at him with smiles.

"Dara LaVie. We are so impressed by your intuition, dedication and skill over this summer. Your loyalty to your friend, quick thinking and bravery saved a camper from a potentially dire situation. For that, we applaud you with the Honorary Seal of Faera."

Dara was stunned. She slowly rose up. Ezekiel was ecstatic for her. He was the first to stand and give her a standing ovation. The campers joined in. Her mouth was dropped in shock, especially as she caught a glimpse at Ethan who was beaming with pride.

The Magnus handed her the plaque shaking her hand.

The campers exited the amphitheater, many lingering giving hugs and handshakes bidding each other farewell as they plunged their daggers heading off home. Ezekiel turned to his friends feeling like crying, laughing and hugging onto each of them. He opted to play it cool in the end.

"Awesome award for saving me," he said to Dara, bumping into her with a flirtatious nudge. The rosy pink filled her dark face.

She pulled out a perfectly folded square of paper and placed it into his camp vest pocket.

"You'll call me?"

"Of course! It's the least I could do for you saving me," he replied feeling incredibly brave.

"And for standing me up at the dance," she joked.

"Ouch," Ethan said laughing with the others.

"Hold on now! I'm not going to let you leave without a dance. I can't have you holding two things over my head." He looked a Miles and raised his eyebrows. Miles pulled his colossal pipe out of his trunk and blew into it a loud pitched sound. He started to play an upbeat tune rocking his head and body into it. From each path leading up to the amphitheater, band campers of each unit marched up totting their musical instruments in a synchronized fashion filling the air with melody.

Ezekiel put his hand out to Dara.

"You're serious?"

"Yep."

He seized her hand, twirling her around, leading her as he was taught. She laughed and threw her head back cracking up hilariously as he lifted her, twirling her and they floated up, circulating the sky and back down. He dipped her and made a cheesy grin as though making fun of himself.

"You still think this is *Camp Strange*?" Dara asked.

"Yes, and I wouldn't have it any other way," Ezekiel replied spinning her in the air.

The band dramatically concluded their tune, saluting and waving each other off as they daggered back home. Miles waved goodbye and vanished.

"See you back home!" Ethan said to Dara as he plunged his dagger into the ground.

Aubrey squished her face like a cute little chipmunk. "Call you later!" With a wink, she was gone.

Kalos pushed his glasses up his nose and gave Ezekiel and Dara a hearty group hug. "See you sooner than later!"

Ezekiel looked at Dara still holding her hand. He gave her a big hug.

"Now I just owe you for saving me," he smiled.

He plunged his dagger into the ground thinking of home and savoring Dara's pretty smile, the friendships he made and the adventure he had.

Epilogue

Ezekiel popped onto the yard in front of the large magnolia tree. The floral scent of the blooms filled his face with a smile as he caught a glimpse of his Mom sitting on the couch waiting for him.

He walked in the front door greeted by hugs and kisses. Before Anne could get a word in he stepped back.

"We need to talk about my dad."

Anne sank slowly into the worn couch.

"Tell me about this. I can handle it."

He pulled out a photo that was folded in his back pocket and handed it to Anne. As she gazed upon it, her eyes filled with tears.

"Is he the Malum?"

Anne stared at the photo, tears streaming down her cheeks.

"Well, is he? Is this why you won't talk about him? Mom?"

After a long pause, she answered.

"He wanted to be."

Acknowledgements

To all those who seek acceptance for who they are, I hope you stop looking.

I wrote Camp Strange because I wanted a story out there that ten year old me would love filled with friendship and adventure. A story where everyone could fit in, no matter how strange, dorky, awkward or weird. I wrote Camp Strange because I wanted to create friends for my autistic son, the REAL Ezekiel, knowing he may never have real friendships, but perhaps could read a story where he did and where those friends were created from my imagination based on his quirks.

I hope those that read this enjoy the adventure but more so look at themselves to be a catalyst of change. Change the way you see yourself and find the magic in being different. We are all so very unique and equipped to create the magic we hope to see in the world, we just need to find it in ourselves!

This is my first novel. Even as I write that, it is still surreal. So thank you, the reader for giving me a chance! Most importantly I thank my publisher, Black Rose Writing for giving me the opportunity to share my magic.

To my husband, I couldn't find the word to emphasize something that exceeded the love, gratitude, support and appreciation I have for you. So schmoozletasticness is the word I am creating (inventing?) to express those feelings without grossing out my readers. Your support of me during this very new, unfamiliar and scary process of being an author is schmoozletasticness. I couldn't imagine I would have been able to do this without you. Will you go to the Summer Solstice Bash with me? (Yes girls, you can ask the guy. I did and then I married him!)

To my daughter, Bianca, you are my star. You have galaxies of potential, a big heart and personality. Don't reach for the stars, you are already there dancing amongst the cosmos. Shoot for Pluto and beyond.

To my personal Uvam, my baby Mateo (yes, you are now six but since you're the youngest you are the baby even when you are twenty-six). You are so talented! Keep drawing, playing, and creating. The world will need another Stan Lee.

To my inspiration, my first born, Ezie. You were named after the fictional detective Ezekiel "Easy" Rawlins, who despite the social injustices he faces, he's always hard pressed to crack the case. No matter what challenges you face, you still find time to laugh at the same YouTube videos. I love your perseverance, laugh and smile.

Fill the world with schmoozletasticness.

Renee

About the Author

As a child, Renee Perez was always drawing the world around her and writing about it. Storylines always followed her. She wrote stories about school, her friends and evil milk cartons. These creative beginnings sent Renee to pursue a degree in English Literature.

Perez is excited to tell the story of Ezekiel Raroso in her debut book, *Camp Strange*, which is inspired by her summer camp experiences and the personalities of her three children who provide her so much joy and inspiration.

Thank you so much for reading one of our **Middle-Grade** novels.
If you enjoyed our book, please check out our recommended title for your
next great read!

Pierre Francois: 5th Grade Mishaps by Lori Ann Stephens

"... an entertaining story with the underlying theme of inclusivity."

—IndieReader

View other Black Rose Writing titles at www.blackrosewriting.com/books

and use promo code **PRINT** to receive a **20% discount** when purchasing.